BREAKFAST IN PARADISE

CARA KENT

Breakfast in Paradise
Copyright © 2024 by Cara Kent

All rights reserved. Without limiting the rights under copyright reserved above, no part of this publication may be reproduced, stored in or introduced into retrieval system, or transmitted, in any form, or by any means (electronic, mechanical, photocopying, recording, or otherwise) without the prior written permission of both the copyright owner and the above publisher of this book.

This is a work of fiction. Names, characters, places, brands, media, and incidents are either the products of the author's imagination or are used fictitiously. The author acknowledges the trademarked status and trademark owners of various products referenced in this work of fiction, which have been used without permission. The publication/use of these trademarks is not authorized, associated with, or sponsored by the trademark owners.

PROLOGUE

THE GOLDEN PARADISE SAT NEAR THE EDGE OF A CLIFF in a quiet neighborhood. It was surrounded by trees and native Hawaiian flowers and still far enough from nosey neighbors that guests felt like they were in their own slice of paradise as soon as they stepped onto the cobblestone driveway. The house, turned bed-and-breakfast, was three stories high with large windows and a library overlooking the ocean.

The library was the main feature that brought everyone to the bed-and-breakfast. A beautiful feature. Guests, primarily couples, loved to sit at the window seat and watch the waves and the vibrant flowers sway in the wind. Flowers that were now kindling for the fire raging in the Paradise. It was at that window Mr. Corey Monroe, a travel writer, stood in complete silence. The other guests had already gone to their rooms, leaving him there reading No matter where he went on the island or in the house, he always ended up back at the window. It was his favorite spot.

The inky black sky seemed to blend into the faraway ocean. Like their little patch of island had been swallowed by nothingness. There was a calmness to it that made him feel better. Just as he thought to himself how he would write about the area around the bed-and-breakfast, beads of sweat cascaded down the back of his neck. His stomach sank, and his chest tightened. He glanced around. He was alone, and the house was quiet, but something was wrong.

He eased out of the room, the wood floors creaking beneath his feet. In the hallway, there was nothing. No, not nothing. There was a slight cracking noise downstairs, but he couldn't place it. The rest of the guest rooms were quiet, without their televisions on, and someone sounded as if they were talking on the phone. It was probably Josie, who had been on the phone practically every minute since she had been there. Mr. Monroe found it annoying as she was constantly saying she was there to relax and take time away from work. Her husband was equally annoyed.

But affairs of the heart were none of Mr. Monroe's business, so instead of heading toward the rooms, he descended the stairs, away from the talking and toward the steady cracking noise.

What is that? he thought. It sounded familiar, but he couldn't place it. His feet touched the floor. He noted the warmness there. It was hot downstairs. Hotter than usual. Mrs. Beth Hardwell usually kept the AC on. Beads of sweat cascaded down his cheeks as he inched closer to the kitchen. It was there he saw it. Small at first. A small puff of smoke.

His first thought was to jump into action. Grab water or a fire extinguisher. Surely, she had to have one. But as he ran into the kitchen, he knew instantly there was nothing he could do. The fire had worked its way from the back, from Mrs. Hardwell's suite, into the kitchen.

Flames licked at the ceiling. Moving, jumping surface to surface. It almost surrounded him. He backed out of the kitchen. Smoke filled the air, thick and heavy. It was billowing all around him now. He glanced to the back of the house.

"Mrs. Hardwell!"

BREAKFAST IN PARADISE

Sweat coated his skin. The heat was unbearable. He called for her again and again. Nothing. Had she gotten out? Was she still back there? Or had she left earlier on an errand? He couldn't remember when he had seen her last. He couldn't think. His chest heaved as his lungs tried to suck in more air. Air not tinged with smoke and fire. He glanced toward the front door, which was not yet marred by fire. He ran to it but stopped. Hand on the doorknob, he looked up the stairs.

"Josie! Armstrong! White! Enriquez!" He waited a moment for any sound of acknowledgment. "There's a fire!" Nothing. He sighed. He couldn't just leave them there to figure out the house was burning down on their own. Well, he could. He really could. And he wanted to. He wanted to run out into the fresh air. Air that didn't burn his lungs. He wanted to scream, but it burned. His throat was dry and the air stung his eyes.

He was running up the stairs before he had time to think. Screaming for them was doing nothing, and he would hate for them all to burn to death. And where was Mrs. Hardwell? The thought still nagged at him. He couldn't remember the last time he saw her. Was it dinner? He must have seen her after that. He banged on the first door.

"Fire!" He ran upstairs and banged on more doors. Shouting fire all the way. The words scraped against his throat. "Fire!" He couldn't scream anymore. He couldn't run anymore. Smoke had snaked through the house. It was everywhere now, and he had to get out.

The rest of the guests had finally made their way out of their rooms due to his shouting. There was more shouting and screams and footsteps. Hard footsteps pounding down the stairs. As he ran back down the stairs, he heard the front door slam. And then another scream. Flames reached out for the door. Josie jumped back.

"The knob is too hot!" She turned and looked back Mr. Monroe. She jumped away from the door and back up the stairs. "What now?"

He grabbed her by the arm and pulled her back into one of the rooms. He closed the door behind them. Smoke eased into the room from the space underneath the door. He could have placed a towel or maybe a blanket at the door. But there wasn't

3

time. They needed to get out now and fast. Mr. Monroe rushed over to the window and opened it. After kicking out the screen, he glanced down at the ground. They were on the second floor. Dread coiled in the pit of his stomach like a snake.

He could break a limb or two, but he it was better than being burned alive. Or suffocating from all the smoke. No, breaking a bone was a much better option. He looked at Josie, huddled across from him in the corner. Clearly frightened, eyes darting from the window to the door. For a brief moment, he wondered about her husband. Who was not in the room with them…with her? Had he left her? Was that the door slam he had heard earlier?

He shook the thought loose from his mind. It didn't matter now. All that mattered was that they got out. He hoped everyone else was able to make it out the front door.

"Come on, Josie, we have to jump."

"Jump?"

"How else will we get down?" He could have been on the ground by now, writhing in agony, but thankful he wasn't dead. "It's either go through fire or go through the window. Pick."

Reluctantly, after weighing her options for longer than Mr. Monroe deemed necessary, she ran over to the window, stood on the edge, and said a short prayer before jumping. He watched as she fell to the ground and rolled a short distance before stopping.

He sighed. His heart stuttered in his chest. Before it could resume its regular beats, he leaped through the window. The fall, or rather the landing, hurt less than he had imagined. He landed more on his side and was able to roll a short distance, like Josie, before stopping near a tree. On his back, after taking inventory of his limbs, he looked up at the house, now engulfed in flames. The sky blazed in bright smears of orange and red.

"Where is Mrs. Hardwell?" he said to himself, hoping she had gotten out. But he wasn't sure if there was a way out from the owner's quarters.

"You okay?" Josie's voice was raspy and hoarse. She held out her hand for him. He grabbed it. Both their hands were slick with sweat, and it took some effort to pull him to his feet without leverage. He sighed; his body already felt sore. And he was so tired. There was a commotion at the front of the house; they glanced at each other for a brief moment before they started walking toward the front.

The neighbors and guests had assembled on the front lawn, framed by fire trucks. Relief surged through him, causing his shoulders to sag. When had they gotten there? He scanned the crowd forming on the lawn. Everyone looked accounted for. Perhaps... He paid particular attention to the faces, searching for ones he recognized. Everyone was there, including some of the neighbors. Everyone except one...

"Where did you two come from?" A firefighter wearing a mask stalked toward them. Mr. Monroe pointed to the window they had just jumped out of. He swallowed the remark about a ladder being useful. Now was not the time for sarcasm. Not with the fire roaring and smoke billowing even higher.

The firefighter led them to the ambulance. He gave each of them a once-over before handing them over to the paramedics.

"They look okay, but check them out to be safe. Was there anyone else in there? Anyone left?"

The urgency in his voice sent a shiver down Monroe's spine. He swallowed hard. "Mrs. Hardwell," he choked out. "I didn't see her, and she's not out here." He scanned the crowd again, looking for her familiar face. Mrs. Hardwell had been a kind host. She had taken such good care of him, especially since he had come by himself. Part of him knew it was because she wanted him to write about the bed-and-breakfast, but part of him suspected that was just how she was with people. Kind and helpful. She treated all the guests the same. And now she was gone.

"Maybe she left before the fire, but I don't remember her saying she was going to run an errand. She always tells us when she's leaving." His heart hammered in his chest. The paramedic took his pulse, sucked her teeth, and shook her head while she started taking his blood pressure.

A gasp reverberated through the crowd. He looked up, his fingers gripping the edge of the stretcher. The front of the house, just above the front door, folded in on itself. There was no door, no windows, no roof. Everything was engulfed by flames and crashing to the ground in a relentless heap.

Firefighters ordered everyone to move away from the house. As they were all ushered away, they still sprayed the house with water. Flames licked at the sky violently. There was nothing anyone could do now. Firefighters could not enter the house, and no one could get out. All they could do now was hopefully stop it from spreading. The fire's fingers reached out and grabbed anything it could. Branches, dried leaves, flowers.

Kindling, all of it, as the fire raged on. How long had it been burning? The question gnawed at him. He picked over it like an open wound, worrying it with his finger. How could it have gotten so out of control?

In the chaos, Josie finally saw her husband. A loud slap drew Monroe's attention to where she stood. Her husband's hand touching his face. It was just as he thought. He had left her behind. Probably shut the door in her face.

He might not have done it on purpose, more instinctively. It didn't look like she cared about his reasoning. She was just angry, and she had a right to be. She could have died, and he'd just left her there. Looking back at the house, it dawned on Monroe.

They all could have died. Mrs. Hardwell was likely dead. A pain radiated through his heart. He had liked the older woman. She was so kind. Tears pricked his eyes, and he was unsure for a moment if it was because of her death or the smoke billowing in the air. Or perhaps both.

They watched in silent awe as the fire overtook the house, their belongings destroyed. A deafening and consuming quiet swallowed the crowd. Monroe couldn't hear the whispers of those around him. He didn't hear the firefighters shouting or the rush of water from the fire hoses. He heard nothing but that awful crackling sound. The fire. Nothing but the fire.

The sun rose slowly as if it, too, was surprised by what happened that night. Slowly taking in the scene before settling behind the clouds. The house was obliterated. Some of the walls were still up—well, the framing anyway. The bones of a home, the meat and muscle burned away.

"We need to check the house once it's cooled. Is everyone accounted for?" A man neared the house and stopped by the rubble of the front door. He was tall and clearly in charge.

Monroe thought him to be the fire marshal. He looked back at them, the crowd of neighbors and the last guests of the Golden Paradise. His mouth was a grim line, his eyes searching.

A paramedic had moved through the crowd gathering names two hours earlier. And they were all accounted for. All except Mrs. Hardwell. She had not walked out of the house, nor had she rejoined the group after a night of running errands.

Mr. Monroe's heart sank into his stomach as dread pulsed beneath his skin. He knew. They all knew, and yet no one had said it out loud.

"No, sir. Mrs. Hardwell still hasn't been found."

The fire marshal stared at the firefighter making the report, his shoulders slowly sagging. "I see." There was a tinge of sadness in his voice. Monroe was unsure if that meant he had known the woman or if it was just a natural reaction to a possible fire death. "Well, let's see if we can find her."

It didn't take long to find her. In her quarters, charred bones twisted due to the heat. She was brought out on a stretcher, but there was no hurry. She was long gone. Mr. Monroe stared at the body as they laid it out on the grass, preparing it for transport. He shuddered, finding it strange how fire could twist bones in such a way.

The fire marshal stared at the bones long and hard. There was something strange about them. He couldn't place it, but there was something not right. He looked around at the rubble that had been the Golden Paradise.

"When was the fire reported?" he asked a nearby firefighter searching through the rubble.

"Call came in just after ten, sir."

"And when did you arrive?"

"Took us about ten minutes. By then, the fire had pretty much taken over the house."

The marshal stared back at the house. How could it have done that in such a short time frame? He looked down at her bones and then the area that surrounded her. There was something not right about it.

"I doubt this was electrical. If I had to make a guess, I would say arson," said the firefighter.

"Yes. I'd have to agree with you. But did Mrs. Hardwell die before or after the fire?"

CHAPTER ONE

Detective Amyra Kahale loved the night shift. More so than her partner, Detective Julio Lister, anyway. While he groaned as the seconds ticked by, she buzzed at her desk, finally getting a jump on their paperwork. Amyra filled in boxes and wrote descriptions quietly and without any complaint. Lister's annoyance and complaints were in his very presence, from the way he sat to the sigh that echoed from his mouth every time he flipped a page.

She ignored him. It was easy enough to do. She just had to focus on the work. Truth be told, they were behind. More so than anyone knew. While they both loved solving cases, the dreaded paperwork always fell by the wayside. Half the department was behind on their paperwork, as the captain had so eloquently stated earlier in the week.

"I don't know why you all find it so difficult to fill out and turn in your paperwork on time, but get it together. From here on out, there will be consequences."

No one knew what those consequences were. No one had dared ask. It was just known that it would happen even if he had to make them up as he went along.

Lister sighed again, and Amyra rolled her eyes. "What is wrong with you? It's just filling things in. You've already done the heavy lifting. Just fill out the report." She turned a page, sat her pen down, and picked up her piping hot cup of coffee.

"You think I remember what happened during this case? Once I move on, my brain does too. Now I have to search my mind for information on a case we worked weeks ago."

Amyra could have taken this moment to point out that if he had done the paperwork immediately after solving the case, he wouldn't have a problem now. She swallowed her retort. He was already annoyed, and now was not the time to pile it on. Amyra and Julio had been partners for years and years. In fact, their tenth anniversary was coming up. They had been partners longer than they'd been with their respective spouses. It was sad when she thought about it, so she tried not to.

She shook her head. It always amazed her how he could move from case to case without any lingering effects. Without the ghost, as her mother called it. Her mother, Sergeant Victoria Kahale, had once been a force of nature within the Honolulu Police Department. She accrued the highest case closure rate in the state during her twenty years as a detective. She was a legend. A marvel. She had told Amyra that there were cases you could move past quickly, but then there were others.

"Some linger. Like ghosts, they attach themselves to you. Hard to shake. You have to find a place to put them. Lock them away inside yourself so you can focus on the work at hand."

Amyra wasn't sure what her mother meant at first. How could a case haunt you? She didn't believe in ghosts...not at first. But her mother was right—some cases haunted. Some burrowed under your skin deep into the bone and made themselves at home there.

One such case haunted her mother from the time Amyra was eight. Her mother never liked bringing her work home, a point she often stressed to her daughter.

"It is important that you find a way to take it off before you walk through the door. Work stays at the office. Don't bring it home with you. Once you start doing that, you'll never be able to stop. And you will ruin everything."

Of course, Victoria never seemed to follow her own advice. She could not leave this case at the office. Even as a child, Amyra knew the boxes at the back of her mother's closet were never to be touched. In those boxes was a case of a young girl and her mother who were murdered. Bodies split open from throat to belly. Bodies positioned to look like they were making snow angels in the dirt. Both naked. The case had never been solved, and it haunted her for years. She always felt like she was close. "I'm so close. I just need one more thing. I'm so close," she would whisper. But Amyra never knew how close her mother was.

Victoria never talked about the case, never went into any details, or disclosed what she had found since she moved the case files into her bedroom closet. It was off-limits. It haunted her and her alone.

Amyra had a few ghosts already, four that haunted her daily. Her dreams. Her waking nightmares. Bodies directed. A little boy quartered and left in a park for a jogger to run upon. An older woman, raped and disemboweled in her living room.

Victoria Kahale bent over a steering wheel, brains splattered on the roof of her car. Gun next to her. Suicide... But her mother would never kill herself. And her mother wasn't right-handed. Everyone knew that... and where were the boxes in her closet?

She shook the thought from her head. She didn't have time to be haunted now. She had paperwork. Her mother would burst into her dreams later. Until then, she sipped her coffee and listened to Lister sigh heavily.

The room went still as the alarm near the front door went off. It was a signal to let someone at the front desk know that a person was coming and to be on alert. Amyra paid it no mind. It was probably an officer nearing the door with a drunk suspect. She took up her pen and started making more notes.

But the alarm sounded again. Lister looked up at her, eyebrows bunching together like two caterpillars bumping into each other. She stifled a laugh. His face was severe. The alarm stopped, but before she could put her pen to paper, it sounded again.

"Kids messing with the door?" she asked. It was an odd thought but a possible one. Bored children could have wanted to drive the officers crazy. Sounded like something she would have done when she was younger.

Lister checked his watch. "This late?"

Amyra checked her watch, too. It was a little after midnight. He jumped to his feet. A man of action, he would rather investigate than fill out the paperwork, anyway. Amyra stayed at her desk and waited. Lister, his hand on his gun, inched toward the front door. Through the glass, he saw them…children. Young ones. He sucked his teeth. What were they doing out so late? Where were their parents?

His hand fell away from his side only to inch back into position when he got closer to the door. There was a large black lump behind the children. They looked dirty and unkempt, with unruly hair and smudged faces…the saddest eyes he had ever seen. His chest tightened as if a rope had been looped around him and pulled. Something was wrong.

He pushed the door open. Three of the children flinched. Outside, the cool night air sent a shiver down his spine. He glanced behind him and saw another officer moving toward the door, curiosity etched on his face. They shared a look before Lister turned his attention back toward the children. Well, not them at the moment, the thing behind them. The children were so quiet and so still like statues. He moved around them toward the bundle of fabric. He kicked it at first. When his foot touched, he knew instantly what it was.

"Get them inside!"

The officer swept the children inside the station. None of them fought him or protested. They crept as if they had practiced the art of silent movement. He didn't know children could be that quiet. He yanked back the fabric, which turned out to

BREAKFAST IN PARADISE

be a black jacket, and saw a man. A white man with dark brown hair and paper-white skin. He bent down to touch him, but he knew already. Before his fingers grazed his cold skin, he knew the man was dead.

The officer rushed outside to join him.

"Who is he?"

Lister shrugged. "That is the million-dollar question."

CHAPTER TWO

THE LOCAL PRECINCT HUMMED WITH EXCITEMENT. Officers buzzed around, trying to secure the body while figuring out where it came from. Had someone dumped him there, or had he brought the children and then collapsed? Lister didn't think the second option was possible. He had touched the man, after all. His skin was so cold. He had to have been dead for a long while before anyone noticed him.

Amyra watched from the doorway as crime scene techs and officers swarmed around the body. Her night shift was off to an interesting start. Mysterious and mute children dropped off with a dead body... Curiouser and curiouser, she thought.

Lister rushed back into the building. "He's been dead for a while. But he couldn't have been out here the whole time. Someone dropped him and the children off and then ran."

She looked from him to the front window and back again. His face was flushed and his coffee-colored eyes were bright and alive. He had that look, the same look he got whenever they were on a new case. She hated that look. That look said no more paperwork tonight.

"Isn't there a camera out there?" She glanced behind her, looking for someone at the front desk. It was empty.

"Vincent is checking. I think Koa is helping him. It's so strange. Did you see the children?" His fingers twitched at his sides. He was ready for a cigarette. She knew that sign well. But he was trying to quit. His lips pressed into a grim line as he stared at Amyra and shoved his hands in his pocket.

A slight smile kissed her lips. She admired his restraint for however long it lasted. And it never did. "I haven't. Are they hurt?"

"I couldn't tell at first. We should get them checked out."

A few officers were two steps ahead of them. The children, nine in total, had already been wrangled and were on their way to the nearest hospital. Amyra wanted to speak to them. Not just speak with them but look at them. Lister seemed shaken by their appearance, and she wanted to know what about them had done it.

"I guess we can table tonight's paperwork," she said.

A smile tugged at the corner of his mouth. She knew that would make him happy. At least for now, until they would eventually have to get it done or else.

The deceased man was fingerprinted and then taken to the morgue. Amyra noted there were no visible signs of injury, and there was no blood on the front or the back of his shirt or black pants.

She thought that odd. There were also no ligature marks around his neck or any markers of injury that she could see from a preliminary once-over. It looked to her that he walked up to the door and then simply dropped dead before he could open it. There was something off about the whole thing. Who dropped a dead body off at the police's doorstep, and what did the children have to do with it?

Her mind raced with different scenarios, but none quite clicked into place. She had to see them. Once the body had been taken care of and the surveillance tapes viewed, the detectives headed to the hospital. Lister preferred to drive, while Amyra preferred to ride in the passenger seat. It gave her time to think, to plan. To sort out the facts that had been nagging at her. On the tape, a truck pulled up in front of the precinct and, when no one was looking, dumped a body by the front door. She figured it had been a man from the way he lifted the body out of the truck. He was tall, although he kept his face hidden. She could just make out a black beard and a scar near his chin. He dumped the body by the door.

He didn't handle him with care or any kind of empathy one should have shown a dead body. He just dropped him and then went back to the car. The children were ushered to the door, and then the man walked away. He got back in his car and drove off before someone could get to the door. He didn't knock or tell the children anything. He just walked away.

She tried to surmise why a person would do that and how the children factored into everything, but nothing came to mind. It was such an odd situation she couldn't think of a logical scenario that made sense.

The hospital was quiet. Too quiet. It was unsettling, but she reminded herself it was after midnight on a Monday. It would be busy Friday night, though.

"The children are being checked out. So far, it looks like most of them are okay. Physically anyway. If we want a more extensive examination, we will need their parents," said Officer Mahoe, pacing the waiting room floor. She looked tired, her eyes fighting to stay open. She kept moving even while she talked, rocking back and forth on her heels.

"Did they say anything?" asked Amyra. Surely one of them had to say something.

She shook her head. "It was unnerving. I asked questions while my partner drove, but no one said anything. I have a lot of nieces and nephews, and children are never this quiet on their own. Not unless they are forced. Something happened to them. All of them."

Amyra nodded. They waited for the doctors and nurses to finish with all nine children. One hour ticked by, and then another. Finally, a doctor, a handsome man with a graying beard and light gray eyes, walked toward them.

"Sorry, that took so long. I was pulled away by an emergency with another patient. Now, about the children. Physically, they have been through a lot—some more than others. There are signs of abuse, and all of them are malnourished. We need to speak with their parents to do a...there might have been sexual abuse."

"Did they say anything?" asked Lister, his eyes narrowing. Anger pulsed from him like a separate heartbeat. He wasn't angry at the doctor but at the person responsible for hurting the children.

The doctor shook his head. "No, nothing. Not one word. We are feeding them. Maybe they'll talk once they've had something to eat." He walked away and left them there to wonder.

Mahoe shook her head. "Why drop them off in front of the police station?"

Amyra shrugged. She had wondered the same thing and had come up with nothing. "All the children need to be fingerprinted. And we need to start running them through the missing persons database immediately. The sooner we know who they are, the sooner we can figure all this out."

One day turned into two, and so on. Amyra visited the children daily, and yet still none of them would speak to her. Something, or rather someone, had them afraid. Even though they had been in police custody for days, they were still afraid. She worried for them. She worried for their parents. She had never had children and never wanted any. She couldn't imagine what their parents had been through. The detectives still didn't know how long the children had been with whoever had dropped them at the station.

"I suspect they had been without food for a long time," said the doctor. "Based on their bloodwork and the state of their teeth, the very little they were fed had little nutritional value. Candy bars. Chips. They haven't seen a vegetable in a while."

On her nightly rounds, Amyra walked into one of the children's rooms. A little girl whose name was still a mystery. She looked like she was about seven, with warm brown eyes, cinnamon-colored skin, and dark hair. As soon as Amyra walked into the room, her eyes never left her. She watched intently as she placed a bag of chips on the table in front of her. She watched as she pulled a chair close to the bed and sat down. She watched her like there was nothing else in the room. Like they had the world all to themselves. Amyra didn't say anything at first.

The quiet nestled between them, and she let it, partly because she didn't know what to say. She had a million questions she wanted to ask but didn't want to bombard the girl with questions when she was so clearly shaken. So clearly afraid of something. But if Amyra could figure out what that something was, maybe she could reassure her that everything was okay now. That everything would be okay. She just needed to start small and then work her way up to bigger questions.

"Do you miss your parents?" she asked finally. It was a stupid question, but then again, maybe it wasn't. If her parents had sold her to someone, then she wouldn't have missed them. If they had hurt her, she shouldn't have wanted to see them again. She waited for the answer, and it came, albeit not verbally.

The young girl nodded slowly.

"Well, we need your help to find them. We need to tell them where you are, but in order to do that, we need to know your name." Amyra gave her as encouraging a smile as she could. It was like a light had finally turned on in the girl's eyes. Like it had just dawned on her she could go home. "We don't want to keep you here any longer than we have to, but we need someone to release you to. Do you know your parent's names? Maybe an address. We need something to get started."

The young girl stared at the bag of chips on the table, her mouth twisted in thought. And then she nodded slowly. "My mom's name is Gini."

"Do you have the same last name?"

She nodded. "Livingston."

"Okay." She wrote it down in her notepad, noting that Gini might have been a nickname. "And what's your name so we can make sure we find the right people?"

She stilled for a moment, uncertainty skittering across her face. Seconds ticked by and then she answered. "Anabelle." For a brief moment the horror movie of that name entered Amyra's mind. She loved that movie, especially how it reaffirmed her dislike for dolls. They were creepy, and the movie solidified that. Even though Lister didn't seem to agree.

"What kind of little girl doesn't like dolls?" he had teased.

She had never liked dolls, not even as a child. They were strange and creepy. Her grandmother had made a doll that looked just like her when she was seven, and Amyra had become convinced the doll was trying to steal her soul so she could become a real girl. Like Pinocchio only much darker and more depraved.

"Dolls are creepy." She had told Lister. "I always thought they tried to steal our souls as we slept so they could then replace us and live as real humans."

Lister had looked at her then, for so long and so intently he veered a little too hard to the left causing the car next to them to honk several times. "That's hella dark, Amyra. And how old were you when you thought that?"

She never answered the question. Partly because she didn't know the answer. She couldn't say why she felt that way. When she thought about it, there was a memory. It was there and then it wasn't. It slipped through her fingers like the finest silk, like water, impossible to hold on to. It could have been the fire that changed her mind. Although she didn't remember the fire, only the nights afterward, which brought about her fear of dolls. The scar that stretched the length of her back ached at the memory. When she saw the doll that looked like her, she became so panicked that it was going to kill her that she grabbed it and slammed it against the wall. Just in case it got any ideas as to who was in charge.

She stared at the girl and snapped back into reality. She hadn't thought about the fire in years. There was never a reason to. "Thank you for telling me your name, Anabelle. Do people call you Anna?"

She nodded.

"Can I?"

A smiled tugged at the corner of her lips as she nodded. "Thank you." Amyra took a moment to text Anna's information to Lister so he could look into it. She tucked her phone back into her pocket when she was done. "Can you tell me where you're from?"

"Chicago."

"I see." She nodded slowly. She tried her best to keep her tone light and fun. Granted, what they were talking about was quite serious, but she didn't want the girl to clam up or to think she was in some kind of trouble. They were just having a simple conversation. "Do you know how you got here?"

A shadow passed over her face then. For a moment, she thought Anna would not answer her. That the interview was over, but to her surprise, the words spilled from Anna like she had been waiting a lifetime to say them. To tell someone, anyone who would listen. And so, she did. She told Amyra about the man who watched her as she played at the park across the street from her house. How nice he seemed, and she knew she wasn't supposed to talk to strangers, but he was so nice, and his puppy was so friendly. How the dog walked right up to her and started licking her face. And she had wanted a dog, but her father was allergic, so she could never get one.

She talked about how she had seen the man at the park for weeks and how she played with his puppy and they would talk. How by the end he wasn't a stranger. They were friends. Amyra's heart sank deeper and deeper into her stomach the more Anna revealed. He took her, although she didn't remember how. She was walking home, and the next thing she knew, she was in his car. And then she was other places with other people, mostly men. She bit her lip then. Anna didn't want to continue with the story nor did Amyra want to know what happened. They bother already knew where things went from there.

"The man that was dropped off with you, was he one of the men?"

She nodded. "He was. Another man came into the building we were in and killed him. And then he took us. He kept his face covered so I couldn't see but he was nice. His voice was nice. He told us to stay in front of the door and wait until someone came out."

Amyra had other questions, but she didn't want to push. She had already learned much more than she thought she would. It was enough for now. She sat with Anna while she ate her chips and dozed off to sleep again. That had become their routine. When she was fast asleep, she got up from her chair and exited the room. She was on her way to her car when she got a call from Lister.

"We have some interesting matches to the fingerprints and DNA."

"Really?" She knew he had learned something interesting. Any other time, he would have waited until she rejoined him at the precinct, but when he learned something fascinating, even though he knew she was on her way back, he still had to call her. He couldn't wait to tell her.

"The children were kidnapped from all over. Not just one state...Florida, New York, Pennsylvania...all over. But the interesting thing...You remember that case from a while back, Dane Wesley?"

Amyra searched her memory. Dane Wesley had been all over the news, not just because of his crimes but his death. He had killed multiple men linked to a child trafficking ring that took his sister. He was later killed in jail before he could go to trial. "Of course. Why?"

"When we took DNA from all the children, one came back a match. The girl, Joy, is a familial match to Dane Wesley and his sister Yumi. Yumi was arrested, but now it appears that she has vanished into thin air."

Amyra's fingers reached for the car door and stilled. "Now that is interesting."

CHAPTER THREE

I OFTEN FOUND IT HARD TO JUST LIVE IN THE MOMENT. MY mind, no matter how hard I tried to relax, would never let me rest. It was always moving and formulating plans and searching for mysteries. It was hard to turn it off most days. But for once, as I soaked in every ounce of sun available to me on the beach as the water lapped at my feet, my mind was practically blank. Jill and Hattie murmured in the background, but my ear wasn't focused on what they were saying. Mostly, I just heard the crashing of the waves and children laughing.

It was nice. A day without murder. Without a mystery to solve.

I glanced to my right at my neighbor Delia, whose face was turned down. She had lost custody of her daughter. Not because she was a bad mother, but because her husband had more money and could offer her daughter a better, more secure lifestyle. That ruling had broken something in her, and I had tried to pull her out for herself. We had gone on hikes and to the beach and out to a bar, to the movies, and everywhere else fun Hattie could think of. But nothing filled that void within her.

Jill finally told us to stop. "She has to sit in her feelings for a little while. She'll snap out of it."

We were giving her time. But we kept inviting her places, and she kept accepting our invitations. So that was something. But she still wasn't out of it yet. I stared out at the waves and sighed. After another hour, we packed up our snacks and towels and headed for the car. I felt drained from the sun and hungry.

We hadn't done anything all day. It was one of the few days this year when we all had the day off. Even Tony, who had elected to spend the time with his new girlfriend. Well, not really new. He and Aisha had dated before, but things had ended abruptly and badly when he said he didn't want to get married. She did, and since neither was willing to change their minds, they had separated. In their time apart, it was difficult to say which had changed their mind. Surely, one of them had to have for things to be different this time around, but Tony offered no details, and I didn't go searching for any. It wasn't my business, and I was determined not to let my curiosity get the better of me.

We piled into Jill's car and headed to our next destination—food. As always, I was hungry, and judging by the growling stomachs in the car, I wasn't the only one. The snacks of fruit and cheese and chips and a few sweets were good, but it was time for real food now.

It was decided a place that served brunch would work best. I wanted a mimosa, whereas Jill and Delia wanted Bloody Marys. Jill knew the right place where the food was good and the drinks were better. As usual, she did not disappoint.

My mimosa was more champagne than orange juice. The bubbles tickled my nose.

"We should do something tonight," said Jill, lowering her menu. She tucked a bright red strand of hair behind her ear. "We could go to the movies or something."

I shrugged. "I have a date tonight, so you can count me out."

Jill propped her elbows on the table and leaned forward, her chin resting in the palms of her hands. "Do you now?" She wiggled her eyebrows, a smirk easing across her lips. I rolled my eyes. She knew I was dating Harrison, and I refused to give in to her teasing.

"Anyway. Maybe another night," I said.

Jill chuckled, and Hattie smiled. The waitress, a young woman with honey-blonde hair, bright blue eyes, and an impeccable memory, returned with our food. I ordered eggs benedict with two crab patties and a fruit cup.

"How are things?" asked Hattie. Jill and I stopped and looked at her. There was one rule for the day, only one—no talk about work. We could do anything and talk about anything, but not our jobs. At first, it was harder than I imagined it would be. I had been surrounded by all things murder for so long that it was all I talked about, all I thought about. It was a little easier now, but there were times I had to remind myself that I needed to find something else to talk about.

"I don't mean work," she said with her hands up. "Geez, I just meant, how is everyone doing?" She said the words slowly so no one could misunderstand her meaning.

I ate a crab cake and thought about my answer. How was I doing? It was a difficult question to answer. I couldn't say why. I should have known the answer right off. I spent the most time with myself, after all. Who knew me better than me? And yet, when I opened my mouth to answer the question, I replaced the words with another forkful of eggs and crab.

Fortunately, Jill answered the question first, saying she was doing well even though she was tired. And of course, the discussion inevitably turned back to work.

"I keep telling them we need more hands in the morgue. People keep transferring out, and then everything falls on me," she said. The last two morgue assistants left Hawaii and settled somewhere else. One, upon the realization of what working in a morgue truly meant, changed her profession altogether. "I don't know what she thought she would be doing in a morgue. Of course, you work with dead bodies. That's the job."

She had only lasted a couple of weeks.

"Maybe she thought there was something else she could do. Like taking care of the paperwork or something. She could do the things that no one else wanted to do."

BREAKFAST IN PARADISE

Jill laughed. "No one likes paperwork, but still…"

We spent the rest of our brunch talking about our lives and how the new year started for us. And what we hoped for. I still couldn't answer the question. I mulled it over the whole time, and yet the answer still wouldn't come to me. I figured I was doing well.

It always annoyed me when people said, "New year, new me." They never meant it. It was a new year, and after a month or two, they would all be back to the same old tricks. Same bad habits.

I had a few goals of my own, but I decided to start small instead of doing a complete overhaul on the first. I wanted to get out more and socialize, so I did. I made a point to get out and do something at least twice a month on my own.

I went on a hike by myself and out to lunch at a new sandwich shop. It was nice getting out on my own, exploring the island that had been my home for almost a year.

My relationship with Harrison had been going well so far. I didn't want to jinx it, but we spent a lot of time together. Either I stayed at his place or he at mine. Almost every night. Except for those nights when he had to stay at the office rather late or I was at work late. Then we usually hung out for lunch or dinner and then went back to work.

"Do all psychiatrists stay in the office so late?" I asked one night over dinner.

He shrugged. "Some do. I like to write extensive notes, and then there is my work at the hospital. Sometimes, I stop by just to make sure everything is still running smoothly. Sometimes everything is okay, and then sometimes it's a… well, a madhouse, and then I'm not getting home until well after midnight."

"Yeah, some nights I don't get home until then either." Those nights, we were too tired to even talk, so we stayed at our respective condos. We hadn't exchanged keys yet, and I wasn't sure I was ready for that. I liked having my own space. I liked knowing when someone was there and when they weren't. If I gave him a key, he could come over whenever he wanted, and then it wouldn't have been my space anymore but ours.

I didn't know if I wanted it to be our space. Not yet, anyway. We weren't there yet.

25

After brunch, I was tired from the champagne and the rich meal. I was ready to go home, but Jill and the others wanted to go somewhere else. Jill wanted to get her nails done, and Hattie and Delia wanted to go shopping.

"I think that's it for me today." They wanted to have a real girl's day, but I was no longer in the mood. I was tired, and I needed to take a nap before my date.

"You want me to take you home?" Jill asked. She finished the last of her Bloody Mary and set the glass on the table.

"No, I'll catch an Uber. You guys have fun." I said my goodbyes and told them all to be careful and have fun. It was still early in the afternoon, and Harrison wasn't picking me up until nine. That was the good thing, I supposed, about living in the same building as my boyfriend. He was right across the hall.

My Uber driver pulled up after the girls had already left. They had offered to stay with me until then, but I declined. I didn't want to stop their fun. And I didn't need a babysitter.

He pulled up in a silver sedan. Before I got in the car, I made sure to ask his name. Mike was a large black man with shoulder-length locs and a gold cross around his neck. When he smiled, he had the deepest dimples I had ever seen. After checking the child's lock was off, I got in the car.

He was nice and mostly quiet. He made a few remarks about brunch and about the music playing on the radio. He was a big Swiftie and even took his daughter to one of her concerts.

"Hard to say who had more fun, me or her," he said.

I smiled politely. Whenever anyone brought the singer up, it made me think of Kasey Swift, the member of the team who had first welcomed me to Hawaii. I didn't know what was going on with her lately. She had needed some time away after a horribly traumatic case, and she still hadn't told us what had happened. I was sure she would someday, but my heart ached when I thought about how much she was suffering.

I thanked him for the ride as we pulled up to my building, paid him, and then got out of the car. My eyes got heavier with every step. Upon entering my condo, I kicked off my shoes, set my purse on the console, and collapsed onto the sofa.

It was after six when I finally rolled onto my side and opened my eyes. I checked my phone for any texts from Harrison. When

I saw there were none, I sent a text asking if we were still on for dinner. A lot of our dinner dates didn't come to fruition. Either he had to cancel, or I did. I would have some crazy case to work on, or he had to leave early to deal with a patient in crisis. It was difficult to be angry when that happened.

He was helping someone who truly needed it. How could I be mad about that? I got up and got a glass of water from the kitchen. My phone pinged from the sofa. My chest tightened as I stared at the screen for a moment, and then everything in me relaxed.

Harrison Rogers: As far as I know, we are still on. (Praying nothing goes wrong) :)

I sat on the sofa and sipped my water. Harrison had a relaxing effect on me that I rather enjoyed. He was easy to be around and to talk to. My mind didn't wander when I was around him, especially when he talked about his work. Our relationship was as easy as it was simple. We were dating, but it wasn't too serious. He wasn't going to meet my parents anytime soon. We liked each other, and we liked spending time together when we could around our work.

And that was it. The ease of our relationship was a welcomed change. Just about the easiest thing in my life at the moment. I turned on the TV. The news blared as I fought to turn it down.

"Yes, you heard that right, Vin. A group of children were dropped off in front of the precinct, along with a body. The identity of the man has not been released at this time, nor are they releasing the names of the children. We know nine children were left outside the station. We don't know where they came from, but we will update this developing story when we receive more details."

I stared at the screen, waiting for the reporter to say something else. I wanted…needed more details. How did the children get there? Where had they come from? And what about the dead body? Who was the man? Did the children see who killed him? Were they there when it happened? Did they do it? How old were they? What conditions were they found in? Where were their parents?

The first thought that popped into my mind that wasn't a question was Dane and his sister Yumi. I wondered for a brief moment if the children found were the victims of the child trafficking ring Dane had tried to put an end to. He killed a lot of people when he figured out who took his sister.

Yumi was taken from their front yard when they were young children. He never saw her again. She was taken by a trafficking ring that dealt in all manners of flesh. Originally, I thought they only dealt with children, but they also dealt with adults and helping people find potential murder victims.

Wherever the children were being held, it was good that they were safe now. I turned the TV off so I could focus on getting ready. I wasn't sure what I wanted to wear tonight. Something slinky, maybe. I glanced down at my watch. I needed to start getting ready, at least.

I took a long hot bath in vanilla and lavender bubble bath. The hot water eased the tension I had been holding in my shoulders and upper back. Outside the tub, perusing my closet, I settled on a blood-red curve-hugging dress. I had never worn it before. The tag still dangled from the tag in the back. I had meant to wear it before now, I just hadn't had a reason. Tonight was as good a night as any.

After I finished getting ready, I checked my phone for the time. It was almost eight-thirty. I completed the outfit with a gold watch and a matching necklace and bracelet. After filling a clutch that I rarely used, I was ready.

Harrison knocked on my door twenty minutes later in a black suit, black shirt, and a red tie, almost the same shade as my dress.

"Look at you!" A giggle bubbled up my throat.

He grinned. "You look as beautiful as ever."

I did my best curtsy. "Well, thank you." We got onto the elevator, and I hooked my arm in his. "Where are we going?"

"A really nice restaurant I heard about from a colleague. He said the food was amazing."

"I'm all for that."

He grinned. "I know."

I nudged him with my elbow. It was well-known how much I liked food. Tony told everyone. I wasn't a foodie or anything. I just enjoyed good food…that I didn't have to cook myself.

BREAKFAST IN PARADISE

The restaurant had a sleek, upscale look with its limited number of round tables set with white tablecloths. The floors were a polished dark wood, and each table was lit by a crystal chandelier.

Harrison pulled out my chair for me, and I sat down. A waiter appeared next to our table with a drink menu. Harrison ordered a bottle of red wine that I couldn't pronounce the name of, and the waiter disappeared.

"Fancy," I said with a grin.

"Figured it would be nice to treat ourselves for the night. Get away from work."

I smiled. It was difficult for both of us to take off our work hats at the end of the day and focus on other things. But tonight, I would give it a try. No work talk. I kept my phone in my purse and refused to pull it out. I read the menu and settled on a steak with roasted potatoes, garlic, and butter string beans.

Harrison ordered the same except he got quinoa and a beat and goat cheese salad. We spent our time between the waiter's visits to the table and our small bites of food, talking, but it was difficult to avoid talking about work. Too difficult. I needed to focus on other things more often.

We talked about our lives and what we wanted for the future. I wasn't sure at first what I wanted for the rest of my life. He wanted to get married and have kids, eventually. I wasn't so sure. Marriage maybe. But I was getting less and less sure about the kids every day.

"I just. With the things I've seen... having children... bringing them into this world... I don't know if I can do that. I mean, their getting hurt is a strong possibility... or them hurting me or hurting someone else. Having a child is like breathing new pain in the world."

He tilted his head. "You could also be breathing new hope into this world. And that's something the world desperately needs."

He had a point. Hope was needed, but I still wasn't sure about it. We talked about our families and how much we loved them. And then we talked about our coworkers.

"Tony seems nice."

"He is. He wasn't when I first met him. Or, I mean, he was quieter."

"Why?" He placed his knife and fork on the plate and wiped the corners of his mouth.

I shrugged. "I think he was testing me, trying to figure out what I knew and how fast I could put things together."

He smiled.

"But he's been nice. A great partner."

Harrison told me about his new assistant, and how he didn't think she would last. "She seems jumpy. Like she's afraid of the people I treat. I can't have that in the office, you know. I need patients to be put at ease the second they walk through the door. I don't think she can do that."

After dinner, we walked out of the restaurant, the night air cool and relaxing. A soft breeze blew through my hair, and I smiled.

"Why don't we go for a walk?" His hand fit perfectly in the small of my back as he guided me down the sidewalk. "I'm not really ready to go home."

I sighed. "Yeah, me either."

CHAPTER FOUR

My hand brushed the pillow next to me, and my eyes opened immediately. The cold spot told me Harrison had been gone for a long while. I glanced at the clock, the bright red numbers blurred at first and then slowly came into focus. It was almost seven.

Harrison always left early in the morning. Very early. Most mornings, he stopped by the hospital before going to the office. I admired how dedicated he was to his work and his patients.

I rolled onto my side for a long moment. I should have gotten up and gone to the gym. I should have gone for a run. The exercise part of my New Year's resolution hadn't yet come to fruition. I still hadn't gotten back into my routine of running and working out before work. It made me feel better when I did it. I just couldn't keep at it.

And I wasn't going to get back to it this morning, either. I sat up. My feet touched the cool hardwood floor, and a shiver ran down my spine. After I glanced at the clock for the second time, I decided I needed to go ahead and get in the shower.

I sent a text to Tony before heading to the bathroom. He had started spending more nights at his girlfriend's place. I never knew when he was staying over or not. When he did, I drove myself to work. I still preferred him driving, but I could if I needed to. And I needed to often lately.

After my shower, I checked my phone. Tony had texted me back, saying he was, in fact, in his condo and would meet me in the lobby in an hour.

This told me two things. That Aisha had spent the night at his place for a change, and that I didn't have to make breakfast for him this morning. That was another one of our daily routines that had fallen away. I wasn't salty about it... well, maybe a little bit.

I got dressed and got all my things together. After a cup of coffee and a slice of buttered toast, I made my way to the lobby. Aisha and Tony shared a lingering kiss by the door before she pushed him back, smiled, and walked out.

"Oh, would you two get a room?"

He spun around, eyes wide. "This is a room."

"Not a common area."

He laughed as I followed him outside. The morning air was cool against my skin.

"Did you hear about the fire?"

I followed behind him as we walked to the car. I didn't know what he was talking about. The only thing I saw on the news was about the children that were left at a police station.

"No, I don't think so. What fire?"

"The Golden Paradise."

I was quiet. He turned around to look at me and noticed my blank stare. I had no idea what he was talking about, and now he knew I didn't. A ghost of a smile touched his lips.

"It was a bed-and-breakfast. I took Aisha there just a few weeks ago. It was beautiful. Outside and inside. Just far away enough from the neighbors that it was like being on your own slice of the island. And there weren't a lot of guests there the weekend we went."

"And it burned down?"

He opened the driver's side door. "It did. From what I heard, it was in complete ruins. There's nothing left."

"Oh, that's a shame. Was it arson?" I asked once I got in the car and closed the door.

He shrugged next to me. "I don't know. Last I heard, arson was suspected. It was such a beautiful place. People around here are real sad about it."

I had never heard of the place, but I, too, was a little sad to see it go. His sadness was contagious. It was a somber drive to the field office.

"How was your day off?" he asked in the elevator.

I shrugged. "It was nice. I went with Hattie and the girls to the beach and then to brunch, where I had one too many mimosas. Then I went home and fell asleep. And then, I went to dinner with Harrison."

"And how was that?" He pressed his shoulder against mine. "What did you guys do?"

I rolled my eyes. I recounted our date while avoiding Tony's smirking face. "And what did you do?"

"Nothing really." He wiggled his hands back into his pockets. "I slept mostly. Aisha had to work, and she went over briefs for most of the day. It was quiet and nice."

"Yeah, it was. Nice not thinking about murder suspects or victims."

He nodded slowly. I didn't realize how much I needed the break until I woke up this morning refreshed and ready for the day. It was nice getting away from work for a while and not thinking or talking about it. Not thinking about it was difficult, but when I had other things to distract me, it was easy enough.

When the elevator doors slid open, Hattie caught my eye, and she walked over to my desk.

"I think you two might have a case. It's being decided right now, so be ready," she said, staring at her tablet.

"What case?" Tony walked over to his desk and sat down. "Another strange murder? Possible serial killer?"

She shook her head for a moment but then stopped. She tilted her head to the side and looked up at the ceiling as if she were thinking about something. "I'm not sure how strange or if it is a serial killer or anything. I suppose it is possible. But for right now, it looks like arson with a suspicious death."

"The Golden Paradise?" Tony stared at Hattie, eyes wide and alert.

"Yup. The owner was found burnt to a crisp, but her body was twisted and in bad shape. Hard to say whether it was murder or not, but for right now, I think they suspect it is."

Tony shook his head. "Mrs. Hardwell was a nice woman. Who would want to hurt her?" He sighed, and his body went limp in his chair. "She was really, really nice." The sorrow in his voice made Hattie look up from her tablet.

"That's what people keep saying. Everyone said how nice and great she was. And that there were no problems that they saw on the property. I don't know if the FBI is taking over the case just yet, but I was told to put you on standby."

She walked over to an agent and left us in silence. Tony seemed shaken by the news. He stared at nothing for a long moment. I left him to it. As the seconds ticked by in silence, I took the time to clean off my desk and finish a report I had been holding onto. I hated filing reports, but we all had to do it. Once done, I filed it away and returned to my desk.

Tony stared at his computer.

"You want to talk about it?" I looked at my screen and waited for an answer. Tony didn't like talking about his feelings. He would if he had to, but he preferred not to. He was the kind of person who liked to sort through their own thoughts alone. I tried to give him that space when I thought he needed it. Now, he looked like he could use a distraction.

"No. I don't know why I'm... it was only a place I had been to once."

I could have told him the answer. Maybe it was all the time I had been spending with a psychiatrist, but I knew why he was so upset. He and Aisha hadn't decided if they still wanted to get married or not. They probably hadn't even talked about it. This caused a lot of animosity in their relationship that everyone noticed.

BREAKFAST IN PARADISE

Every time she was in the same room as him, it seemed like she hated him. Like it was difficult for her to be in the same room as him. It had been clear to me that they had a history, and it hadn't had a happy ending. Their time at the bed-and-breakfast was their first getaway since they had gotten back together. I suspected that was why it had such a special meaning to him. I could have told him that. I could have also mentioned that he might view the building going up in smoke as a warning of how their second-chance relationship might end. I swallowed my comments. It was none of my business, really, and he didn't ask for my input.

"Do you want to go to the crime scene?" If it was going to be our case in the end, we should probably get a jump on the investigation. And I wanted to see just how much of the building was left. Tony made it seem like the entire building had been burned to ash. I wasn't sure if that was possible. Surely, even in a fire fed by an accelerant, there had to be something left behind.

I had never investigated a fire before, and I was curious. He regarded the question for a long moment, his head slowly nodding.

"Sure. Might as well."

I told Hattie to call us once she knew whether we were getting the case or not, and we headed to the bed-and-breakfast. I didn't have to tell Tony the address because he already knew it. Like he had it memorized or something. The scene laid out before me was far worse than I had imagined. I hadn't seen it on the news like Tony, and walking up to it now was distressing.

It might have once been beautiful. A gorgeous hideaway for couples, but now it was black rubble. Burnt wood. Scattered ashes. It was hard to look at. Police still roamed the area, although I couldn't tell what they were looking for. There was nothing there.

A crime scene van sat next to a large truck near the driveway. Crime scene techs sifted through the remains of the building. Some of the bones of the house were still up, but most of it had fallen down. Tony inhaled sharply as we neared the remains of the home.

"It was so beautiful. I wished you could have seen it before..." He gestured to the scene around us. "This."

I could see it...the beauty that might have once been there. The house was in ruins, but the gardens around the house, the area that had not been kissed by fire, was beautiful. Greens, purples, pinks and reds. Bright and lush and out of place with the charred mess before me. It looked like, when the bed-and-breakfast was standing, the views must have been beautiful.

I turned around and saw the ocean. The sounds of the waves crashing against the cliff below us were calming. Amazing sound to go to sleep to.

"It seems like it would have been beautiful," I said mostly to myself.

"Can I help you two?" A tech walked over to us with an evidence bag in his hand.

I held up my badge. He nodded slowly. "I figured the FBI might be taking over the case. We don't really have anything for you. Not since the body was taken away."

"Was it just the one body?" asked Tony.

"As far as we could tell. Sometimes, if the fire was hot enough, the bones could...mold together, for lack of better words. If they are in close proximity. But I don't think that happened here. It seems like everyone else made it out. But we are still sifting through the remains for any signs of bones or other signs another person might have been caught in the fire. So far, nothing."

"Okay. Thank you."

He walked away. My eyes scanned over the ruins. The sound of car doors slamming behind me jolted me back to reality.

CHAPTER FIVE

"I take it you two are the FBI agents." A woman meandered toward us, a cigarette between her fingers unlit. She wore jeans and a white tank top. A dragon's head tattoo poked out from her shoulder.

I looked at her and her partner, another woman with fiery red hair and light brown eyes.

"We are," said Tony.

The women exchanged a knowing glance.

"I'm Detective Branson, and this is my partner Detective Dumas." Branson used her cigarette to point at the woman next to her. They resembled each other slightly. I figured that was what happened when two people were partners for such a long time. Dumas was taller, while Branson had a more voluptuous body, but they wore identical facial expressions. "I hear you two will be taking over our case."

I stilled for a moment, trying to read her tone. Even though there had been an emphasis on *our*, there wasn't an ounce of animosity in her tone. Local detectives usually hated it when the FBI butted in and started taking over their cases. They were quite territorial about it. It was understandable. I would have hated it if someone had come in and tried to take over all my hard work. Some agents did so gingerly, while others lacked the tact or empathy.

"I guess we are," I said. "Hope that won't cause any problems."

Branson smiled. "Not a one. I figured it would happen judging by the list of suspects. All out of state. You have better resources to deal with them. Just makes sense."

"So, what are we dealing with?" Tony rocked back on his heels, his hands deep in his pockets. The fire had long been put out, and yet heat still radiated from the ground.

"Fire started in the owner's quarters. Beth Hardwell owned the bed-and-breakfast. It's a shame. She just really got it off the ground." Branson explained that the place hadn't done so well in the beginning. It needed a lot of work. More than Beth had anticipated, and she and her husband ended up doing most of it.

"Just started to take off. Became a main attraction on the island recently after a tourist magazine or something wrote about it. But anyway... one of the guests was the first to notice the fire, and he ran through the house, knocking on doors to let everyone know. He ended up having to jump out of the window with another guest to get out."

"And everyone got out?" I looked back at the charred remains of the house.

"Everyone except Beth Hardwell. A body was found, but it was pretty burnt. The fire marshal suspects arson. He said there was something wrong with the body, but he couldn't figure it out before she was taken away."

"What do you think?" asked Tony. Like Tony, I wanted to know their first impressions of the case and the scene, especially if anything stood out to them.

Her eyes roamed over the burnt scene as if she was searching for something. There was nothing there, not really. The house had practically burned down completely. The door and

BREAKFAST IN PARADISE

most of the windows were gone. The earth around the house was black, and it was hard to discern what was on the ground, burnt wood, glass, luggage. It was all one.

"I just find it strange that the bed-and-breakfast burned down without those guests in it. And how it got so out of control so quickly," Dumas said.

"I'm not sure if the guest did it or not. I mean..." She lit the cigarette and took a long drag before she continued. "It would make sense. The owner was dead, and they were, for all we know, the only ones there. I just find it strange that they would come all the way out of state to kill this woman and burn down her bed-and-breakfast. I just can't picture someone going out of their way like that... and not leaving. Like I would have done it and then ran out of the house while it was on fire."

"But all the guests are accounted for?" I asked.

She nodded slowly. Smoke billowed in the air, and it seemed so strange. Hours ago, smoke blanketed the area, and then here she was adding to it. And from the looks of it, she thought nothing of it. "All guests were accounted for. Sure, they could be covering up for someone, but I believe the records have been burned."

"So we don't know truly how many guests there were. We just know what they tell us." I shook my head. It didn't sit right with me. Surely, she could have had electronic records as well. Not just paper ones. It would have made more sense. These days, everything is done through the Internet. Guests would have had to book a room online. Well, unless they stop by to look for vacancies. But who did that?

"What about a computer or online booking system?" I asked.

A smile tugged at Branson's lips. "We can't find her computer. It could be with the remains of the house, but it would be charred. I'm sure the FBI could figure out a way around that, though."

I sighed. Love might be able to do it. I wasn't sure how, but it was worth asking her. I shrugged. "Maybe. Have to ask our tech department, and they both love and hate it when we bring them difficult tasks." Love loved being challenged. Even though she groaned before agreeing to take it on, she always agreed.

"Good." She tossed her cigarette on the ground and stamped it out. "Let's see... what else can I tell you... The files are already on their way to your field office. Along with our initial notes and a list of her family and friends and who you might want to talk to."

"Is there anyone in particular you think we should speak with?" asked Tony. He glanced back at me, and then his eyes searched the rubble before settling back on her.

"I would put her ex-husband at the top of my list." She smiled at Tony. "You know there are no secrets around here, and Mrs. Hardwell was well known. Her first husband left her because of this place. I always thought that was why she was so determined to make it work. To show him it wasn't a waste of time. That's why I was rooting for her and was happy to see it doing so well lately. I heard they didn't part on good terms. There was a lot of animosity there on both sides. She sunk a lot of money into this place... his money. Their savings, and then there is her second husband who kind of disappeared."

I blinked. My ears perked up. "Disappeared?"

"Rumor has it... he left her. He was tired of working on the place and renovating it, and he just up and left in the middle of the night. There is also a rumor that he left her for another woman. My mother believes that last one."

Dumas shook her head. "The rumor mill on the island moves fast. There's no truth to most of it."

Branson shrugged. "I don't know. Isla, in the property room, said he was having an affair and that he left with the woman in the middle of the night. Her aunt lives close by."

"Please! Isla wouldn't know the truth if you beat her with it."

A chuckle bubbled up my throat. We said goodbye to the detectives. They turned around and walked back to their car. The area was quiet and peaceful. It smelled of burnt wood and burnt plastic. The remains of the bed-and-breakfast had been sifted through already. I assumed that whatever they found would be sent to our lab for our techs to look over.

I moved around the burnt rubble. I wasn't looking for anything in particular. I just wanted to walk around the crime scene. My eyes roamed over the scene, not settling on anything. Not searching for anything, just looking. I wondered, for a brief moment, what it must have been like for Mrs. Hardwell. I tried to stop my mind from going there, but I couldn't help it. Had she been dead before the fire was started, or did she die from smoke inhalation? Had she been passed out before the fire consumed her body? It was a horrible thought.

A shiver coasted down my spine. I didn't want to think about it. Burning alive was a horrible way to die, conscious or unconscious. If her body was as charred as they said, we would probably never know what really happened to her or if she was alive when it happened. Her lungs were probably gone, burned to ash. Jill wouldn't be able to tell if she was still breathing when the fire went up.

"Horrible way to die." Tony's voice snapped me back to reality, back to the moment.

"Right? Horrible. I hope she was dead before the fire touched her."

"But that would make it a murder," Tony pointed out.

"Well, we're better at solving murder than arson, right?" I glanced around what remained of the building. "What could make a fire burn this fast and this hot?" I asked mostly to myself. I wasn't looking for an answer, but then one presented itself.

"Well—"

I jumped. My heart raced as I turned around. I had forgotten the fire marshal was still there. He smiled.

"Didn't mean to startle you. But to answer your question, there was an accelerant used."

"Gasoline?" I asked once my heart rate had calmed down.

He shook his head. A mop of strawberry blonde curls moved about his head, shimmering in the sun. "No. if it had been gas, we would have smelled it. Didn't smell any gas at the scene last night. If I had to make a guess, I would say paint thinner. Still need to check to be sure but she was doing some repairs and painting."

"She was?" Tony stepped forward, hands still in his pockets.

He nodded. "One of the guests told us. He said they were going to be the last guests until she finished the repairs and repainting some of the rooms. She might have had paint thinner lying around. And he said she was going to paint in her bedroom, which is where I believe she was found. Or at least on the side of the house."

"How fast did the house burn?" I asked.

He regarded the question for a long moment. "When I got here, the fire was already out of control. Firefighters had to back out of the house because there was nothing left we could do. The structure was falling apart. I would say thirty minutes."

"Is that unusual?" I inched closer to him.

"It did go up quickly. And the plants around here didn't help any. And there was a lot of wood furniture in the home. I know because my wife and I came here last year for a weekend away. There was a lot of wood furniture and easy kindling for the fire. By the time the guest noticed it...the back of the house was already engulfed. It was moving into the kitchen, and then, he said, once it got there, by the time he went upstairs and started banging on doors, the entire downstairs was on fire. It was like someone left a trail of paint thinner or another accelerant throughout the house so it would catch faster. So naturally, this is being ruled arson."

"Electrical panel is okay? No way this could have been an accident, not the murder but the fire?" asked Tony.

He shook his head. "No." He was adamant. "I've been at this a long time, and nothing about this scene reads accident. And the electrical panel had been replaced already. It was one of the new upgrades she had done. There was nothing electrically wrong with this house." There was an edge to his voice. He was not happy about having his expertise questioned. Tony meant no harm. I knew that. The fire marshal did not.

"Just needed to be sure before we started the investigation. We trust your judgment," I said. He looked at me then, eyes softening, before he gave a curt nod.

"I understand. I guess I'm still on edge. This could have been a lot worse than it was. There are some dried branches around the house. If they had caught fire...it could have easily jumped around. Moved to the other houses. We are all lucky it stayed here. It's a horrible thing to say since someone has died, but still. We are."

Before he walked away, he told us he would send over his reports once they were finished. I thanked him for his time. At

BREAKFAST IN PARADISE

that moment, I wanted nothing more than to get out of that burnt field. Everything was dead. A chill ran through me. A chill so deep I felt it in my bones despite the bright sun that hung over us. The sky was blue and bright with no clouds or promise of rain. Birds sang and the wind blew pleasantly, eerie and unnerving as a backdrop to the charred bones of a home.

I stepped away, inching towards the car. His footsteps followed close behind me. Back in the car, Tony's hand stilled over the ignition. "I really liked this place. Wanted to come back, eventually." His eyes seemed to glaze over as he stared out the window. As he settled back into himself, the car roared to life, and he pulled out of the driveway.

Why would someone go through the trouble of killing Mrs. Hardwell and burning down the bed-and-breakfast?

I didn't want to say it was the husband, but it was almost always the husband or the boyfriend. Her husband, or rather husbands, might have had several reasons to kill her. I would have said both of them, initially, but her first husband might have had more of a reason to have her killed. If he had life insurance on her and on the house, it might have been worth killing her.

And what about her second husband? Where was he? The thought nagged at me the entire way back to the field office. How could he just disappear? Did he leave the island? It was so strange I couldn't stop thinking about it.

It plagued my mind as I entered the building and when I got to my desk. I sat down and sighed as I wondered how we could find him. Did he care about his wife and her death, or was he somewhere else snuggled under his mistress without a care in the word?

But more importantly, I wondered if they were still married. Whatever prompted him to leave, surely she must have divorced him by now. How long had it been? I knew all too well that just because they had separated, just because he had left her, didn't mean she would divorce him.

My Aunt Tamara's husband left her years ago. They had an argument one night when I was twelve. It was loud and violent. The children were made to stay upstairs. My parents had tried to stay out of it, but after what felt like hours of screaming, I heard my father. First his footsteps pounding down the stairs and then his voice. Loud, octaves above theirs. His voice had silenced them. His words after that were muffled. He did it on purpose. He spoke in a way only they could hear, and then it was quiet. The front door slammed shut, and then a car door. And then nothing.

My uncle never came back. But my aunt never divorced him. They were still married on paper even though, last I heard, he lived with a woman in Miami and had two children by her.

I couldn't say why my aunt never divorced him. He had clearly moved on. She never did, though. Never dated either. Now that I was older, I figured it was because she still had hope. She loved her husband and hoped one day he would come back to her. I doubted it. Everyone in the family doubted it.

I sent a text to Love asking if she could hack into the website for the bed-and-breakfast and see who else might have booked a room. She sent a text back and said she could try. I sent her the information. I was staring at my phone when a folder was dropped on my desk.

"And what is this?" I looked up. Hattie stood next to my desk, smiling.

"The files from the local PD. They sent them right over. We also have the guests' locations. Put them up in a hotel nearby. All their belongings that were in the house during the fire are gone. Which, for most, includes their phones."

A gasp escaped me. I hadn't thought about their phones and what they had lost in the fire. Their wallets. Their IDs. They had lost everything they had brought with them. Most probably hadn't thought about grabbing anything on their way out. I wouldn't have.

I ran through my routine as soon as I walked through the door of my condo. I took off my shoes, took my wallet and phone out of my pocket, and placed it on the console by the door. I usually didn't think about them again until I was leaving. If I ever lost my phone, I wouldn't know who to call or how to call them, their numbers not locked in my memory. The only one I knew by heart was my mother's. And she was back home. "They must be horrified," I said.

Hattie shook her head. "Very shaken. They were all so busy trying to get out that they didn't think about their stuff. Who does when the house is on fire? If it wasn't in their pockets, most of them wouldn't have it. I read through some of the notes, and one person didn't think about anything until they were already outside, and by then, they were too afraid to go back in. Can you imagine?"

I shook my head immediately. I had never been in a fire. Thank God. And I prayed I never would. It must have been horrifying. A million things would have run through my mind if my building caught on fire. But the most immediate one, the thought that would scream louder than all the rest, would be *run*! And to look for Tony would probably be the second.

I would have been terrified. Perhaps too terrified to move. Maybe that was what happened to Mrs. Hardwell. She saw the fire and was too scared to move, to run. Maybe that part of the crime was an accident. The fire might have been started on purpose, but maybe she was just an accidental casualty.

It didn't matter though. The person responsible for the fire was still guilty of her death, accident or not. Hattie was called away by another agent while I stared at the folders. Even though the two detectives had just gotten the case, it was only two days old, they had collected a lot of evidence and conducted a lot of interviews.

I was eager to know everything they did and saw and everyone they spoke to. But more importantly, I was eager to learn who Beth Hardwell was and why someone would burn down her business.

CHAPTER SIX

Instead of going over the file at this very moment, I wanted to go back to the scene. I asked Tony if he wanted to join me, and we could go to lunch after or before. He said before.

Aunt Mai's was busy during lunch, as usual, but we were able to find a table in the very back. Once we sat down, a waitress hurried over to take our drink orders.

"Sorry. I just want to go ahead and get it in before things get too out of hand," said the young waitress. She looked new, maybe in her early twenties or still a teenager with big doe eyes and purple hair. She smiled, but her eyes said she was tired.

We ordered our drinks and our food. I opted for a sandwich, while Tony wanted a poke bowl. We both tried to keep it simple.

"Why do you want to go back to the house?" he asked as he leaned on the table.

"Just something I didn't think of until we had gotten back and I was at my desk. I thought it would have been nice to talk to the neighbors. I don't know if Branson did or not, but I wanted to hear what they had to say on my own." Learning information secondhand during investigations worked most of the time, but sometimes, it was best to hear it for yourself when possible.

We learned so much from interviews. Sometimes, it wasn't just what a person said but how they said it. Their body language and eye contact while they spoke. There were several factors that helped us understand what was being said. I wanted to see the neighbors. I wanted to know what they thought of Mrs. Hardwell and the bed-and-breakfast. Did they like it? Did they want it to move to a different neighborhood?

Did they like Mrs. Hardwell? Did she like them? Was there someone who hated her? Where did her husband go?

The neighborhood seemed old the last time we were there. Tony had said it was mostly retirees that lived there, which was why it was so quiet.

"It's filled with retirees, which was a good idea. People come to the bed-and-breakfast to get away. It's a nice, quiet place. Secret hideaway. There are no young children in the neighborhood. Not that I've ever seen. I read a review when I was looking into places we could go, and one of them said that the neighborhood was quiet because everyone was fifty or older, retired, and had grown children."

If you wanted to spend a quiet weekend with your boyfriend or girlfriend, a quiet place in a quiet area was ideal. I figured since they were retired, they might have spent a lot of time looking out their windows. For a moment, I remembered a neighbor we had once. He was in his sixties and lived alone. Never married and never had any children. Mr. Henry Lester was an ornery old man who seemed to hate everyone. Especially children. When we walked by his home, he was always in the window staring daggers at us. Like he dared us to touch, to even look at his property. I never did, though. I hated his house.

I hated his entire lot. It was always so dark, like the sun, too, was afraid to touch his property. But he was always home and rarely ventured out except to get groceries and go to the post office. When one of the houses across the street had been vandalized, everyone turned their attention to him. Not because they thought he had done it but because they knew he had seen who it was. He never told our neighbors who drew the obscene pictures on the house. He wouldn't even answer the door when they walked over to ask. But he stood in the window and watched. He was always watching.

If the neighbors around the bed-and-breakfast were anything like Mr. Lester, they knew something. Something about the fire. Or something about Mr. Hardwell.

The waitress returned without food. We ate quickly, not wanting to hold up the table. A line was forming outside, and the people looked restless.

"I wonder if they liked having a bed-and-breakfast in their neighborhood."

Tony's eyebrow raised slightly as he chewed his food.

"I mean, as you remember, you didn't like living next to the Airbnb that your neighbor turned their house into. That was why you moved. I wonder if the neighbors, any of the neighbors, had the same feelings on the bed-and-breakfast."

His head tilted slightly as he pondered the statement. "I never thought about it. When I was there, it was just us and another couple. It was so quiet it was almost like we were the only ones there. I guess there could have been some rowdy guests that might have upset the neighbors. You think that was why this happened?"

I shrugged as I finished my sandwich. "I'm not sure. It was just a thought, really. Could be why the building was burned down, so there wouldn't be a bed-and-breakfast in the neighborhood anymore. Maybe her death was an accident."

He nodded slowly. "Yeah, I guess that could be possible. I know I came close to burning that house down a couple of times. Especially in the middle of the night with the music thumping." He shook his head. "Noise-canceling headphones didn't even work."

"Good thing it's over."

He finished his food, and I paid the tab this time. We rotated paying for lunch. That way, one of us wasn't always paying for it.

BREAKFAST IN PARADISE

Tony always wanted to pay, and that made me feel bad. As soon as we stood up, there was a sharp inhale from the patrons waiting near the door. We left, and someone took our place. They seemed really excited about it.

"Aunt Mai is really taking off," I said as we walked back to the car.

Tony chuckled. "Yeah. I told her the other day she was getting too famous for us. She laughed and agreed."

That made me laugh. I could hear her voice agreeing with him in a partly sarcastic way. Her diner had really taken off lately. It wasn't surprising, though, because the food was amazing, and the staff was always so friendly and filled with people who had lived on the island for years. It was one of those places where, when you walked in, someone either knew you by name or knew you from around the island. It felt homey.

The neighborhood was surprisingly quiet. There had been a fire, and yet no one was outside walking around. No one was on the front porch watching the crime scene tech vans drive away. We drove through the neighborhood and then stopped in the driveway of the Golden Paradise. Techs were still combing the scene.

Best not to bother them. Instead of going near the house, we turned around and started to walk. I stopped near the closest house to the Paradise.

The two-story home was painted light gray with black trim and a bright, almost magenta door. It was beautiful. The door popped against the gray and black and blended with the array of pink flowers in the yard. It was gorgeous and made me wish I had lived there or had that kind of home. Someone took great care of it, especially the flowers in the yard. They must have spent every morning in their yard.

I walked up to the door, and Tony's footsteps followed close behind. I knocked twice. After a long moment of silence, the door opened. Slow at first. I held up my badge, and then the door opened wider. A woman with light gray hair wearing a pair of bright pink jeans and a gray and pink top stood in the doorway. Her cat-eye glasses were pink-rimmed and matched her pants. She was striking. In her fifties, maybe, but it was clear she took care of herself, probably by doing yardwork every morning. She smiled slightly.

"Is this about the fire next door?"

I smiled and nodded as I tucked my badge back into my pocket. "Yes, ma'am. I am Special Agent Storm, and this is my partner, Special Agent Walker. If you don't mind, can we come in and speak with you for a moment about your neighbor?"

"Of course. Come in. I was just making some tea." She ushered us into her home and closed the door. "Follow me to the kitchen." Her home was warm and inviting. It looked lived in but not overly so. There was a faint scent of something burning, but I suspected that it was because of the fire.

Underneath the slight smell of smoke, there was vanilla, sugar, and butter.

"You're just in time. I made some sugar cookies to go with my tea."

We followed her through the house into the kitchen. It was a straight shot from the front door to the back door in the kitchen. Rooms branched off from the long hallway. I caught glimpses of brightly colored walls and equally bright furniture as I followed her.

"What is your name?"

She laughed. "Sorry. Excuse my manners. I'm Judith Oakley. Were you able to find Beth?" She gestured to the round glass table. There were four bright teal chairs around the table.

The walls were a bright pink, but everything else was teal: the color of the chairs, even the appliances. I didn't know they were made in that color. The cabinets were black, and the backsplash had different hues of pink. There was a lot going on, yet it all seemed to work together. It was quite beautiful. I didn't think I would do it in my kitchen, but it worked for her and her style. Pink was clearly her color.

I sat at the table, and Tony sat across from me.

"Cookies smell amazing," he said.

A smile bloomed on her lips. "My favorite kind. Well, these and strawberry shortcake with white chocolate chips and pecans, but I'm trying to cut back on my sugar." She looked down at the plate of cookies she carried to the table. "As best

I can." She grinned. "Can't cut all the sugar out of my diet. It would make me very angry."

"I get that," I said as I eyed the cookies. Tony shook his head and smiled. The tea kettle screamed as steam billowed in the air above the stove. She ran back and took it off the burner.

"I hope you don't mind chamomile."

I smiled. I liked chamomile tea. It was my favorite because it was nice and calming. Cups, saucers, and a container of sugar and cream were arranged in front of us. I put a little cream in my cup first and then poured in the tea. I liked cream or milk with more floral teas like chamomile and jasmine. It made it taste better to me.

"Now, your questions." She sat at the head of the table and placed a saucer in front of us with two cookies each. They were still warm and crunchy around the edges but soft in the middle. I moaned despite myself with the first bite.

Mrs. Oakley giggled. "What do you want to know about Beth?"

While I finished chewing, Tony started talking.

"We just want to know anything you can tell us about her. Anything that might seem important. What kind of person she was, or if there was anything strange going on at the Paradise."

Mrs. Oakley's eyes narrowed at Tony. Her face softened for a moment. "I can't believe she's dead. She was so kind. Such a kind woman. I don't know who would want to hurt her."

"Well, we aren't sure whether it is murder."

"But it was arson?"

I nodded and then sipped my tea.

"The Paradise was beautiful. She did all that work herself, you know?"

"Herself?" I glanced at Tony who chewed on a cookie.

Mrs. Oakley waved a hand dismissively. "I don't mean she got a hammer and nails and went to work. I just mean that she mostly paid for it herself. She oversaw the work, and she designed everything. She was very hands-on. I told her she could just hire someone to design it and do all the work, but she didn't want to do that. She knew what it looked like in her head, and so she had to be the one to guide them."

"Sounds like a lot of work," said Tony.

"Sounds expensive," I added.

Mrs. Oakley pointed at me like I had given the right answer to a silent question. "It was hard work and expensive. She sank a lot of money in that place. Part of me is happy she's dead, so she didn't have to see it all go up in flames. Assuming she was dead before the fire." Her eyes flicked between us expectantly, but neither of us confirmed her suspicion.

A smile bloomed on her lips. "Her first husband left her because of all the money. Beth never told me the whole story, I don't think, but I heard bits here and there. She wanted to make it into something beautiful, and I think at first he wanted to make her happy."

"When did that change?" I asked.

"Early on. When it became clear that she cared more about the house than him. She loved that place, and she wanted to make it the best it could be. Unfortunately, her husband kept a tight leash on their bank account. But she still found a way. Almost wiped their savings out completely before he realized it. Their marriage was over soon after. He was so angry. I heard him yelling all the way over here."

"It's understandable if she wiped out their savings without talking to him about it. That's a level of disrespect and selfishness that's difficult to get past," said Tony. Mrs. Oakley nodded in agreement.

"I know. I know. I never understood her fascination with it. I think at first it was supposed to be a place of business, you know? She knew early on she wanted to use it as a source of income. But after he left, and after their big blow-up... I think then she was more determined. She was determined to make it a success just to prove him wrong."

"And by then, she had already sunk so much into it that it was too late to turn back. She had to keep going. If she didn't—"

"She would have looked like a fool," said Mrs. Oakley. "And she still, in some ways, looked like a fool until her second husband. Then it was like she found someone who finally shared her vision... but then he left too. I guess nothing is ever as it seems."

CHAPTER SEVEN

SHE HAD A POINT. EVERYONE HAD THEIR SECRETS. AND nothing was ever what it seemed. People often had two versions of themselves, if not more. One, they showed the world and then who they really were. Mrs. Hardwell could have been holding parts of herself back.

I found it interesting that both of her husbands left her for different reasons. Or it might have been the same reasons. Her second husband disappeared in the middle of the night. He could have left because she was sinking all their money back into the business, and maybe he was tired of it.

"Have you seen anything strange around here?" I asked, nibbling on the crispy edges of a cookie.

Mrs. Oakley stared off, her eyes set on the teapot but not really seeing it. It was like she was there, but she wasn't there for a long moment. She pressed her lips into a firm, thin line while she thought. I sipped my tea and looked at Tony. He shrugged.

"Well," she said finally, "I did see something strange last night. At first, I thought nothing of it. I thought it might have been one of the guests walking around. They do that, you know. But after the fire..." She shook her head.

"Anything you can remember helps," I told her.

"I saw him; at least, I assume it was a man. I didn't see his face. He wore all black, and he walked around the property. I was worried about it. I guess I should have been."

"Did he have anything in his hands?" asked Tony.

She regarded the question for a moment and shook her head. "Not that I can remember. He just looked like he was walking around. Getting some air. His hands were in his pockets, and his body was turned away from me." She sipped her tea. "You know who might know? The neighbors across the street."

The houses in the neighborhood were not directly next to or across from each other. They were all off center. The neighbor might have lived across the street, but it was across the street and a few steps to the left. It gave all the houses room to breathe, to grow.

"What makes you think they know anything?"

She smiled at me. "If you think I'm a gossip, where do you think I get all my information from? They know everything."

I thought she was the neighborhood gossip, but she was just the receiver of the information. At least she baked you cookies and made tea while she gossiped. It was like a nice warm treat with a side of information. We left Mrs. Oakley after she packed us both Ziploc bags filled with cookies. I was giddy about my cookies, and Tony thought it was funny. I insisted on locking them up in the car before we went to the house across the street.

"Locking up your cookies." He shook his head as we headed back.

"Don't want to leave them anywhere."

A ghost of a smile kissed his lips. He was always making fun of me about my love for food. I took my free cookies and set them gently in the backseat. He laughed harder.

"Shut up."

BREAKFAST IN PARADISE

The neighbors across the street lived in a drastically different house from Mrs. Oakley. The outside looked like engineered wood. Smooth and sleek with large floor-to-ceiling windows. The door opened before we reached the house. They must have seen us walking up through those large windows. I couldn't see inside the house, though, from the street.

A woman stood in the doorway, her long black hair pulled into a high ponytail. She pushed her black-rimmed glasses up her nose. "You the police?" Her eyes darted between us expectantly.

I held up my badge, and Tony pointed to it, not wanting to fish his own out of his back pocket.

"Oh! FBI... is that about the Paradise?" She grabbed at my arm as I nodded and pulled me into the house. "Come in. Come in. We've been waiting to hear what was going on over there. Can only see so much through the window, you know. Come in. Come in." She closed the door behind Tony before ushering us further into her home.

The house was cluttered, but not really. She had a lot of things, but everything had its place. Her home was neat and smelled of lemon-scented bleach.

"Hideo!"

We followed her down a long hallway that branched off in three directions. We entered a large room with high ceilings, large windows, and books tucked into every corner. A man sat in an oversized brown leather recliner, staring at a book. He sat up straight when he saw us.

"Who do we have here?" His voice was rough and deep enough to drown in. He was an older man, older than me anyway. His slate-blue eyes seemed to dance in the dim light of the room. He glanced from me to Tony and back again, a smile eased across his face.

"These are FBI agents," said the woman.

"Oh, they've come to tell us about the fire."

I blinked. "Not quite. We've come to ask you about your neighbor."

He frowned for a brief moment and then shrugged. "Same thing, really, when you think about it."

"Not sure if that's true," I said.

This remark made him smile so hard the skin crinkled around his eyes. "Well then, what questions do you have for us?" He gestured to the leather sofa across from him. "I'm Hideo Nakamura, and this is my wife, Miko. I'm sure you've probably guessed it, but we are retired, so we spend a lot of time home and watching the neighborhood."

Mrs. Oakley was right. They might be able to help us. Miko sat on the arm of her husband's chair. He wrapped his arm around her as if to keep her in place. It was weird. I couldn't say why, but it was a little strange. The way they looked at each other. The way they looked at us. Like we were prey or something. Like we had all the answers they were looking for, and they would stop at nothing to get them. They wanted to know more about the fire, but so did we. And I would win.

"Well, for starters, the night of the fire, did you see anything strange?" I asked.

The two exchanged a look. "Besides the fire...no," answered Miko. "Not that I remember. Seemed like a normal night until I saw the smoke." She glanced at her husband. "This is so fascinating. I'm a bit of a true crime buff, myself. First crime scene in the neighborhood."

It was like a light bulb had gone off. It explained why they were so happy to see us. It explained their excitement. True crime had become America's favorite pastime. True crime novels. True crime podcasts. True crime TV shows. Everyone, or rather almost everyone, was fascinated by murder. It was then my eyes roamed the room. Really took everything in. There were books in every corner, stacked high. My eyes scanned the titles, all true crime novels.

"What can you tell us about Beth?"

Miko frowned. "Makes me so sad. I mean, I love true crime, but I guess it is different when it's someone you know. She was so nice. It was probably the husband."

"Which one?" remarked Hideo.

Miko looked at him and smiled. "Fair point. I would say it was the first one, but who knows."

I sat perfectly still and waited for one of them to say something. They wanted to talk. I could see it on their faces. There was so much they wanted to say. We just needed to give them the opportunity. I sat back and waited.

"Well, you know about her husband. Her first one. He left her penniless and destitute."

I blinked. "I thought she had gone through all their money before he left."

"True." She smiled, satisfied I knew that much. "But what was left, he took with him. Left her nothing but what was in her bank account. I figured he thought he was owed what was left in their savings since she had taken so much of it. In my opinion, he was right. Still felt sorry for her, though."

"Do you know if he still lives on the island?" asked Tony. It was the only thing no one had mentioned so far. I was curious if he stayed or if he wanted to get as far away from her as possible.

Usually, when a person suffered a betrayal, they wanted to get as far away from the person as possible. I would have. Most divorces, from what I knew, had something to do with money. Either one person made all the money, and the other one did nothing but spend it. Or one or both partners were selfish with money, only considering their needs. I wasn't sure which category Beth fit in. How they funded their savings hadn't been mentioned, but I figured it was money saved from both their jobs. Where he was trying to save, she just wanted to fix the bed-and-breakfast. She had become so fixated on what Paradise could have been that she wasn't living in the moment. She wasn't thinking about the state of things—her marriage, for starters, and how her fixation was affecting it.

"He does," answered Hideo. "But from what I hear, he wants nothing to do with Beth or the bed-and-breakfast. I don't want to say he hates her, but he strongly dislikes her."

"That's putting it nicely," remarked Miko. "I would definitely say that he hates her. Rightfully so. She ran through his inheritance before he could spend a penny of it, and then she started digging into their savings. Mostly, his savings. She had a job working for a cleaning service before they came here. She didn't add much to the account, and yet she took most of it to make her dream come true. He hates her. I would hate her."

I nodded slowly. I would have hated her, too. I would have sued her although I would have to look into how the property was split between spouses and if I could sue her. But if it was possible, I would have and taken the Paradise away from her. It sounded mean in my head, but...

"Have you seen a man stalking the property?" I asked.

They exchanged a knowing look. "I wouldn't say stalking the property," said Miko.

"Right," added Hideo. "More looking for something."

"I thought he was out for a walk. A lot of the guests walk around at night, after dinner, to get some air. It's a beautiful walk. She let the neighbors walk around on her property, walk through the garden, along the ocean's edge."

"So, it wasn't unusual?" asked Tony.

She shook her head. "No. Common, actually."

"But there was another man," said Hideo. He and his wife exchanged a long look.

"You're right." She looked back at us and leaned forward. "There was another man walking the property. Not last night." Her eyes cut to the corner of the room for a moment. "I don't think it was the same man. But there was someone a few nights walking around. He didn't look like any of the guests, you know. He looked like he was hiding. He was looking for something but trying not to be seen. But Beth—I think she was just getting home from somewhere—she saw him."

Hideo nodded. "She looked scared. She yelled at him, and then he walked right up to her and got in her face and was shouting. I tried to hurry up and open a window so I could hear, but by the time I did, he scurried away."

"She looked shaken by his presence," Miko finished.

"And you can't tell if it was the same guy as the one from last night?" I asked.

They both shrugged. "I couldn't say," said Miko. "He was in all black. He might have been the same guy, but the other one...looked like he was looking for something. Like he had dropped something on the ground and was searching for it. The one from yesterday looked like he was on a stroll. He wasn't looking for anything in particular. He was just walking. I don't think we are helping." Miko looked back at her husband.

"What is her first husband's name?" I asked.

"Victor Giroux. I'm sure he'd have no problem talking to you," said Hideo. He squeezed his wife's hip. "I'm sure he probably knows she's dead by now."

"And what about her second husband, Doug Frazier?" Asked Tony. He leaned forward, resting his elbows on his thighs. "Does anyone know what happened to him? Any ideas?"

I leaned forward, too. I was eager to know anything they could tell us about him. We were all focused on the first husband, and I almost forgot about the second one.

They exchanged another look, and Miko shook her head. "I really thought this marriage would work. Doug was nice, and he treated her well. And he did everything she asked, and what wife doesn't love that? I thought they were perfect for each other, and he seemed to enjoy working on the house, which was what she needed. He was willing to do a lot of the work himself, and that saved her money."

"I'm sure she was happy about that." I looked at Tony, who smiled.

"She was. Relieved, really," said Miko. "It was a weight off her shoulders, and then…I don't know what happened. They started arguing all the time. And loudly."

"We could hear their voices across the street. Couldn't make out what they were saying sometimes, but they were loud."

While Miko and her husband told us about Beth's constant fighting with her second husband, I wondered if they had told the police about the man who yelled at Beth. If it wasn't her first husband nor her second, then who else could Beth have pissed off so much they would have stalked and killed her?

CHAPTER EIGHT

Beth Hardwell

TWELVE YEARS AGO...
 The house was in a good spot, she thought. It had taken the better part of a day to talk her husband into looking at the house with her and their realtor. The bed-and-breakfast was more her idea than his, but he had come to understand that it was a good business idea. Or maybe he just wanted to appease her. It was hard to tell with him. Sometimes, he said something was a good idea, and then he quickly put it out of his mind and never brought it up again.
 "We could market it as a piece of paradise," or something like that. She wasn't really sure how to market it. She just knew she wanted it. She wanted it more than anything. Needed it.

BREAKFAST IN PARADISE

More than she needed air to breathe. This idea had roamed around her brain for years. Ever since she and her husband had visited Honolulu on a rare family vacation, she had talked him into it. She had to talk him into most things. Victor was a man who could be persuaded if you worked hard enough. And she did. She made sure he never had to lift a finger to do anything at home, and he caved to her occasional whims.

She wanted to get away from the cold in Chicago. Some place warm and sunny and beautiful. What better place than Hawaii? It was her dream vacation, even after his sister pointed out they had no reason to go on vacation.

"What do you need a break from?" Cate had asked one night at dinner. She came over for dinner every week, even though she hated Beth's cooking.

"It's just some time away," said Beth. She had glanced at her husband before she answered and noted his expression, grim. His brows furrowed as he stared at his phone, his lips set in a grim line. She would get no help from him, as usual, when it came to the snide remarks of his family.

"Time away from what? This beautiful house?" Cate gestured to the dining room. "My brother slaves away at work so you can live in this big beautiful house. And all you have to do is take care of it, and now you want to drag him to some island so you can get away."

"It's not just me. It's a vacation. It's not a big deal." She looked at Victor again, not sure why. He didn't look at her or Cate. He sat in his chair at the head of the table, chewing slowly.

"I just can't figure out what you need time away from. It's not like you have noisy children to take care of it."

And there it was for the millionth time. Cate, who had six obnoxious and ill-mannered children, always made a point to bring up the fact that Beth had none. And could have none. It was a constant jab that she should have been used to, yet... tears pricked the corners of her eyes as she stood up and excused herself from the table. Her inability to have children was the one thing Cate could use to hurt her. And use it she did.

She should have been used to it by now, five years after her last miscarriage. But the wound was still raw, gaped open, unable to close. To heal properly. And Cate poked at it every chance she got. If Victor cared or even noticed how much it hurt her, he never said anything. He never soothed her or tried to help her heal. He never corrected his sister or his mother on her behalf.

Well, even with their constant prying and underhanded remarks, she was right where she wanted to be—Honolulu, Hawaii. She had made it back after all those years. Victor had finally decided to retire. It had taken some coaxing, but she got him back to the island and then to look at properties.

"We will have to have some kind of income now," she had said. "This could help us. We can't live on our savings for the rest of our lives."

It was something he knew, yet he didn't want to admit it. Contrary to what people thought of him, Victor Giroux was a planner. He had most of his life planned out before he was twenty. He would get married, have three children, and work in the family law firm that he would eventually pass on to his children. He did get married, and he did work in the family law firm, but he had no children to speak of.

While not all the plans came to fruition, he continued to make them. He planned for their retirement, too. So, he knew his wife was right. She never had a steady job, so contributions to their savings weren't steady. Mostly, it was based on what he contributed, and that would only last them so long. They would need another business, but running a bed-and-breakfast was not what he had in mind.

But the more Beth talked about it, the more he thought about it. If it was in the right location, it could do really well. As he stared at the house, he realized it was, in fact, the right location. Overlooking the water, the house sat on the edge of the property with large windows and beautiful plants and trees. It had potential. While somewhat neglected, it was clear that someone, sometime, had cared for the property. Had loved it.

He could already picture what needed to be done to get it up and running. But what he had in mind was different from what Beth had in mind. While Victor thought of adding a hammock out front and perhaps a pool overlooking the ocean below, Beth thought of structural changes. Adding a third story.

BREAKFAST IN PARADISE

Bigger windows and adding an owner's quarters near the back of the building for them to live there.

 She wanted to live there all year round. But she wasn't sure if Victor had the same idea, and she didn't care. Not really. Not like a wife was supposed to. She had lived as the ever-obedient wife for years, and she was quite done with it. She would only do what she wanted to do from here on out. And he would just have to go along with it. She knew he would. That was his way with her. The consolation prize of their marriage.

 Victor never loved her. Not really. He liked her well enough, but he wasn't in love with her. It was something they both knew but never talked about. She didn't have to talk about it. She never had to ask or find clever ways to bring it up. She knew. It was clear in the way he talked to her. The way he touched her, never loving but neutral. It was made even clearer by the way his family spoke to her. The way he allowed them to speak to her. It was clear they didn't like her, but he never stood up for her.

 When they spoke, he seemed to withdraw into himself. He never uttered a word, but later, he felt terrible. He always felt bad. It was like cause and effect with them. His family made her feel like she was nothing and then would swoop in and buy her things to make her feel like a person again.

 No one had ever done that for her. Bought her nice things to make her feel better. She used his guilt. Maybe a little more than she should have, but he was using her. It was only fair. Tit for tat, as they say. He wanted a wife, and she was that. She waited on him hand and foot, put up with his judgmental family, and had done anything, and everything he wanted the way he wanted. The least he could do was buy her nice things. It wasn't asking too much. Not to her, at least.

 And this would be the same. He would buy this house for her, but she had to play it right. She could play Victor like she could the piano. She always knew the right keys to push and the right time to push them. The house had been on the market for a while, over a year, which was strange to her and the realtor. It was in such a great spot overlooking the water. Most people would have killed for that location. But the location was not the problem. The market and the condition of the house were two of the biggest factors.

"I know the inside is...leaves a lot to be desired. But with renovations, you could do it." Mina, their relator, strolled into the house like she had walked the path a dozen times. "With the location, it is a great investment. With the right upgrades, and you would make your money back in no time."

Beth didn't know a lot about business, but she knew enough to know that it wasn't always true. Just because it looked easy didn't mean it was. It was never as easy as they made it seem. Sure, the location was great, but she still might mess it up. There was no guarantee they could make a profit due to location alone. But Beth didn't say anything. She swallowed her words and followed Mina around the house.

When they were finished with the tour, she stood outside the front door. A few feet away from Victor as he talked to Mina. She heard what they were saying, but she wasn't paying attention to it. It didn't matter. Nothing else mattered. She wanted the house. She wanted to make it hers in a way only she could. It had to be this house. Not because of the location or anything. But the bones. She stared at the bones of the house and saw everything. What it could be. What she could make of it if he would only let her. She would have this house, and he would pay for it. She just had to play the right note.

"It's expensive," he said. Mina stepped away and headed toward her car. He must have told her they couldn't afford it. No point in lingering after that.

"I know," she said.

"Maybe one day. But now is not the time."

Beth swallowed her words again. They weren't right. They tasted wrong. They wouldn't bend him to her side, and therefore, they were not the right words. She had to wait for the right words to come to her. She had spent a lot of time waiting and planning. She could do it a little longer.

She would live there without him if she had to. He didn't share her vision, and that was fine. He never did, and he never had to. But she saw it. She knew what it could be. A lush, beautifully decorated bed-and-breakfast. A quiet slice of paradise. She even had a name picked out. Golden Paradise, because the setting sun over the gorgeous waters cast everything in a golden glow. She sighed and moved toward the car. There was nothing left to say.

On the way back to the hotel, she began to curate a plan. A plan that would get her what she wanted.

"Your mother wants us to come visit," she said as she gazed out the window.

"I know. You don't have to come. I know how hard it is on you."

She shrugged. "If I don't, it will be much harder for you. You know how they get. It'll be fine."

And it would be. She knew it. She felt it deep down in her bones. In her marrow. That house would be hers, and if she had to suffer through his mother's snide remarks or his sister's boasts about her children, then so be it. She could have had children if she really wanted to. But she didn't. If she had a child, then his attention would have been somewhere else, and then she wouldn't have gotten the gifts that made everything more bearable. A child was not worth that. She was glad she didn't have any.

But she would suffer through them, too, Cate's spoiled children who thought the world revolved around them and their mother. She would suffer through it all. And when it was over, and Victor felt so badly that she had been forced to spend the weekend with his family, he would buy her that house. And if there wasn't enough money to do so, she would make sure that somehow, some way, there was. It was just that simple.

Because Beth had made up her mind. She wanted the house. She wanted the bed-and-breakfast, and she wanted the money to do with as she liked.

And she'd be damned if she didn't get all three. With or without her husband.

CHAPTER NINE

I found myself desperately wanting to meet Victor Giroux. Not because I found him interesting or saw him as a suspect but because I wanted to know more about Beth. I wanted to know what she was like during their time together and how he really felt about her. Others had surmised, but I wanted to hear it from the horse's mouth. I wondered if he hated her or if he even cared that she was dead. How did he feel about her remarrying? There were so many questions. Did he have insurance on the house, since he had technically been the one to buy it?

No one knew exactly where he lived, but I was able to get a phone number for him from Miko. Her husband and Victor kept in touch solely through the phone. They mostly talked about the bed-and-breakfast. He kept him informed as to what was going on around the neighborhood. He didn't care to hear about Beth but liked hearing how the business was doing. It doing so well seemed to make him happy. This fact piqued my interest. If he still got a share in the profits, then, of course, he would have been happy the business was doing well. This also made him unlikely to want to burn the place down. If it were putting a steady stream of money in his pocket, he wouldn't want it to go away.

Maybe he wanted to run the business himself. That seemed unlikely. Even so, it could have been true. We went back to the field office, and I called Mr. Victor Giroux. He sounded annoyed from the first time I opened my mouth and said my name.

"I know she's dead. And I don't care. Talk to her second husband. I'm sure he knows more than I do."

"And that might be true, but I can't find him. I can find you, and since I have you, I have a couple of questions to ask about your ex-wife. Could you come in?" Silence on the other end told me he was thinking about, or trying to figure out, the best way to say no.

"Or we could come to you. Where do you live? We want this to be as convenient for you as possible, but we still need our questions answered." I waited. The ball was in his court now. I figured he was the kind of man who wouldn't like the FBI showing up at his home in front of his neighbors or in front of his coworkers. That was most people, actually. However, some would find it exciting.

After a long moment of silence, Victor sighed. "Fine. I will come by tomorrow. I can't tell you anything, so it will be a complete waste of time, but I guess I have to do it anyway."

"Thank you so much. I look forward to speaking with you." I hung up the phone and sighed, sinking deeper into my chair. I could have just asked my questions over the phone. We did it all the time. But there was something about this...about him...I wanted to see his face. I wanted to ask my questions and look into his eyes. I wanted to watch his body move with discomfort, or his face contort with rage.

A lot is learned from a person's voice, but even more can be learned from their body language. I preferred my interviews this way, although sometimes it's just not possible.

"He sounded so helpful," said Tony, his tone laced with sarcasm.

I shrugged. "Of course. He's eager to find the killer of the ex-wife he left because she stole most of his money." I could be just as sarcastic when I really put my mind to it.

"There is something about that situation that really bothers me. How did she steal all the money? How long before he noticed, and why did it take so long? And why wouldn't he have gotten a lawyer to deal with it?"

I thought about it for a moment. My parents had a shared account that they both put money in. Their shared account was for the mortgage and the household expenses like bills and repairs. And then they had their separate accounts to do whatever they wanted with. Maybe they had a joint account too. A joint savings account. I was still uncertain as to how that worked.

I made a note to ask my dad about it later. He would know more about it than me. I had never had a joint account for anything. I was fairly certain that Victor would come into the office, but part of me was less sure. He could run off. I flagged his name at the local airports.

"You think he might run off?"

I shrugged. "He didn't sound too eager to come in. I don't know if that's because he did it or if he really doesn't care about her anymore. Either way, I would rather keep him on the island."

Tony slid over one of the files on his desk. "This is from the detectives. Everything they have learned so far."

Detective Branson and her partner were very neat. Not just their handwriting, but the way they organized their notes. Each of the guest's interviews had a photo of the guest attached, along with information on where they came from, and where they have been staying since the fire. They hadn't gotten to all the guests yet. The ones they hadn't talked to yet were in our interview rooms. The ones they had were put up in hotels, awaiting further instruction.

Josie Dennis sat at the metal table, her arms folded across her chest. The scowl on her face told me she did not want to be there. I couldn't blame her. If the hotel I was staying in had been burned down, the last place I'd want to be is a police station. But then I thought, where else would I go?

"Thank you for staying to speak with us," said Tony as we sat down.

Josie cut her eyes at him. "I'm sure I had a choice." There was an edge to her voice, sharp and pointed. I couldn't tell if it was because of the fire or us.

"Fair point," I said.

She sighed, and her shoulders fell slightly. "Sorry. It's been a long few days, and I just want to go home."

"That's understandable," I said. "Did you and your husband make it out unscathed?"

She rolled her eyes. For a moment, I thought I had discovered the source of her irritation. What could he have done that irritated her more than losing her stuff in a fire?

"Yeah, my husband got out unscathed. Left me to die, though."

I blinked. I felt Tony stiffen next to me. "I'm sorry. And how did he do that?"

She explained that it was Mr. Monroe who had discovered the fire. He ran through the house, yelling and trying to get their attention. He knocked on their door, yelled about the fire, and then moved on to the next.

"I turned around to get my purse, but he rushed out the door. I was right behind him on the stairs. He ran out and then closed the door behind him, trapping me inside. The other guests were ahead of him. What kind of person thinks to do that? Close the door on their way out in the middle of a fire?"

I swallowed a laugh. It wasn't funny. And she had a point. Who thought of that and why? If there was a fire in my apartment or hotel, the last thing on my mind would be closing the door. Especially if I knew someone was behind me.

"I had to jump out of the window with Mr. Monroe. We were the last ones in the house, and I couldn't get the door open."

I shook my head. For the briefest moment, I wondered if we were on the wrong trail. What if her husband wanted her dead and was using the fire to kill her? Maybe Mrs. Hardwell had gotten in the way, and he had to knock her out. Maybe she wasn't the intended target.

"I see," I said. "I understand you being pissed off. I would be."

"Did you ask him about it?"

She sucked her teeth. "He said he wasn't thinking. And he didn't know I was behind him. I told him, 'Really? If you didn't know I was behind you, you at least knew I wasn't in front of you.' So, either way, he was just going to leave me in the burning house with no thought or care as to where I was. What kind of husband does that?"

Another good point. He either wanted her dead, or he just didn't care about what happened to her. Sad. "Aside from the fire, did you notice anything strange around the house?"

She shrugged. "Not really. It had been pretty quiet. It had just been us, really. Mrs. Hardwell and the staff."

"There's staff?" My back straightened. I hadn't heard of any staff up until this point. Her files were all burned up, and Love was trying to get into the online website to look for booking dates. However, the staff wouldn't have been on the website.

"Yes. Um... there was a cook and a maid. She turned down the rooms with Mrs. Hardwell. It was bare bones. I think Mrs. Hardwell liked doing the work herself. She liked cleaning up and taking care of the guests. That's why she kept such a small staff and lived on the property."

That made sense. If she had spent so much money on the property, keeping staff to the bare minimum and doing a lot of the work herself, kept costs down.

"Did the guests have any problem with her?"

She shook her head. "Of course not. Mrs Hardwell? She's so sweet. She's always been so kind to us. This is the second time we've been here. I don't think anyone could want to hurt her. It had to be some kind of accident or something. No one would hurt her on purpose. I won't believe it."

I smiled. She really liked Mrs. Hardwell. Tears bloomed at the corners of her eyes. She tried to wipe them away before they fell.

"She gave us great advice and told us the best sights to see and the best places to go and to eat. She was always so helpful and was there when you needed her. She really loved what she did. You could see it. Always had a smile on her face."

The rest of the interviews were much the same. The guests loved Mrs. Hardwell. She was kind and helpful and could have done nothing that would have caused her death. No one had anything mean to say about her. It was…strange. How could she get along with everyone? I didn't think that was possible.

No one mentioned a man stalking the property or whether Mrs. Hardwell seemed bothered by anything. She was her chipper self right to the end. That being said, they also couldn't remember the last time they saw her.

"I think I saw her after dinner. No…wait…during dinner. She was definitely there during dinner. The cook preps dinner and then leaves. Mrs. Hardwell finishes it up and serves it. So, she had to have been there then, but I'm not sure where she went after. Maybe someone else saw."

But no one else had seen her after dinner. No one remembered if she had left or gone back to the room. She served them dinner, and then she faded into the background. After a day of interviewing and learning nothing, we decided to call it a night.

"We'll need to interview the guests who are now at the hotel," said Tony. "Not that I don't trust their interviews. I just want to hear for myself what they have to say."

I agreed with him. I wanted to speak with them, too. Maybe they had more information about Beth than the ones we interviewed today. We went home to prepare for our dates.

Since Tony started dating Aisha again, we'd gone on a few double dates.

They've been… cordial might be the best word. I didn't think Aisha liked me at first. And that feeling was still there. She was still a little standoffish toward me even though Tony tried to smooth things over. Harrison and I were meeting them at Tony's for dinner.

I wasn't sure who first suggested we have double dates together. I couldn't remember who brought it up first. I knew it wasn't Aisha. I was against it at first because I didn't think she would like it, but Tony assured me it was fine. We went bowling and then to the movies and out to dinner. It was fun. But we weren't making a habit of it.

I knocked on Tony's door. I heard steps nearing the door just as Harrison kissed my shoulder. Tony opened the door, his eyes narrowed. The smell of onions, garlic, and meat wafted into the hallway.

"Hey, man. Smells great," said Harrison.

Tony smiled. "Come on in." He closed the door behind us. "Dinner is almost ready." Harrison followed him into the kitchen with a bottle of red wine. I went into the living room, where Aisha sat on the sofa, typing on her phone. She glanced up when I sat in the chair across from her.

Her smile was tight, but at least she smiled this time. I smiled back. She averted her eyes.

"How have you been?" I asked, trying my best to make conversation. I remembered what Harrison had told me just barely an hour before.

"You are Tony's new partner. That...she might think that you guys at one point had an intimate relationship."

I blinked. "What? We never—"

"I know. I know. But she doesn't. You got close to him while she was out of his life. She might be threatened by that. She's just figuring out again where she stands in his life. She might be worried about your relationship with him."

Just because I was female didn't mean I was sleeping with my partner, and it annoyed me that it might be the reason she was so mean to me.

It annoyed me even more because I would have. If he hadn't said he wouldn't date a coworker, I would have gone out with him. I never told him, but...it didn't matter anymore. I wasn't her rival, and I needed her to see that. I didn't want her not liking me to affect my relationship with Tony. So, I needed to play nice.

"Pretty good. Just working on a tough case. I should be reading over briefs." She glanced at Tony in the kitchen. "But he wants to relax."

I cracked a grin at that. "Sounds like Tony. He keeps telling me I need to do other things outside of work. It's hard, though. Work is the first place my mind goes, especially if we are stuck on a case. Hard getting it out of my head."

"Exactly. I don't know why he doesn't understand that." She tucked her phone underneath her thigh. "He told me about the bed-and-breakfast."

"Yeah, he said you guys went there, and you really liked it. It was beautiful."

She leaned forward. "It was. It really was. The views from the room were gorgeous. It was heavenly." Her voice was light and joyful. She looked radiant as she spoke. She smiled, and her eyes sparkled. It was nice seeing her like this. It must be what she's like when she's with Tony.

Her bright red lipstick matched her off-the-shoulder top and her red heels, which were sitting neatly next to the sofa. Her hair was pulled into a loose bun on top of her head. She looked casual but still ready to go out on the town. Her phone dinged, but she didn't look at it.

"It was a great weekend. A girl in my office suggested it. Well, T brought it up. But I told her about it, and she and her partner had been there, and they loved it. She said it was a beautiful place just to relax, and she was right. It was. I didn't even take my work with me, which is a first for me."

"That sounds nice. I have a hard time relaxing. It's like it's so foreign to me my body doesn't know how to do it. But I think I might try this year to really give it a try.

"What about the owner? Beth Hardwell."

She shrugged. "She was a little weird. She was nice and very attentive. Made sure we had everything we needed, but she was…you know, you just get feelings about people." She held my gaze for a long moment. "Something about her was a little odd. Maybe she was just a little quirky."

I smiled. "Maybe. Everyone seemed to like her. They keep saying how nice she was."

"Stop talking about work!" shouted Tony from the kitchen.

Aisha rolled her eyes. She shook her head. "Good luck. I'd be curious to learn who would want her dead."

I was curious, too. Dinner went without a hitch. Aisha seemed to relax a little and opened up a little more. We talked about our lives and how we grew up.

"I envy you with siblings," Aisha said. "It was always just me and my friends. But the house was pretty quiet without them. I always wanted a sibling."

"I keep telling her she can borrow mine anytime," said Tony. His right hand kneaded the back of Aisha's neck. "She can take my brother right now."

I shook my head. He was always trying to get rid of King. King was Tony's brother, and to me, he was nice. He cared about Tony a lot. I saw it when Tony was shot and in the hospital. King stayed by his side. But he didn't want Tony to know about it.

"Your brother loves you," I said.

He rolled his eyes. "No, he doesn't."

"Stayed by your side when you got shot."

Tony blinked. "I didn't know that. I just remember you and Mom. He was there?"

I nodded. "The whole time." I sipped my wine.

"Oh. Well, she can still borrow him from time to time."

Everyone at the table laughed. I shook my head.

"I like my brother. I don't like that he's dating my once best friend. But we had some good years together. I guess it doesn't bother me as much as it used to. But still."

Aisha nodded. "I wouldn't be able to talk to her like I used to. It would change our whole relationship."

"Exactly. Like whatever I tell her, I know she's going to tell him. So, unless it's something I want him to know, I don't tell her. And I used to tell her everything." I straightened in my chair. I hadn't talked to her in a long time. Our relationship changed drastically after I found out she was dating my brother.

"I don't think it matters," said Tony. "I think as long as you have your boundaries and make sure she knows what they are, everything should be okay."

I shook my head. "So if I dated your brother, our relationship wouldn't change?"

Tony's eyes narrowed. His body straightened, and his hand dropped from Aisha's neck. "What?"

"You and I are friends. If I dated your brother, would it change our relationship?"

Harrison nudged me with his elbow. "Uh, should I be worried?"

I laughed. "It's just a question."

BREAKFAST IN PARADISE

I stared at Tony and waited for him to answer. For a moment, I felt sorry for putting him on the spot. Aisha stared at him, too.

"I guess it would change a few things," he said slowly. His eyes never left mine. He looked hurt by the question. I wouldn't actually date King. He was nice, but he just wasn't my type. I think. I hadn't spent enough time with him to really say that.

I smiled slightly. "Exactly. It changes things," I said just as slowly.

CHAPTER TEN

Victor Giroux looked nothing like the way I pictured him. From the way people talked about him, I pictured a soft pushover that was easily taken advantage of by his wife. The kind of man that could be easily talked into things and easily led by a woman. Not that there was anything wrong with that. But that wasn't what walked through the door.

Victor was in his late fifties with dark hair, graying along the edges, broad shoulders, and a strong jaw. He had the most beautiful light green eyes. He followed me into an interview room wordlessly. He sat down, and I sat across from him.

"I don't have much time."

"I understand. This is really to…better understand your former wife. What kind of person was she, and would anyone want her dead?"

He chuckled. "Other than me?"

I nodded. "Yes. Or you, if you'd like to go ahead and confess."

He chuckled again. "As much as I wanted to, I didn't kill her. I would have loved to have gone through with it. I'd be in a lot less debt today if I had. But no, I didn't kill my ex-wife. I didn't have a reason to."

"She stole your savings. Although if you two were married, it wasn't all yours. I mean, she shared some of it, right? It wasn't just your money."

He sighed. "It was mostly mine. Some I saved after years of working at my father's law firm. Some was an inheritance, and she put the rest of it in. Her contribution was under five thousand. She was never good at saving money. And once she saw something she liked, she had to have it. It was a compulsion. I knew that. But once I understood it, I couldn't be angry at her. Not fully. But I also couldn't stay with her. I had worked too hard, thrown too much of my life away at a job I hated, to die penniless."

I leaned back. There was a sadness in his voice I wasn't expecting. He had loved her. Or rather, he had loved her once, but he couldn't put up with her anymore. "Did you want to start the bed-and-breakfast? Or was it solely her idea?"

"I was never really sure about it. She had wanted to do it for years, but I...you'd have to spend money to make any, and I was never comfortable spending that much. Not like her."

My mouth twitched. "It wasn't her money. Easier to be loose with it when you aren't the one working for it."

His eyes lit up then, and he smiled. Like it was the first time anyone had understood his frustration with her. This was something my father had taught me early on. When you work hard for something, you take better care of it. Beth hadn't worked hard for the money, so spending it wasn't a big deal.

"Exactly. That might have been my fault. When we got married, I told her she didn't have to work. So, she didn't. Not unless she was bored. And she wasn't bored often."

"Did you two have any children?"

He shook his head. "Three miscarriages. Doctor told her during the last one she would never get pregnant again. And she didn't."

"What kind of person was she?"

He sighed at the question. "She was a good person until she became fixated on something. Money or the bed-and-breakfast. Those two things were her main focus. Her only focus. She seemed to care about nothing else. I was surprised she got married again, and then I heard he worked in construction, and then I knew why she married him. He could help her dream come true and at half the cost."

"You make her sound so cold and calculating."

"She wasn't. Not at first. But like I said, when she was focused on something... that was it. Nothing could get in her way."

"Do you know of anyone that wanted her dead? Any family? Friends?"

He shrugged. "She could be nice when there was something in it for her. She didn't really make friends. She had a sister, but I don't know if she's still alive or not. I've never met her. She preferred to keep people at a distance. Just far enough away to be friendly but not close enough to really know her."

"You never met her sister? How does that happen?"

"I don't know. Not everyone is close to their family. I figured there was a reason, and one day, she might want to talk about it. That day never came."

"Do you know her name? Anyone else in her family?"

"Um... her name was Savannah Hardwell. She probably married, but I don't know her married name. Their mother died when Beth was a young girl. Savannah helped raise her sister and her brother, and then her brother was killed in a car accident. She said her relationship with Savannah was pretty strained after their mother died. Her sister resented having to take care of them. She said they never recovered, and then her brother died, and they grew further and further apart."

"That's sad."

"Yeah, I thought so. Death usually brings families closer together, but not them."

It was so strange. The Beth he described didn't fit with the one everyone else described. They all said how nice she was. Although he said, she was nice, too, when she wasn't fixated on something. And she liked to keep people at a distance. Maybe that was what she did with her neighbors. She kept them at a distance. That was why they didn't really know her.

"I'm sorry she's dead. I really am, but I can assure you I had nothing to do with it. I didn't even hate her anymore. Now, don't get me wrong, I still didn't like her, but I didn't want her dead." He sounded so sincere. I searched his eyes, and I believed him, but I still had to ask.

"Can I get your whereabouts for two nights ago?"

He took a deep breath. "I was at work. I work at a flower shop. We have a wedding we are getting ready for, and that has caused a lot of late-night hours. It's been draining, but it's a lot of money for us, so we are happy to do it."

"So, you left the law firm to work with plants?" I rested my head in the palm of my hand.

A smile bloomed on his lips. "I did. Much to my father's objection. He told me to come back to the firm. He said I could make all the money I lost marrying Beth, and I could be happy."

"Why didn't you take him up on his offer?" Going home would have been the first thing I did. I would have surrounded myself with familiar faces.

He sighed. "I wanted to be happy. I was never happy at the firm. I did it because it was expected of me. I married Beth because it was expected of me. Well, I was expected to get married even though I wasn't sure it was what I wanted. That's just how my family is."

"Did they like her?"

After a sharp exhale, his head tilted slightly, his eyes roaming the ceiling. "No. If I'm being honest, they strongly disliked her. My sister, my mother, my father, and cousins. My grandmother hated her. They told me not to marry her and that it wouldn't end well. And they were right."

"Why didn't they like her? Did they just have an idea of who you should marry, and she wasn't it?"

His head wiggled from side to side. "There were a variety of reasons. My mother didn't like the way she looked or carried herself. My father didn't like that she didn't come from a prominent family. My sister and my grandmother hated that she couldn't have children. And they thought she was selfish and lazy."

"Was that why you married her?" My fingers drummed against the table. He seemed to dislike his family. Marrying someone they hated was an interesting way to get back at them. A way to go against them. The one thing he could do that wasn't for them. But their disdain for her must have been hard on her. It could have been why she wanted to get away from them.

"I guess. In a way, it was. Which was wrong of me, and I know it was hard on her. But I think that was why I gave her whatever she wanted. I tried my best to make it so she wanted for nothing because I knew the difficult position I was putting her in. And I couldn't say anything against my family, so I bought her things. And did what she wanted."

"So, you spoiled her and created a monster."

"And then I had to let it go. She was so fixated on that place. Like she was possessed or something. The second she saw it, she had to have it. And then she had to make it better. She added the third story, you know."

"Really?"

He nodded. "She had an idea for adding extra rooms, and it did make the place better. More rooms, more money. She was right. But the money we had to put into that place... It was too much. Too much, and it took too long to make it all back." He shook his head. "I hope she was dead before it all burned to the ground. That would have broken her. It would have killed her. If I really wanted to hurt her, I wouldn't have killed her. I would have burned the place down, or I would have taken it from her. That was the way to hurt her, not to kill her."

He might have had a point. She loved the house. She had worked hard on it and sank a lot of money into it. She would have been devastated to watch it go up in flames. I believed him. I believe he didn't do it.

"Was there anyone that hated her? Anyone that wanted to hurt her?"

"She never let anyone get that close to her. Maybe a contractor she didn't want to pay. But other than that, I can't say. Maybe her second husband would know. He would know more than I did. I had little contact with her. I still have a stake in the business and get a small percentage every month. That's all deposited in an account. I don't talk to her or see her if I don't have to."

"Right. Yeah, we need to find him. He seems to have disappeared off the face of the earth."

"That's weird but understandable. He might have wanted to get away from her and thought going underground was the best way to do it."

My back straightened. "Why would he want to get away from her? Was she violent?"

"She could be if she didn't get her way."

It was so strange to hear him talk about his ex-wife that way. It was an honest conversation, but there was a contrast between how he spoke about her and how others spoke about her. He knew her in a way they didn't. Up until now, all we had heard was how nice she had been.

But Victor said she was nice when she wanted to be or when she thought she would get something out of it. Something nagged at me. I had the worrying feeling that I had forgotten something, but I couldn't remember what it was.

"I might have more questions for you later, but I think that's it for now." I stood up, and he followed.

"Well, I'm not going anywhere, so you know where to find me."

I walked him to the elevator and then met Tony at my desk. I told him everything I learned about Beth from her ex-husband. I believed he was telling the truth about most of what he said. But he was her ex-husband. Could we really trust what he had to say about her?

Tony wasn't so sure.

"I don't know. Everyone talks about how nice she was, and he says she was a bad person…I mean, it could be true, but it could also be him shifting the blame."

"She stole their savings without talking to him about it. I think the blame is right where it should be."

He shrugged. "Maybe. But when someone leaves you, or you leave them, it changes your perception of that person. I'm just saying his…the lens he sees her through might be a little cloudy."

"Good point. But I believed him. I do believe him. The way he talked about her. I could tell there was a little love there. Like he did at one point love her. He just couldn't do it anymore.

It felt honest. He answered all my questions, and he told me about her family."

"What about her family?"

I told him about her sister and brother. "Could you go for a long time without speaking with your brother or sisters? I don't think King would let you."

"Right? He would call me just to annoy me and make me talk to him. I don't think I could do it. Especially not my sisters. They must have really been upset with each other. After all these years... I wonder if she knows she's dead."

"I don't think anyone knew to call her. I just learned about her myself. I don't think she talked about her sister. I don't think she mentioned anyone in her family, which is so strange to me. But her sister should know. If we can't find her husband, then we will have to notify her next of kin. And that would be her sister."

"Also true. We still need to make sure that the body is hers."

"Who else would it be?" I asked. If it wasn't Beth, then why hadn't she shown up by now?

"Well, let's go see Jill and see if there is anything she can tell us."

I jumped up. "Maybe it's her husband, and Beth is on the lam."

"On the lam? Really?"

"Shut up."

Jill stood in the middle of the exam room with her arms folded across her chest, lips pressed into a frown. I didn't trust the look on her face. Something was wrong. Something was always wrong when Jill stood in the middle of the room or when she paced, trying to get her thoughts together.

Tony nudged me with his elbow.

"You alright over there?" I inched further into the room. She looked at me as if she just realized we were there.

"Oh, you two. Are you taking over the Golden Paradise case?"

I nodded. "Yup. That's why we are here. I was hoping you had something for us. Something that could tell us if the body belonged to Beth Hardwell or not."

She shrugged. "I'm... I can't say. All I know for sure is that she was dead before the fire."

I frowned. "So it was murder."

Jill nodded. "Take a look here. There's a huge bludgeon on the back of the skull. That's what killed her. Somebody came and bashed the back of her head before the fire."

"Someone did this to Mrs. Hardwell?" I asked.

Jill raised a finger. "Well, that's the thing. The body appears to be female, but it's so charred that it's hard to tell who she was. It could have been Beth. But until we get an anthropologist down here and some DNA to compare..." She threw her hands up in the air.

She sounded annoyed or irritated. Something was bothering her that she clearly didn't want to talk about.

"Is there anything else you want to tell us?" I asked.

She shrugged. "I don't know what I can or can't say. So I'm not saying anything. I'll try to have something on Mrs. Hardwell for you. I would like some of her DNA, but... I mean, I have her bones, but I have nothing to test it against. The place is..."

"Disintegrated. Yeah, we've seen it," said Tony. "I don't think you'll get any DNA from the house. I can't think of where else you could get it."

"What about her sister?" I looked at Tony. "If we can find her sister, then you can run the DNA samples and see if there is a familial match."

Jill nodded. "I could do that. If you could get it, I could test it."

"Now we just need to find her." I spun around and headed toward the door. As I walked to the car, I noted that Beth didn't have her husband's last name. "Did she take her second husband's name?"

Tony stopped near the car door. "His name isn't Hardwell, so I don't think so. It might be her maiden name."

"Well, that might make her sister easier to find. Even if she got married."

We went back to the field office to do some research. After a long two hours and several calls to women who seemed both annoyed and intrigued by my calling, I found Savannah Long, previously Savannah Hardwell. She lived in Savannah, Georgia, of all places.

I assumed she was the right Savannah—It was amazing how many there were—because of two things, her name and the fact that she favored Beth. Also, because she was the last one on my list, and the rest were a definite no.

This Savannah Hardwell did not answer my call, so there was hope. I left a message for her to call me back. I informed her who I was and that I was calling about her sister. Even if she didn't like Beth, she might still be intrigued enough to call back.

I hoped she hadn't changed her name from Savannah, but I put that out of my mind. I tried to think of different scenarios that could have happened on the night of the fire. What was Beth doing when it started? Was she sleeping? Did someone break in, and she caught them? Was it planned? Did someone want her dead?

We needed to know more about Beth, and we needed to find her second husband.

CHAPTER ELEVEN

SOME ARSONISTS LIKED TO RETURN TO THE SCENE OF A fire and admire their handiwork. While I slept, curled up next to Harrison, the thought entered my mind. The arsonist might return to the scene. Crime scene techs had gotten everything they could from the scene. Everything was burnt to a crisp.

When I mentioned it to Tony the next morning, he said it was possible.

"Assuming this was about arson and not killing Mrs. Hardwell, then yeah, sure. The arsonist could return to the scene. But if it is about Beth, then he wouldn't return."

"I wonder if it's about something else."

He pulled into the driveway of the Nakamuras. As I got out of the car, I saw the curtain in the front window fall back into place. The retired couple truly watched over the neighborhood.

I imagined them taking shifts to look out the window and watch what was going on. Perched on the windowsill with a notepad and pen in hand, writing license plate numbers of all the cars that drove by slowly or stopped.

As a neighbor, it would be annoying. As an agent, it would be helpful. Before I could touch the door, it opened. Mrs. Nakamura burst through the doorway. "Did you find anything?"

I opened my mouth to speak, but she grabbed my arm and yanked me into the house. Tony followed, chuckling.

"This has been the talk of the neighborhood. Everywhere I go, people talk about the fire. Do you know anything more?"

I followed her into the room where her husband sat in his recliner. He sat up when he saw us and smiled. "You're back!"

"I am! With a few more questions." I didn't even sit down. I just had a few things that I wanted to know. I wasn't even sure if they could answer them, but of all the people in the neighborhood, they would have been my best bet. "Did Beth ever mention her family? Maybe a sister or a brother? Her mom?"

Miko sat on the sofa instead of her husband's lap this time. They exchanged a look. Miko shook her head. "I think this was a long time ago. She might have mentioned her sister and mother died... I can't remember how, though."

"A car accident," said Hideo. "She said they were driving one night from church, and the roads were icy. She didn't like talking about her family or her life before Honolulu."

I frowned. "Her sister died?"

They nodded.

"Not her brother?"

They both shook their heads.

"Second question. Have you seen anyone hanging around the charred remains of the house? Anyone that shouldn't be there?"

Miko shook her head. "And I've been looking. We've been looking in shifts, trying to keep an eye on it since the police have gone. I would hate to think about a person trying to take a souvenir from the scene. Some people do that, you know. It's horrible. Disgusting."

The way the words jumped out of her mouth made me think she had been one of those people. She had taken something from the crime scene and hidden it away. I glanced around the room. Her eyes followed mine, and she smiled.

"But no. We haven't seen anything like that. No one except the police has been around." She looked at her husband. "We take turns so one of us is either looking out the window or working the missing persons case."

My ears perked up. "What missing persons case?"

Surprise took shape on her face. "Oh, well, there have been some missing men in the area. Just men. They come here, and then they disappear without a trace. I'm surprised you haven't heard about it. Well, it is a local PD case. When I heard about it, I thought about Beth's husband Doug. He disappeared without a trace. I wondered if somehow it was connected. I even asked Beth about it."

"And what did she say?" asked Tony, who leaned against the door frame.

"She didn't seem to care. Or rather, she didn't believe there was a connection. She didn't want to talk about him leaving her. She didn't want to talk about him."

"Huh." I thought that was curious. I gave Miko my card and told her to let me know if she saw anyone around the crime scene. I also stressed that it was important for her not to go over there either. She smiled coyly.

"Of course not."

But I knew she had already been. We left the house and headed to the field office. We still needed to find Doug Frazier. Beth's second husband had disappeared without a trace. Maybe he left the island altogether to get away from her. And while that was possible, something about it gnawed at me. It was possible, and yet it didn't sound right.

But that wasn't the only thing nagging at me. Why had Beth lied about her family? Why did she keep them a secret? And who did she lie to? She had told her husband her brother had died in a car accident, but her sister was still alive. But she told her neighbors her sister and her mother died in a car accident but never mentioned having a brother.

Which was the lie? And why lie? If she didn't want to talk about her family, then she didn't have to talk about them. But to tell people they were dead... her sister was alive. At least I hoped the woman I called, who still hadn't called me back, was her sister. As soon as I got to my computer, I searched for Doug Frazier. And I found nothing.

There was no movement on his social security number or passport, nor did he have a cellphone, social media, or record of a job. All we had was the name of his last employer. I sent them a follow-up, but didn't expect much of it since it had been so long since Doug had disappeared.

Since I found nothing about Doug, I moved on to the missing person cases Miko talked about. After a quick search, I found the names of three men who had gone missing near the bed-and-breakfast. From what I found online, there wasn't a lot of information. They were last seen in the area but then were never heard from again.

"That's so weird," I said mostly to myself.

"You want to go ask them about it?" Tony was already opening the drawer and grabbing his keys before I could answer him. I did want to talk to the detectives working on the case. I wanted to know more about the men, but more importantly, I wanted to know why Doug was not considered missing by the police. That question raised a lot more within me. Why was Beth so sure her husband had left her? Did he leave a note? Was there an argument, and he stormed out? Who would know?

At the local precinct, cops buzzed around us. There were some quick glances, but most of the officers seemed to pay us no mind. We were taken to a small, empty interview room and told to wait. As I followed Tony down the hall, I saw a little girl. Jet black hair and light-colored eyes. She looked at me with the saddest eyes I had ever seen. When I smiled, she quickly looked away. It was odd. She reminded me of someone. The memory slipped away before it could fully form. Staring at her was like staring at another sad face, but whose?

It dawned on me when I walked into the interview room. The cold air, sharp and bracing, knocked something loose. Dane. She reminded me of Dane Wesley. They had the same eyes and the same nose. The thought of him curled within me. Taking on a new shape. Before, when I thought of him, I felt sadness with a tinge of anger. Now, it was just sadness, complete and never-ending. I felt so sorry for everything he lost, everything he couldn't get back. Never being able to find his sister. And yet, if he hadn't killed all the people he did, she might have never come back to the island.

"What does the FBI want with us?"

The loud and playful voice shook me back to reality. I couldn't help Dane, but I could find justice for Beth, and that needed to be my focus for now. I looked up at the man standing in the doorway. He entered the room with his partner following close behind. One, the loud one, was older with graying brown hair and warm brown eyes. He smiled so wide the skin around his eyes crinkled in delight. He seemed in love with life and his job.

The younger one, a man with dark hair and light eyes, seemed more timid. He hung back while his partner's personality took up the room. He introduced himself and his partner while he shook our hands. Detective Arnold Carey and Detective Wynn Brockless.

Detective Brockless leaned against the wall. "They didn't tell us why you wanted to see us?" There was a hint of an English accent when he spoke.

"I was curious about something and needed more information about it," I said.

A smile bloomed on Wynn's face. When his partner opened his mouth to speak, the smile quickly dissipated. "Heaven help us when a woman is curious." He chuckled at his joke, but he was the only one.

"Anyway. The missing persons cases you two are working. The three missing men—"

"Right," said Arnold. "The men who went missing around... well, I guess the bed-and-breakfast isn't standing anymore. Horrible. It was a beautiful place. Took my wife there last year. She loved it."

I was surprised to hear that he was married. For a moment, I felt sorry for his wife. I glanced at Wynn as the thought eased out of my mind. It was like he could see what I was thinking. His lips curled into a smirk. "Right. We are investigating the fire. And we are looking for Beth Hardwell's second husband."

"Doug Frazier," said Wynn.

"Right. Did she ever file a missing persons report on him?"

Both men shook their heads. "Why would she?" asked Wynn.

"Well... he's missing." Did he really not see that, or was he just trying to be a smart ass? Doug was missing and had been for months. And no one was looking for him. Maybe that's why I was thinking about Dane. His sister had gone missing, and no one had looked for her either. She had been gone for years, and no one cared. No one but him. But Doug didn't have anyone that cared about him, it seemed like. They all acknowledged his existence and his abrupt disappearance, but that was it.

"He's not missing. He ran off to be with his mistress."

"Great," said Tony. "Where?"

"What?" He looked back at Wynn, but he stared at Tony.

"Where did they run off to? Point us in their direction so we can ask him a few questions."

He sighed. "Listen. He ran off and left his wife. That was it. It's nothing more," he said with a chuckle.

"How do you know he ran off with his mistress?" I asked. If I knew who had told him, then I could ask how they knew and if they had seen it. No one we talked to had seen him leave.

He glanced back at Wynn again, looking for some backup.

"Mrs. Hardwell told us," said Wynn. "She was shaken and crying because her husband had left her. She said he ran off with his mistress after packing a bag. It was one night after an argument."

"And you believed her?" I asked.

"Why would she lie?" Wynn looked offended at the suggestion.

"Well, if she killed her husband, it would have been a great way to get you off her trail before you even found it."

His eyes went wide. His partner stumbled back. It was strange to me that the thought never occurred to them. It just occurred to me, and I'd only had the case for a couple of days. And I wasn't even looking into their case. But it made sense. If she killed her husband and told everyone that he left her, no one would suspect anything. Well, some people would. But not the ones around her, apparently.

Wynn chuckled. "I can't imagine old Mrs. Hardwell murdering her husband or anyone else for that matter."

"I guess my imagination is better than yours. No one has seen or heard from him since that night. He hasn't gotten a job, used his social security number, or touched his bank account since that night. Where could he have gone?"

A shadow passed over his face for the briefest moment.

"Listen, I don't know who you think you are to come here and accuse us of—"

"I'm not accusing you of anything. I'm trying to understand. How did this happen? How could you not even look for him? How could you take her word for it? Did you even look at the bed-and-breakfast when those men went missing? Did you even ask her about it?"

They both laughed. And the sound of it grated my nerves raw. My hands clenched into fists. I wanted to hit them, both of them. Not because they were laughing but because they didn't do their damned jobs. If they had, maybe we would have some answers now. It was infuriating. They couldn't be bothered to do their jobs.

"There is no way that sweet lady killed those men. She isn't capable. Wasn't capable," said Arnold, a laugh on the edge of his voice.

I shook my head. Tony placed a firm hand on my shoulder, grounding me.

"About the three missing men, what can you tell us about them?" Tony's tone was light, but it was forced, though.

Arnold folded his arms across his chest. "Nothing. It is our case, and we will work it to the best of our ability."

"So nothing at all then."

Tony squeezed my shoulder. Arnold's eyes cut at me, but I didn't look away. I meant what I said. Were they even capable of closing the case, or working it at all, because it didn't sound like it?

"I think you two should leave," said Wynn. He opened the door and gestured toward the opening. "If we find anything or solve it, we will let you know."

With a tight grip on my shoulder, Tony guided me out of the room. They weren't going to tell us anything, not now. Anger, red and hot, pulsed in my veins. I had to get outside. I allowed him to guide me. I didn't struggle against his grip even though I wanted to. I needed him to keep pushing me, so I didn't turn around and go back into that room. I felt eyes on me, but I didn't look at them. I kept my eyes on the beige-colored tile floor.

The air outside was cool against my skin. He let go of my shoulder, but I kept moving. We got into the car. He was about to put the key in the ignition but stopped.

"You think she killed him?"

I shrugged. My shoulder tingled with the movement. I could still feel his hand there. "I think it's a pertinent question to ask. And they should have asked it. But now I doubt we will ever know."

"If she did, the body might be on the property. But we will need a reason to dig it up. And a feeling won't cut it."

I knew that. The thought of her killing her husband didn't enter my mind until the detectives started talking, and now it was the only thing I could think about. It was like a puzzle piece had finally fallen into place. It felt right. I couldn't explain. And because I couldn't explain it, Davies would not go along with it. I nodded slowly.

We went back to the field office. Before I could sit at my desk, Hattie ran over.

"One of the guests wanted to speak with you. He said he saw something that might not help, but it seemed important."

CHAPTER TWELVE

TONY FOLLOWED ME INTO THE ROOM. A MAN SAT AT THE table in a light blue shirt and khaki shorts. He looked up when I walked in and set his phone down.

"Are you two working the Paradise case?"

I sat down. "We are. You have something important to tell us?"

He sighed. "I'm not sure how important it is. Or if it can help, but I've been thinking about it and…" he ran a hand through his light brown hair. "I felt like I should say something and let you decide whether it was important or not."

"Good call," I said. "So what is it?"

"It might be nothing, but I saw Mrs. Hardwell one night, a few days before the fire, arguing with a man. He was shouting at her, and she was shouting back."

I leaned forward. "What was he wearing?"

"A dark hoodie...black, I think. Or dark blue. It was in front of the house but off to the side a little bit. It was like they didn't want to be seen."

"Do you know how the argument started?"

He shook his head. "I was out for a walk, and when I started back toward the house, they were...talking at first...I think. Their voices were hushed, you know. I couldn't hear what they were saying. And then I think she said something, and he just started yelling. I walked faster. I was worried about her. Mrs. Hardwell was so petite. I thought he was going to hurt her. It looked like he wanted to."

"Did you hear anything that was being said?"

"Um...I think he was looking for someone. He kept saying 'I know you've seen him.' And then she said she didn't know what he was talking about and told him to go away. I said I would call the cops. I think the man got spooked and ran off. I told her I would still call the police. I already had my phone out as he was walking away."

"What did she say?"

"She said don't bother. She said she had already talked to the police about him. It wasn't the first time he had come by the Paradise. She said he was following her. I thought that was strange. She didn't explain why he was following her. But she said she spoke to the police, and they didn't seem to care. They couldn't do anything to him until he hurt her. And so far, he hadn't."

They didn't mention that. The detectives made no mention of someone following her. My fingers tapped against the table. "Do you remember what he looked like?"

He picked up his phone. "I took a picture as he was walking away. I snapped it just as he was looking back at us. It's not a good picture, I'm afraid. Cheap phone." He handed me the phone after pulling up the picture. The man had light brown or reddish stubble on his chin. I couldn't make out his eyes. He looked familiar, though, but I couldn't place it. After sending the picture to myself, I handed the phone back to him.

He was one of the guests we hadn't had the chance to interview yet. Detective Branson and her partner had, though.

"What was Mrs. Hardwell like?" I asked.

"She was kind." His eyes lit up while he talked about her. "She reminded me in some ways like my grandmother. She was always willing to help, and if you had a problem, she would sit with you and help you figure it out. When the airport lost my luggage, she stayed up with me all night making coffee while I made calls."

I smiled. She certainly sounded like the kind of caring person so many claimed she was. Or was that just a front she put up for the guests?

"I can't imagine anyone wanting to hurt her, but then again...do we really know people? I only had contact with her at the house. Anything outside of that, I wouldn't know."

"Can you think of anyone that would?" I asked. We needed to find someone who knew her. That really knew her.

He shrugged. "Other than the other guests and the staff, no one came there. None of her friends visited or anything. She might have met them outside of the house because she wanted to stay out of our way, but...I never saw anyone."

"Did she leave the house often?"

He shrugged again. "She appeared when we needed her and then fell into the background when we didn't. Most of the time, she told someone when she was stepping out. But she could have left without us knowing. I wouldn't know. I spent most of my time sightseeing."

"Okay. Is there anything else?"

"No. That was everything. I just thought it was something that you should know."

"Thank you for coming in."

Tony walked him out of the room while I stayed sat at the table. Beth was nice, or she was manipulative and money hungry. It just depended on who you asked. I sat back in the chair and tried to decide which was the real Beth Hardwell.

More people said she was nice than not. But did those people really know her? It could have been a front. A nice woman could have been what she wanted them to see. But Victor saw the real her. He had to. He saw her every day while they were married. He knew a side of her they didn't get to see.

There had to be someone else out there that we could ask. Who else did she talk to? I felt Tony standing in the doorway behind me before he said anything.

"Why didn't they mention the stalker?"

"That's a good question," I said. "Good question." My fingers drummed against the table for a long moment. Instead of going back and talking to the same detectives, I called Detective Branson. She was nicer and better with people than Arnold.

"You need our help already?" Branson's voice on the other end of the line was playful and teasing.

I laughed. "Yes, yes, we do. I figured you were the best one to talk to."

"Who else did you talk to?"

"A Detective Arnold Carey and—"

"Oh."

I could practically hear her eyes roll. I swallowed the laugh bubbling. "Right. So, I figured I would try again. Umm... we are looking into Beth Hardwell, and we just learned that she might have had a stalker. When we talked to the detectives, they didn't mention it."

"Interesting. I hadn't heard anything about it, but I'll look into it and let you know."

"While I have you. Do you know anyone who knows Beth? Not neighbors but her friends. She didn't seem to have any."

She was silent for a moment. I didn't even hear her breathing. I wondered for a moment if she had thought the same thing while she was investigating.

"I see. I thought that in a few hours, we would have the investigation. She seemed to live a lonely existence. Just her and her husband, and then he left her. She seemed to isolate herself. Don't know if that was intentional or not. Her neighbors were all I could find who spoke to her almost weekly, if not daily. She didn't seem to talk to anyone else. Not that I could find, anyway."

"Okay. It was worth a shot. I just figured I'd ask. Thank you."

"Sure. I'll let you know what I find. And from now on, call me, or Detective Kahale is really nice and helpful. She does great work. She's just like her mother. But find us if you need help. Better still, we are going out Friday night. Well, not really out. We play poker at her house. I'll send you the address. We'll pick your brain and get you drunk."

She hung up before I could protest my objection. I didn't know them. I didn't know her. Why would she want me at her house? You don't invite someone you don't know to someone else's house. Who does that? My phone pinged with the address. I stared at it. When did I give her my phone number?

You said you wanted to meet more people outside of work. But was this really outside of work? I shook the thought out of my head. It had been brought to my attention several times that I read too much into things. I was always looking for hidden meanings that weren't there. Dissecting sentences, looking for the truth. I needed to stop doing that, but it was a hard habit to break.

I had a few days to think about it. As of right now, I don't have any plans for Friday night. It might be nice to meet some of the female detectives.

"She said she'd look into it and let me know."

"Good."

The day ticked by, and I busied myself doing searches for Doug Frazier. A few minutes before I was ready to call it a night, two officers walked over to my desk.

"Are you Mia Storm?" asked one officer.

"Special Agent Mia Storm," corrected Tony.

"Right," the officer shot a look at Tony. He didn't like being corrected. The smile that had been on his face when he walked up fell for a moment. "Sorry. It's been a long day. Detective Branson said you were looking for us."

I looked at Tony. "Was I?"

"About Beth Hardwell and a stalker?"

I jumped to my feet. "Right. I asked her if she really had a stalker because no one mentioned it until today."

"Yes, ma'am. I wouldn't say stalker, really. He never got violent or anything. We were called to the house because of a guy creeping around her property, but by the time we got there, he was gone. He didn't hurt her. He just looked like he was looking for something. She didn't seem to want to press charges or anything. It was weird."

"In what way?" Tony didn't stand up. Instead, he leaned back in his seat.

"She wasn't the one that called us. It was one of the guests at the time. Mrs. Hardwell didn't want the police called. She just wanted the man to go away. There was nothing we could do anyway because he didn't do anything. Except yell."

"What did he say?" I sat on my desk.

The officer rocked back on his heels. "He screamed at her about someone. Like…he knew she knew where he was or something. Beth didn't tell me that. The guest did. She didn't want to talk about it. It wasn't the first time he had wandered onto her property either. But she still couldn't tell me what he looked like."

"What did you think?" asked Tony.

"In my report—"

"I'm not asking what you put in your report. I'm asking, what you thought was going on."

He was silent for a moment, weighing the question. "I thought…to me, it felt like she knew him. She knew who he was, and she knew why he was there. And whatever was going on, she didn't want the police involved. She didn't want us there. She didn't want our help. The guest was offering more details than she was. I figured she knew the guy and wanted to handle it herself, or she didn't want to get him in trouble." He paused for a moment and sighed. "But when we got word she had been killed in that fire…I thought about the guy on her property. I felt bad. I wished there was more we could have done, but we had no name, no description. We had nothing."

"It's not your fault," said Tony. "There was nothing you could have done."

The words did not make him feel better. It was clear by the look on his face. He still blamed himself. He tried to smile it away, but it was there. Just behind the eyes. *What more could I have done?* I felt bad for him. He might be stuck with that feeling for the rest of his life.

With a curt nod, he walked away. His partner followed close behind. Beth Hardwell had a stalker, but she probably knew him. What could she have done that would have made someone follow her? Stalk her property. And why would she protect him?

"You think she might have owed someone money?" I looked back at Tony, who shrugged.

"You think this was about building materials?"

I chewed on the questions. Beth had been working on the house. These guests would be her last until repairs were done. "What if she didn't pay the contractor and refused to give him the materials back? Maybe that pissed him off, and he tried to get them back. Or maybe he thought burning the place down would teach her a better lesson."

He sighed. He didn't believe my little scenario. I mostly didn't believe it either. Lost materials weren't worth killing someone over. But then again, if it was your livelihood, the sole way you put food on the table, and someone cheated you out of not only the work but the money and materials... I'd be pretty pissed off. Maybe not burn a building down pissed, but I'd be pretty close.

"Maybe. I guess that is possible. If he was pissed enough, and after trying to talk to her to get her to pay him so many times wasn't working...yeah, I guess I could see that."

"Well, he can't get the materials now."

"In the morning, we should look into the contractors that worked on the house in the last couple of years."

"Yeah. First thing in the morning." I was exhausted. All the talking and thinking had taken a toll on my mind and body. I just wanted to go to sleep. Curled into my nice, warm bed and sleeping for hours. I'd take a shower in the morning. I was at my front door when my phone vibrated in my pocket. Part of me didn't want to answer it. I was tired and ready to just be done with the day. But I did. The voice on the other end sounded panicked.

My chest tightened. "Who is this?"

"I'm Maise, Dr. Rogers' secretary. Is this Mia Storm?"

Panic coiled beneath my ribcage. "Yes. What happened?" My heart stuttered in my chest, unable to catch the same rhythm again.

"I was told to call you. There was an incident at the hospital. He was stabbed by a patient."

My blood froze in my veins.

A thousand questions ran through my mind: How does that happen? How did a patient get something sharp enough to stab him? Shouldn't precautions have been taken? Where was security?

But all I said was, "what?"

My pulse rushed in my ears like a raging river, loud and never-ending.

"We're bringing him to the hospital and we had you as his emergency contact."

"Give me a minute," I said. I couldn't hear her. My pulse was too loud, and my heart stammered. I grabbed the door frame to steady myself. "Breathe," I told myself. "Just breathe."

CHAPTER THIRTEEN

CALMED MYSELF DOWN ENOUGH TO HEAR THE ADDRESS from his secretary. Harrison had been rushed to the emergency room. The wound didn't nick any arteries, but there was a lot of blood. She told me it seemed like he was going to pull through. That helped me relax. It was good to know that he was okay. But I still wanted to know how it happened. I shoved that out of my mind for the moment. I needed to focus on getting to the hospital.

I made it there in record time, surprised I never got pulled over. He was sleeping when I got there. The doctor had given him something for the pain and to help him sleep. He was worried about the wound on the back of Harrison's head. From what I gathered from the police, who were still outside his room, a patient was angry at Harrison for something. Neither officer knew what it was that set him off, but he grabbed a pen and stabbed Harrison in the throat. He fell back and hit the edge of a table on his way down.

"He'll be out for a while. If you want to go home and get some sleep," said a nurse, a tall woman with dark eyes and dark brown hair.

"I'll be here," I told her.

"Could be a while," the woman said.

"I know."

She shrugged, then checked his vitals and made a note of the readings before leaving the room. I didn't want to go home and get some sleep. I wanted him to wake up. I wanted to know what set the patient off. I wanted him to open his eyes and tell me everything was going to be okay. I wanted to believe him.

I moved the chair from the corner closer to his bed and sat down. I held his hand tight at first. I wanted him to know that someone was there. That I was there. I wasn't sure when I fell asleep.

My head snapped up, and my eyes opened instantly. Sunlight filtered into the room. My phone vibrated in my pocket. I checked the time before I pressed the green phone button. It was almost eight.

"Yeah?"

"Hey, are you in your apartment?"

"No. I'm at the hospital. Harrison was attacked by a patient last night. I've been sitting with him all night."

"Shit. Is he okay?"

I nodded even though I knew Tony couldn't see me. "Yes, he's okay. So far, anyway. He hasn't woken up yet, though, which has me a little worried."

"You want to sit out today? I could cover for you."

The concern in his voice was touching. "No, I could use the distraction. The nurse said it would be a while before he woke up. I'll drive home and change and then meet you at the field office."

"Okay. If there is anything I can do, let me know. Let me know if there's any change."

"I will." I hung up and shoved it back in my pocket. I watched Harrison for a long moment. The rise and fall of his chest. It was steady, which I took as a good sign.

"I'll be back later," I whispered with a squeeze of his hand.

§

Tony was waiting for me outside the office with a concerned look on his face.

"Is he okay?"

I shrugged. "I honestly have no idea. I'm not next of kin, so they can't really tell me anything. But he's breathing. He just hasn't woken up yet. And he got stabbed in the throat."

"Shit! Patient must have really hated him. Did they arrest them?"

I shrugged again. I had no idea who did it or if they were arrested. Knowing Harrison, he wouldn't even want to press charges against the person. He really cared about his patients. It was hard for me to imagine a reason one of them would stab him. Maybe they were having a mental break or weren't taking their meds. It could have been for so many reasons. And he wouldn't say. Even if he were awake, he wouldn't say anything. He took doctor-patient confidentiality very seriously. Even if they hurt him, he wouldn't say anything unless he had to.

Whoever the patient was, they proved they weren't only a danger to themselves but to others as well.

"We going in?" I stared at the doors. I didn't really want to spend the day in the office. I didn't feel like sitting. Not right now.

"You want to talk to the contractors who worked in the house? I made some calls while I was waiting."

My ears pricked up. "Sure. I'd prefer that to going in the building right now."

He nodded. "Figured as much. Let's go."

I followed him to his car. "If you get a call to go to the hospital, I'll take you." I nodded slowly.

"Thanks." I wasn't sure if they would call me. His secretary did, probably because she knew about me. She knew he had a girlfriend and that I might want to know about it. But what about his family? The thought didn't even enter my mind last night. I didn't think about his adoptive parents or anything. They should know, but I had no way to get in touch with them. Where was his cell phone?

His secretary would know. She would know who to call. I shouldn't worry about it. I couldn't do anything about it. Not now. And maybe he didn't want his parents to know. We drove to the address written on a slip of paper in the console.

The contractor was already working on another building site. A house, I thought at first. It looked like a house, the framework anyway.

"Are you Hoang Thien?" asked Tony as he walked up to an Asian man with short black hair and dark brown eyes. One eye had an angry red scar underneath. It looked fresh.

"You the FBI?"

I nodded.

"Okay. Let's go over here." He gestured to a dark blue truck parked in front of the site. It was clear whatever he was going to tell us, he didn't want to say it in front of his workers. The site was busy. Workers buzzed around us. I followed the men to the truck.

"Now, what is this about?" He leaned against the truck and folded his arms across his chest.

"Beth Hardwell," I said.

He straightened. "I was sorry to hear what happened to her. Horrible way to die."

"You think she was alive when the house burned down?" I asked.

He shrugged. "People been talking about it, but no one knows everything. I hope she wasn't. She loved that place. Obsessed with it, really. She would have gone insane if she saw it go up in flames."

"Was there any bad blood between you two?" I asked.

He glanced at the work sight. "Not really. She paid me what she owed me, but... I hate to speak ill of the dead."

"But..." I said to coax the words from him. He wanted to tell us. He wanted to say something. He just needed the right encouragement.

"She was crazy. She was and her husband, too. They were two of the strangest people I have ever met in my life, and I would never want to work for either of them again, even if she wasn't dead."

My eyebrows shot up. I hadn't been expecting that. But his words sounded genuine. There was no animosity behind them.

"What made you think she was crazy?"

He looked at me for a long moment, weighing my question. "It's hard to describe. She was so fixated on the bed-and-breakfast. By the time I was working on it, most of it was already done. I did mostly cosmetic work. You know, painting and changing out the dated fixtures. Simple stuff. Beth was particular about how she wanted things. It was like she could see it in her head and wasn't going to stop until the two matched, which was fine. I've had picky clients before. I'm used to it." He glanced at the work site again before he continued. "So, my guys and I put the flooring in. She wanted to change the wood tone. We do our jobs, and then the next morning, we come in to look at the kitchen, and the flooring in the sitting room was destroyed."

"Destroyed?"

He looked at me and nodded. "It was like someone took a hammer to it. I was shocked, and it pissed me off. We did good work on it, and I didn't see any reason for her to do that. If there had been a problem, she could have just told me the next day. She didn't have to take a hammer to the floor. It didn't make any sense. But she told me it wasn't right. Not the right wood tone and that we needed to do it again."

"Why did she mess up the floor?" I asked. It didn't make any sense. Surely, it would have been easier to just tell him that the flooring wasn't the right color.

He shrugged. "To prove a point, I guess. Never got a full explanation about that. We had to redo it. I was never sure if it was her or her husband that did it. I want to say it wasn't her, but she had some cuts on her hands, so maybe."

"What can you tell us about her husband?" The fact that we still hadn't been able to find Doug still nagged at me. Everyone knew he was married to Beth, but they couldn't tell us anything important about him, like where he was. It bothered me. It felt impossible. It also felt like they were both hiding something, but without them, we couldn't figure out what it was.

"Hmm... He was a little strange, too. More the silent type. She was the main talker. And I think she was the person who really had the ideas for the place. You know what I mean. It was her dream, and he was just going along with it. Whatever she wanted. I really feel like he would have done whatever she wanted. That's why when I heard he had left her, I was surprised. This was after I was done working on the house. I never thought in a million years he would have walked away from her. She could leave him but not the other way around."

"Why would she leave him?"

He leaned back against the truck. "How can I put this? She was a flirt. We see it all the time, you know. Usually, women make our food while we're working and whatnot. It's nice, but sometimes it goes a little too far. I think some of them believe they can get a discount if they flirt with us. The food is nice, but then they want to stand around and talk, and then they're touching you. I had one woman grab my foreman's ass in front of her husband. She acted like it wasn't a big deal. Beth didn't grab anyone. Not that I saw, at least—but she stroked some of their arms and leaned in a little too close. He either didn't notice it or overlooked it."

How odd. The thought must have been written all over my face because he smiled.

"It was weird being in that house. I wish I could better explain it. I'm not an articulate man, and I don't think weird is a strong enough word. Something wasn't right. I was glad when our contract with them was up, and I didn't have to go back. She asked us to, but I said I had too much on my plate. I could have used the work. I just didn't want to go back in that house."

"What was it that bothered you?"

A shadow passed over his face. He stared at the ground for a long moment. I wanted to know more about the house. It was our crime scene, but we couldn't walk through it like we could with the others. It was gone. Nothing but the charred remains were left. The burnt bones of what used to be. I needed to know more about what the inside of the house was like. The guests seemed happy there. All of them said how much they enjoyed their stay. A few of them had been there more than once. What had he seen that they didn't?

BREAKFAST IN PARADISE

"It was dark, you know? Even with the blinds open, letting in all that sunlight. It was still too dark. Like a heavy dark cloud just moved around, room to room. There was something not right. I don't know a better way to describe it. Whenever I walked into that building, I got a pit in my stomach. An uneasy feeling that never left me, not until I was in my truck and pulling out of the driveway. I can't place it, but I just got the feeling that something was wrong."

"Did you ever see anything wrong?"

He sighed. "Not really. The cook or the maid might know more."

"Yeah, we are going to see them soon," said Tony. "We just wondered if it was possible that she might have owed the contractors some money for finished projects."

He straightened again. "I can say a lot about Beth Hardwell, and I have. But she never stiffed us. Or any other contractor she worked with. If that woman didn't do anything else, she paid us. And her husband helped with a lot of the work, so that cut down on costs. She made sure she paid the workers. She wanted the work to continue, so she had to pay. And we all talk to each other, so word would have gotten around if she didn't pay someone."

"I see," said Tony. It wasn't the answer he wanted. He wanted it to be one of the contractors. I could tell by the way his shoulders fell. We had finally gotten what we thought was a promising lead, but it slipped through our fingers. We thanked him for his time and then walked back to the car.

"We are meeting with the staff?" I asked once I got in. Apparently, he had done a lot while he was waiting for me at the field office. I didn't think I was that late. My shower had taken a little longer than I thought. I just stood there and let the hot water beat against my back while I zoned out. Maybe he couldn't stop thinking about the case either and got an idea in the middle of the night. Happened to me a lot.

He took his phone out of his pocket. "I told Hattie to text me when she found their information. She did while we were talking to him. What do you think?" He shoved the key into the ignition. The car roared to life.

"I think something was going on in that house. And I think the only people that can tell us are dead."

CHAPTER FOURTEEN

The cook, an older woman named Piper with big blue eyes and blonde hair, stood in her kitchen, squeezing a dish towel. She squeezed so hard that her knuckles turned white. It was clear she didn't want us there. I could see, so I knew Tony could, too. What I couldn't figure out was why. What was she afraid of?

We sat in her small kitchen at a round table. Her home was sparsely decorated. She had the essentials and nothing else. There were no pictures of family on the wall. But I couldn't hold that against her. I didn't have any, either, and I was close to my family. I studied her home as we walked to the kitchen.

Ever since I had been fooled by Yumi, I have paid more attention to my surroundings. She had fooled me. For months, she had been my neighbor, a woman I thought needed protection from her abusive boyfriend. But it was all a ruse. She worked for the child trafficking ring. She was taken by them, and then she worked for them. I had walked into her house and known something wasn't right, but I let it slide. I'd noticed things, but I hadn't been really paying attention. I didn't trust my gut. I couldn't let that happen again, so now I let my eyes linger over everything as we passed, taking in every detail I could. It seemed strange to me that such a mature woman would have little to no furnishings.

"How long have you lived here?" I asked.

She had been staring at the wall but seemed to snap back into herself at the sound of my voice. She smiled slightly. "Not long." She still gripped the dish towel firmly in her hands. "I used to live in another apartment, but…my son…" She sighed, long and deep. The weight of it filled the room. "He was on drugs—is on drugs," she corrected. "He took just about everything I had. Beth was helping me start over. This is what I could afford, and somewhere, I don't think he would ever think to look for me. So far, I've been right."

"I'm so sorry," said Tony. "Addiction can be difficult for everyone."

A ghost of a smile touched her lips. "Thanks for that. It is difficult. But I have to keep telling myself I am not responsible for his actions. It's about him and him alone, and I cannot be the reason he gets clean. If he doesn't do it for himself, he'll never stick to it."

"That's true." There was a hint of sadness in Tony's voice. At first, it sounded like he just felt sorry for her. But then I thought maybe he knew someone dealing with addiction.

"But you're here to talk about Beth Hardwell. What is it that you want to know?"

"More about her. Other than her ex-husband, we've been hard-pressed to find anyone who really knew her. That talked to her every day. That she confided in."

"She wasn't the confiding type," Piper said. "She kept things to herself, or she told her husband. Things might have been different with the last cook but not with me."

"Did you notice anything strange going on in the house?"

She thought about the question for a long moment. "I'm not sure. I was only there when there were guests, and I was

BREAKFAST IN PARADISE

only there for breakfast and lunch. Mrs. Hardwell wanted me to prep for dinner, but she would serve it. It cut down on costs. She wanted to bring me in full-time, but she wanted to wait until things picked up."

"The business wasn't doing well?" It seemed like they had many customers, and everyone who stayed loved it.

She shrugged slightly. "Not as well as she would like." She drew in a deep breath. "Mrs. Hardwell loved money. I wouldn't say she was obsessed with it, but she liked it. A lot. More importantly, she liked spending it more than anything. If she saved most of what she brought in, there would have been money to hire me full-time. That money just passed through her fingers. Sometimes, it didn't even touch them before it was gone again. She bought a lot of stuff. Mostly clothes and perfumes and pretty sparkling things. I figured it was because she grew up poor. Poor children usually have a hard time managing money. I should know."

My ears pricked up. "Did she tell you about her childhood?"

"She mentioned it a couple of times. I think she felt a little comfortable with me. We're both from Georgia and moved here looking for a new start. I wouldn't say she confided in me or anything. No deep, dark secrets. But she said she and her sister and her mother were so poor growing up."

"Did she mention a brother?"

Piper shook her head. "Nope. She said it was just her, her sister Savannah, and her mother. Her father ran off when she was little, and she never saw him again. She said she promised herself she would never be that poor ever again. She said she came close a few times but never that poor. I think that's why it was so important to her and also why she couldn't resist spending it."

"What was her relationship like with Doug?" I asked.

She blinked. "He worshipped the ground she walked on. He would have done anything for her. All she had to do was ask. And she asked a lot. He helped her renovate that place even though it was clear, at least to me, that he didn't want to. He didn't care about it, not like she did. I figured that was the final straw, you know. Why he left her in the end? He just couldn't take that building taking up so much of her life. It was all she thought about. Ways to make it better. But then..." She paused, stuck. Like there was a glitch in her programming, and she didn't know how to get started again.

"Then?"

She blinked several times before she looked at me. Coming back into herself, our conversation slowly registered. "Right. I was never sure he left her, you know. Or...that is to say, I never thought he would. She was his whole life. He didn't have friends. He wasn't close to his family, not after meeting and marrying her. He had no one else, and they had no children. She was everything to him. You could see it. The story that he ran off with another woman has never sat right with me."

"Did you see him leave?" I asked.

She shook her head. "I came in the next morning, and she was sat at the dinner table crying her eyes out. Her face was red and puffy. And one of the guests was sitting next to her, consoling her. The woman said she saw him leave. They had a horrible argument, so loud she heard it in her room, and he stormed out and got in his truck. She said Doug had said he was going to see a real woman." She shook her head again. "That didn't sound like him, but I had never heard him angry. We say the meanest things when we are angry. Horrible things. He never came back. I always thought he would."

"How long had you been there before he left?" asked Tony.

"Two weeks. Maybe three."

"Do you know his family? Or where can we find the guest who watched him leave?" I asked. If we could learn more about him, then maybe we could figure out where he would have gone. Part of me thought he was dead. And part of her, too. Piper talked about Doug as if what people said he did was not possible. It was like she wanted to say he was dead, but she wasn't sure. Not really.

I felt the same way. Deep in my bones, I knew something was off. I couldn't say if he was dead or not, but we didn't have the full picture. Not yet.

"I have his sister's number. She called me a while ago asking me about him. Asking if I knew anything about where he went. She sounded desperate. Frantic. No one was looking for him because of what Beth said, and that angered her. She was his sister, and she said he was missing. But it didn't matter compared to what Beth said."

"I understand how infuriating that could be," I said. She knew her brother. Maybe he wouldn't have left without telling them.

She hurried into another room and then emerged with a slip of paper. "She'll be happy to hear from you. It's not a local number, though. I don't think she lives on the island anymore. Or if she ever did. Their mother did at some point. She might have moved, though. I'm not sure. As far as the guest... I really can't remember. Local police might know."

We thanked her for her time and went back to the field office. I wanted to call his sister in the car, but I stopped myself. I was eager to speak with her. A million questions swarmed my mind. While I called her, Tony called the local precinct to see if they had the information on the guest who saw Doug leave the house.

"Hello?"

"Hello, this is Special Agent Mia Storm. Is this Doug Frazier's sister?"

A sharp inhale followed by a slow exhale told me it was. She was bracing herself. Bracing herself for bad news, but I didn't have any news for her. I was contacting her looking for information. I sighed. I felt bad that I had nothing to tell her, but I needed to know more about her brother.

"Have you found him?"

"I'm sorry. Ms. Frazier, but no. We haven't."

"Chelsea is fine. So why are you calling me?" There was a slight edge to her voice. It wasn't sharp or pointed but dull and worn down. She sounded tired.

"We are actively looking for him. Especially since... I don't know if you've heard about the fire at the Golden Paradise."

There was another sharp inhale. "What!"

Her voice was shrill. I pulled the receiver away from my ear for a moment. The shock in her voice was surprising. She hadn't heard about it. This told me she no longer lived on the island. "Yes. It burned down, and Beth Hardwell was killed." I waited. Braced myself and ear for another shrill shriek... but there was nothing. A sea of silence deep enough to drown in. Her silence wasn't an empty void. There was something she wasn't saying. I could almost hear it. I could almost hear the smile spreading across her lips.

"What a pity." Her tone was flat and dry, without an ounce of emotion, not for Beth. Piper was right. She didn't like her. I needed to know why.

That was it. Nothing else came after those words. If I wanted to know more, I needed to find the right words to ask. "I've been told that you weren't fond of Beth. I was curious about why. What did she do?"

There was a small laugh. "What didn't she do? She was a horrible person. Did you know her?"

"No. I did not. But I've heard she was a nice and helpful person." This comment elicited a full laugh.

"Nice. Helpful? Who the hell said that? No matter, it isn't true. She was not nice or helpful. She was a mean, money-hungry bitch who only thought about herself and no one else. Not even my simple brother, who loved her more than anything."

"I heard he lived for her. She was his everything."

"Yeah. She was his everything. But he wasn't hers. She only cared about money. Making and getting more money. It was never enough for her. She always wanted more. Needed more. Did you know my mother died after my brother went missing?"

"I didn't know that. I'm sorry for your loss."

"Guess who the beneficiary was on her life insurance policy. I'll give you two guesses."

I knew the answer. It was painfully obvious. I suspected she just wanted to vent. She had been the only person who cared for her brother, who had been missing for so long. She would take advantage of an audience now. And I wouldn't…couldn't deny her that.

"Beth Hardwell."

"My mother didn't even like her. She hated Beth about as much as I did. More even. Beth consumed Doug. She wouldn't let him come over for Sunday dinner. She knew we didn't like her, so if she wasn't invited, neither was he. I still can't figure out how she did it. How did she get her name on the policy? Not that I care. It's not about the money, but I just…the fact that my mother's money went to her makes my blood boil. It would have pissed her off so much."

"Do you have any idea where your brother would have gone? It is believed that he ran off with a mistress."

"Doug didn't have a mistress," she spat. "He never would have left Beth. You know how hard we tried to get him away from her. We even kidnapped him once. Kept him in the house for days, trying to deprogram him. He still got away from us. She had a hold on him. A vice grip. She wouldn't let go. He would have killed himself before he left her. He would have killed someone else before he left her. He loved her too much."

It sounded less like love and more like obsession. It sounded like they were obsessed with each other. I swallowed my comments. "What happened when you tried to look for him?"

There was a slight pause, and then the words rushed out of her like a faucet had been turned on and couldn't be turned off. Like she wanted to get everything out before I changed my mind and decided I didn't care anymore.

"I called looking for him. And she, pretending to cry, said he left her. I told her he would never do that, and I asked how long he had been gone. It had been a few days. I told her he was missing and, as his wife, she needed to file a missing persons report. She hung up on me. I waited a couple of days, and I checked to see if a report had been filed. She hadn't done it."

"But she did talk to the police."

"Yeah. She did. But she had told them he ran off with his mistress. When I filed the report, I told them he didn't have a mistress. He didn't do anything that didn't involve Beth. He was rarely away from her. I told them I knew my brother, and what Beth was saying did not make sense. But they didn't believe me. No one believed me. She was his wife, and therefore, she knew him better than me. What she said mattered, and what my mother and I said were just the ramblings of family members who couldn't let go. It wasn't fair."

She spoke more about Beth and how she destroyed their family. When I got off the phone with her, I felt worse than I did before. I brought her no answers and no comfort.

I hung up the phone and sighed. When I looked up, and saw Tony staring at me. A smile crept across his lips.

"You won't believe what I learned."

CHAPTER FIFTEEN

Whatever he learned, it had to be good. He looked excited, like a little kid in a candy store. It was both adorable and annoying at the same time. Especially since my conversation wasn't really fruitful. Before I answered him, I ran through what I had learned. Beth had made herself the beneficiary of her mother-in-law's life insurance policy.

How did she do that? If neither the sister nor mother liked her, how could she have initiated that? Did Doug help? Or was the policy a forgery? Or was her mother not in her right mind when she made it?

His sister said Doug would have never left Beth, and he loved her too much. They were consumed by each other. So, if he didn't leave her, then where did he go?

And no one was looking for Doug. No one cared. Beth had said he left her, and everyone took her word for it. And no one listened to his mother. It was a sad thought. I pictured his mother going to police stations, trying to get someone to listen to her. Holding on to the hope that she would see her son again.

Tears pricked the corners of my eyes. I blinked them away. Tony's smile softened.

"So, what did you find?"

He perked up. "Well, sadly, Brenda Jackson was killed a few months ago. She was the guest who saw Doug leaving the house. She lived in Oregon and was killed in a car accident. So, we can't talk to her. But the Nakamuras installed a ring camera and some other security cameras around their property."

"I'm honestly surprised they didn't have any before now. I mean, truly."

He chuckled. "Yeah, me too when I really thought about it. Seemed like something they would have had long before now. Anyway, one of the cameras picked up someone walking on Hardwell's property. Guy in a black hoodie. He was picked up, and they are bringing him down here."

Now, it was my turn to smile. It was the first bit of good news I had gotten all day. Now, we could speak to her suspected stalker. I was curious about so many things.

The officers arrived twenty minutes after Tony got the call and was taken to an interview room. He was quiet and calm. He didn't seem tense or worried about being in FBI custody. He leaned back in his chair, wrists cuffed in front of him.

"What is your name?" I asked.

"Julius Gabriel," he replied in irritation. Who wants to know?"

"Special Agents Mia Storm and Tony Walker. We have been looking for you. Why were you stalking Beth Hardwell?"

His right eyebrow lifted slightly. "I wasn't stalking her. I was looking for answers."

"Answers to what questions?" Tony had taken his usual lean against the back wall behind me.

"I'm...I'm looking for my brother. Darius Gabriel." He sat up straight for a moment and then leaned on the table. "I need to find him."

I blinked. The information slowly registered. That was one of the names on the list of missing persons we'd been trying to track down. "You think she did something to him?"

"I've been saying this—"

"You haven't been saying it to us. And now is your chance because we are actually listening. So, please say it all again."

He sighed. His hard, narrowed features softened. He glanced behind me at Tony, but his eyes settled back on me. I smiled, trying to make it as reassuring as possible.

"Wait," said Tony. "First, give me your alibi so I can run it down and clear you for the fire."

His eyes went wide. "You think—I didn't do that. I didn't kill her either. She knows where my brother—" He drew in a shaky breath and then answered Tony's question. He had been around the house looking for something. He didn't know what he was looking for exactly, but after walking the property for the millionth time, he went to get something to eat. He was at a burger place waiting for his food when people started talking about the fire.

He told Tony the name of the place, and Tony left the room.

Julius looked at me, his features softening the longer he stared. "Darius was here for a job interview. He was excited about it. He really needed a change, and this was just what he was looking for. He came here, and as far as I know, he went to the interview. He called me on his way back to the Golden Paradise. He sounded excited, like he was sure he'd be offered the job. And then…nothing. I tried calling him. He never answered. And that is not like him."

"He was last seen at the bed-and-breakfast?"

He nodded. "Yeah. He said he liked it there. It was quiet, and the owner seemed nice. He liked her. He liked being here. It was the new start he needed."

"What did Beth say when you confronted her?" Up until now, we'd only heard one side of the conversation—what he said to her, not what she had said to him.

"She kept saying she never had a guest named Darius. I knew that was a lie. I knew he checked in. I saw his reservation. I can't pull it up now because he's not here, and it was on his computer, but I'm telling you…he was at the bed-and-breakfast. He was there. But she refused to acknowledge that he even existed. It was so strange. Why wouldn't she acknowledge it? It didn't make any sense. I can't leave until I find him."

His eyes were wet, his face red. "I can't go home to my mother until I find my brother. Alive or dead, I can't go back until we know."

Tony entered the room and closed the door behind him. "You must have made a lasting impression. The waitress remembered you. She said you looked so sad. You were the saddest person in the joint. She remembered wondering what made you so sad. What could have happened?"

"Cute girl with green and blue hair?"

Tony nodded, a smile dancing on his lips.

"I thought she was flirting with me. I can never tell. Darius used to make fun of me for being socially awkward. He was always trying to set me up with pretty girls. He said..." He swallowed the words and the memory and said nothing else on that subject. "Are you really looking for him?"

"He's one of the missing men from the area," I said.

"Right. There were three. All missing in the same area. I thought that was strange. The Golden Paradise seemed, at least to me, to be at the center of it, and no one else was paying attention. That doesn't make any sense. How can they not see it? How does she have them so snowed?"

That was a great question. It was like Beth had put a spell on everyone. No one that came in contact with her believed she was capable of anything bad, but those on the outside hated her. How did she do that? How did she have them so enthralled, so captivated by her that they believed everything she said? There had to be more to it than that. There had to be something we were missing. Something I was missing. It didn't make any sense. She was the common denominator in so many things.

How could they not see that? Surely, that was cause to at least look into it. Ask a few questions. I shook my head.

"I can't say why people believe her more than everyone else. Maybe it's because she's an old woman, known for her sweet demeanor, and they don't want to believe she was capable of doing anything wrong." They didn't want to believe she was capable of murder or getting rid of their bodies. It was understandable. I had seen a picture of her.

Beth Hardwell had graying brown hair, kind eyes, and a warm smile. She was shorter than me and thin. She was in her late forties, closer to fifty. She looked just like that sweet aunt we all had in our lives. The one we went to for help and guidance. The one we trusted to take care of us. Trusted with our secrets, our children. Our money.

When I looked at her, I didn't see a killer. But I had been at this long enough to know that just because I didn't see the murderous rage just behind the eyes didn't mean it wasn't there. That it hadn't been there all along. Hiding in the darkness. Hiding just beneath the surface of the facade she wanted the world to believe she was.

My parents used to say that everyone was divided into two people—the one they showed to the world and the one they were at home, in private.

"You never really know a person. You only know what they show you, and they will never show you everything."

Beth had been hiding a piece of herself away. She wasn't showing anyone everything. She showed some people one thing, her nice and kind side, and she showed her manipulative, money-hungry side to others.

"She's dead, so I doubt we will ever fully know what was going on. Feels like our suspect pool just really opened up."

Julius nodded. "People hurt by her. That's where you should look. I'm pretty sure my brother isn't the only one who was last seen at the Golden Paradise."

He was right. Whatever she was doing, she had to have been at it a long time. We needed to look at other missing persons' reports to see where they were last seen in the area. If someone was sure she had something to do with the disappearance of their loved one and was tired of being ignored, they might have taken matters into their own hands.

It wasn't what I would have done, but I could see it. I heard it in Chelsea's voice when she talked about her brother. Her frustration was palpable. Her anger a living, breathing thing moving in and out of every sentence.

It was there with him, too. Julius' frustration filled the room. His anger wasn't as strong as hers, though. It had been replaced, slowly, by sorrow. His hope of finding his brother alive was now gone.

He sat at the table, slumped in his chair. I watched him for a long moment. He wanted to know where his brother was. I doubted he would have killed her. If she was dead, she couldn't tell him where he was. And that was more important to him than anything. He had to know so he could go home and tell his mother. He said he wouldn't leave until he knew.

And he had an alibi. He didn't kill her. He didn't burn the place down. I believed him. I believed everything he said.

"Can you tell us if you can remember the name of the company where his interview took place?"

He nodded slowly. "Yeah. I do. It was a computer company. He loved computers. Always tinkering with one."

I tried to ignore the fact that he already spoke about his brother in the past tense. He knew he was dead. He knew it. He had to. I knew it. I mean, I didn't know it, know it. I wasn't a hundred percent certain, but I knew it all the same. I had a feeling in the pit of my stomach when I thought about those missing men. A pit hard and black. They were all dead. I didn't know if she did it or not, but I knew in my gut they weren't coming home. Not now. Not ever.

I wasn't as sure about Doug, but I had a feeling about him too. But maybe, just maybe, if we found them or found Doug, we might find the person responsible for Beth's murder and the fire.

CHAPTER SIXTEEN

Beth Hardwell

EIGHT YEARS AGO…
"How can you say that?" Beth screamed. She was tired of hushed voices and swallowing her screams. Victor never shied away from pissing her off, so why did she have to stop herself from yelling at him. It was stupid, beyond stupid. And no one was in the house, so it didn't matter. They had been yelling at each other for what seemed like forever.

It wasn't really. It wasn't a continuous fight. It was a bunch of little fights throughout the day, and that just made it feel like it was never-ending. No sooner had one argument ended than another one began.

He didn't like her ideas, and she didn't like his. And he didn't understand that her ideas were the only ones that mattered. She wanted the bed-and-breakfast. He didn't want any of it. He was only doing all of this to please her. But he wouldn't listen to her. She knew what it should look like, not him. He didn't dream about it. He didn't research how to draw floor plans so she could show the contractor what she wanted. Why couldn't he just go away and let her create the place she wanted?

"It's my money."

Beth rolled her eyes so hard she felt like she had strained something in her head. He always made that point. It was his money. Everything was his money.

"It's *our* money. I contributed too." She folded her arms across her chest. They were married, and what was his was hers. He always acted like he was the one doing everything, but he wasn't. She made sure he had a good home to come to every day after work. She kept herself quiet, polite, and easygoing so that he didn't have a lot to deal with.

"No man likes a loud, ill-tempered wife. You remember that," her mother had always told her. And she had. She remembered every lesson her mother taught her down to the letter. And she had done it. She gave him what he needed when he needed it. Anticipated his needs and wants before he could verbalize them. She made herself into the image of the woman he wanted. The woman he needed. Bent and broke herself until she fit next to him and nowhere else. Wasn't that enough? Didn't all that work entitle her to some of their savings? She wasn't even spending all of it.

He laughed. She hated his laugh. It reminded her of her father, cruel and dismissive. Like she was so stupid, all he could do was laugh at her.

"Seriously? What you contributed was gone six renovations ago! I put most of the money in, not you. My inheritance... everything is in that account, and you keep spending it!"

She blinked. Her hands slid from underneath her arms and rested at her sides. How dare he... All the rage Beth had been holding in her body... All the feelings she pushed behind a big metal door threatened to burst through. She swallowed. Pushed it further down. Added yet another lock. Now was not the time. She could still get what she wanted. She still had time to soothe her husband in that way only she knew. She sighed.

"I just wanted to make this house the best it could be. The better it looks, the more we can charge and the sooner we can make our money back. Surely you see the benefit of that." She softened her eyes and her stance. She made herself seem smaller, and his eyes softened. "We will make your money back and put it back into the account. But to do that, this place has to sparkle, and right now..." She gestured to the mess before them. "It doesn't."

He looked around. She could see it. She could always see it the moment his resolve softened. Became malleable like clay in her hands, ready to mold into what she willed.

"It's too much," he said softly.

"I can try to revise the plans. Trim some of it down."

He nodded slowly as his eyes drifted to the far corner of the room. "That might be better. At least for now."

She smiled. "Good. I'll get on that." He nodded as he walked away, shoulders dropped, head hung, resigned. She liked it when he looked like that. A hurt puppy stalking off to lick its wounds. Nothing would change. She was changing nothing about her designs. Everything would stay precisely the same, and he would have to deal with it. She could make him deal with it. Bring him round to her ideas. She was good at that, but she was tired. So very tired of having to do the same thing every time she wanted something.

Soothing him and stroking his ego. Why couldn't he just let her do what she wanted?

"You're so selfish, Beth. Selfish and spoiled, and one day that is going to bite you in the ass."

She blinked the thought away. She hadn't thought of her sister in years. She was in her head now. So real, she heard Savannah's annoying small voice blaring in her ears. She was not selfish nor spoiled. She had to work her ass off for everything she had. She didn't have a father who visited on the weekends. She didn't have someone to give her money for no reason, not like Savannah. She had everything handed to her. They gave her everything, and she barely had to lift a finger.

Beth's fists clenched at her sides at the memory. Her last memory of her sister; the smug look on her face. How she hated it. How she hated her and everything about her. Everything that reminded her of the sister she hated, and always would.

She never wanted to see them again, either of them. She could have gone the rest of her life without acknowledging their existence. And she intended to do just that.

Dinner was calm and quiet. Victor had nothing left to say, and Beth was too busy thinking—or rather plotting how she could get what she wanted from her husband. She thought of several different scenarios that might work. That might bend him to her will, but she still wasn't sure. She shouldn't have to go through all this work to get what she wanted. It was her money, too.

Beth wrapped her mind around this thought. It was her money, too. She held on to it. Clutched it close to her chest. It was her money, too, and he couldn't keep it from her. She didn't have to ask his permission, not anymore. He said he wanted the bed-and-breakfast to work. And this was how they were going to do it. She had to put money into it. Most of the work was done already.

The rooms had been renovated along with the bathrooms, and they had added the third floor, which had a library and a rec room. But she wasn't finished. She wanted to add an owner's suite, and she wanted to renovate the parlor, dining room, and kitchen. That would truly make it a great bed-and-breakfast. She didn't mention what she wanted to do on the outside.

New plants, new trees, a seating area and a pool. All of that would take years, and wipe out their savings, but it would be worth it. And she had tucked some money to the side. But she wasn't going to dip into it unless she really had to. She glanced across the table at her husband. His head bowed over his phone while he ate.

"You will have the life you deserve," said her sister the last time they spoke. She hated that thoughts of her family kept bubbling up. Beth had to keep those thoughts to herself. She had told Victor when they married that her mother and brother were dead and that she and her sister didn't get along. But none of them were dead, not really. They were dead to her, but that wasn't quite the same thing. Victor wouldn't have understood. He disliked his family, but he kept dealing with them. He kept letting them invade his life and hers. She had done what he couldn't. She hated her family, and she had walked out of their lives without a second thought. They didn't deserve to know her, let alone claim relation. She didn't claim to be related to them. Not if she could help it. She didn't even know where they were anymore. At some point, after she left, everyone spread. She used to keep tabs on them, but now, living in Honolulu, she doubted she would ever see them again.

Her sister had come to Chicago once. She wasn't sure why she was there. Beth saw her at the grocery store picking up snacks, for what she overheard was a long drive. Savannah hadn't seen her, and she ducked out before she could. Last she heard, her sister was back living in the south with her family, a daughter and a son. If Savannah was anything like when she was a kid, she was probably a horrible mother. Lord knows she was an awful big sister.

Her brother Terry had joined the Marines and had since retired and lived with his wife and daughter up North. Last she heard, he lived in Maine. Her mother was somewhere in the South. She might have lived in Georgia to be close to Savannah and her kids. But she also might have moved somewhere else to get away from her. Beth didn't really care.

Savannah was right about one thing. She would have the life that she deserved, and she would do whatever she had to make it happen. In the months that followed, things did not get better. If anything, it got worse. Beth didn't think it possible, but it did. And it kept getting worse.

"I can't believe you did this." Victor stood by the front door. His bags packed, and his keys were on the console by the door. He was tired of yelling. Tired of screaming at her and not being heard. Tired of her ignoring his feelings. Ignoring him. He was tired of her sneaking and scheming, but more importantly, he was tired of her. Who she was as a person was not something he wanted to deal with anymore. It was like still being around his family. Being smothered by them and their wants, having to ignore his own completely. And he was done.

"You're leaving me?" She laced her voice with just enough pain to make it believable. She didn't care. Not really. She knew this was going to happen eventually, and so she planned for it. She planned for this moment, and she would happily give him what he wanted.

"Yes. Yes, I am. I have to. I can't do this with you anymore. You're sucking the life out of me."

That last part was a little uncalled for, but she let him have it. She let him vent. Whatever it took to get him out the door.

"You took everything. All my savings."

"It wasn't just yours. And I didn't take everything. I left..."

"You didn't add anything. Half a million gone! You took everything! You left fifty thousand and see that as a kindness?" He threw his hands up. "I'm done. I hope you find what you're looking for in this place."

As she watched him leave, she knew she would be happier in the house than she had been before. And she still had at least two hundred thousand dollars to do something with.

CHAPTER SEVENTEEN

Julius gave us the name of the company his brother was interviewing with. His alibi checked out so we had to release him, but we made a point of telling him not to go anywhere. He smiled slightly at the remark.

"Where would I go?" The sadness in his voice was gut-wrenching. I believed him when he said he wouldn't leave without his brother. He couldn't leave until he knew. In my mind, he had an idea of what happened to his brother. He knew he was dead. I think we all knew that. But he still wanted to know where he was. Where the body was. Only then could he go home and tell his mother what happened.

It was sad and infuriating. Anger hummed beneath my skin. Buzzing in my veins. It was infuriating that this had gone unchecked all this time. Why was no one looking for those men? Beth Hardwell...how had she fooled them? I collapsed into my chair.

"We don't know that she did something to them. We don't know for sure, so we can't blame her right now. Not until we find concrete proof," said Tony as he sat down. He was right. I knew he was. Yet I was still angry. In my mind, she had something to do with it. In my mind, she killed Doug, too, because he was trying to leave her. While Tony researched the company and called them to speak with their HR, I looked up the other missing men in the area.

"I wonder how far this goes back." I did a search for the area around the bed-and-breakfast and searched for any men that had gone missing in that area. "Seriously." In the last four years, twenty men had gone missing including Darius. It was a wonder no one put it together. It didn't make any sense.

For the briefest moment, an image of Dane flashed in my mind. No one was looking for his sister. No one had put everything together. No one but him. I shook the thought from my head. I didn't want to think about him, not now. I needed to focus on Darius and Beth and all the others.

"HR said we can come in any time tomorrow. She's going through their records. She said the name sounds familiar, but she'll know more once she checks her records."

"Twenty men have gone missing around the bed-and-breakfast in the last four years."

His eyebrow raised slightly. "More than I was thinking. Any of them have families on the island? We could stop by."

After another quick search, I found two of them had a brother and an aunt who still lived on the island. Tony grabbed his keys out of the drawer while I wrote down the addresses. We were still working on the Beth Hardwell case, but we were just taking a quick detour. I wanted to know if anyone else thought she had killed someone. I wanted to know if there was a connection between the bed-and-breakfast and Beth.

The first house was the aunt of Oliver Chase, Beatrice Chase. She welcomed us into her home once she saw our badges. Her eyes sparkled when we mentioned her nephew but dimmed when we started asking her questions. It was clear we knew nothing about his whereabouts.

"I'm sorry to get your hopes up. We are looking into his disappearance and wanted to know more about him."

A ghost of a smile touched her lips as she nodded. "I figured I'd be hearing from you or someone when I heard about the fire. It's been all over the news, and I thought surely, they found his body among the remains. I guess not."

"What made you think he was there?"

"That was the last place anyone saw him." She looked from me to Tony, confusion creasing her brow. "You didn't know that."

"We don't know anything other than he's missing, and he went missing in the area." I tried to be as honest as possible with her. There was no point in hiding what we did or didn't know. "We need to know everything that the police were told. Is his mother around? Maybe she can help fill in the blanks."

She flinched when I mentioned his mother. It was slight, but I saw it. Her eyes drifted to the corner of the room. We sat on the sofa in her small living room while she sat in an oversized recliner. She was a small woman with grayish-white hair and large expressive eyes. The sadness in them so deep, I could drown.

"My sister died two years ago. That's why I moved here, so I could keep looking for her son. She was exhausted in the end, and I was the one mainly searching for him, anyway. She could barely get out of bed."

"Was he staying at the bed-and-breakfast?" I asked.

"He worked there. Or rather, he did work there occasionally. Plumbing mostly, but he fixed some of her electrical problems as well. He went over one night because she was having a problem with the plumbing, and he never made it home. My sister called me distraught. He always came home. They found his car, but he wasn't in it."

"Was the car on the property?"

She shook her head. "It was miles away. Beth said she hadn't seen him that night. She said she called him about the sink and tub in one of the bathrooms. I think it was backed up or something, but then, thirty minutes later, she called him back. She said it was working again, and she didn't need him to come out. My sister said that he left right after she called the first time."

"So, thirty minutes later, he should have been there by then."

"So, she had no reason to call him back. She tried to act like he never made it there, but I knew better. We knew better. There was no way it took him more than thirty minutes to get there, and that was the only place he was going that night. He was tired, and he just wanted to get into bed. But he liked Mrs. Hardwell, and he wanted to do right by her."

I could have pointed out that he was a grown man and might not have told his mother everywhere he was going. Maybe he had other plans that night, and they ran a little longer than he had anticipated. There were many other things and scenarios that I could have mentioned, but I didn't. I kept my words and my thoughts to myself. They weren't important. They weren't needed. This was about her nephew and what she thought happened.

I was determined to listen because no one else was, and I had seen first-hand how frustrating that was. How frustrating it could be to feel like no one was listening to you even though you knew you were right. So, I listened.

"Beth knew what happened to him. I knew she knew it. There was something strange going on in that house."

She was the second person to mention that. My ears perked up at the words. The contractor had said the same thing. There was something strange going on in that house. I was curious about the something strange. No one could tell us what it was, though. "What do you mean something strange?"

Mrs. Chase thought for a moment, she opened her mouth to say something but then stopped.

"You're the second person we talked to that said that. But the other person couldn't give us any specifics."

Her shoulders dropped. "I suppose I can't either. I had come to visit a week or two before he disappeared. He was off. He was fine one night when he went to work for her but when he came back...he was jumpy and ...strange. He kept looking out the window like he was being followed or something. He didn't leave the house for a few days, and then she called him, and everything was fine. Not fine but...he was less jumpy. He seemed less stressed about whatever it was. It was so weird. My sister and I kept asking him what was wrong. But he didn't want to talk about it. He never wanted to talk about it. When he went missing, she was the first person I thought of."

"What did the police say when you spoke with them?"

She laughed. There was an edge to her laughter. "They were dismissive. I think she does the little old lady routine really well. I think many of them visited the place. They knew her, and they didn't know me. They trusted her. And she used that to her advantage."

"Did you bring up the conversation they had that seemed to calm him?"

She laughed louder this time. "She told them she caught him doing drugs, and that's why he was paranoid. He didn't want anyone to know, and he thought she was going to turn him in. That call was about her reassuring him that she wasn't going to tell anyone. And that it was okay for him to come back and finish the work."

I leaned back. That kind of made sense. If he had been using drugs at her home and she caught him, he would have been paranoid about that. He would have been wondering if she would call the police. Half expecting the police to show up at his door and cart him away. It made sense. It could have happened, and yet there was something about it that didn't sit right. It didn't fit. It was too convenient.

"I take it that was impossible," I said.

She smiled then, weakly but a genuine smile. "Right. His father was a drug addict, and he swore he would never touch the stuff. Wouldn't even drink. Not to mention he was terrified of needles. Always had been. He wanted a tattoo but was too scared of the needle to get one. As soon as she said she saw him shooting up in her bathroom, I knew that was bullshit. And so did my sister. And then we started thinking why would she lie unless she knew something."

"What did the police say?"

She rolled her eyes at the question. It was nothing good, judging by her reaction. Her fists were clenched in her lap. "They believed her. His father was an addict, and some of them knew him. I guess they figured he was like his father. An officer told my sister that he was probably high and would come back, eventually."

I shook my head. They were judging him based on their interactions with his father, and that wasn't fair, especially if he didn't have any history of drug use.

"What do you think happened to him?" asked Tony. He leaned forward and rested his elbows on his thighs. "You've sat with this all these years. What do you think happened to your nephew?"

Tears pricked the corners of her eyes, but she didn't wipe them away.

"He's dead. I know he is. There's no way he would have stayed away from his mother all this time. They were like best friends. No matter where he went, he called her and checked in. She was dying. He knew she had cancer before he disappeared. He never would have just up and left her, not like that. He has to be dead. And I think Beth Hardwell knew more than what she was telling. He saw something that night when he was jumpy and scared. He saw something. I don't know what it was or what it could have been."

She wiped the tears away now on the back of her hand. "I wish that bitch was still alive so you could ask her."

"Me too," I said. I wished she was alive so we could ask her what happened to the men who disappeared around her property. And her husband. Where did he go? I thanked her for her time and gave her my card in case she thought of something that could help us. I didn't think she was a suspect in Beth's death. She needed Beth alive to figure out what happened to her nephew. Her being dead didn't help her at all.

We headed to our next destination. Elias Sampson's brother, Sam, worked as a mechanic. We caught him on his break. His eyes were the size of saucers when I showed him my badge.

"Did you find him?"

I shook my head and his shoulders fell. "We are investigating, and we need to know more about your brother. Anything you can tell us about the day he went missing." We followed him outside and away from the cars and the fumes of the garage.

"Not sure what I can tell you. He had been staying the Golden Paradise for a week. He and his girlfriend were supposed to meet there. He was there for two days and then she was supposed to join him on the Wednesday. She called me Wednesday night asking if I knew where he was."

"Had you heard from him before then?" asked Tony.

"Yeah. He called me a couple of times after he checked in so I knew he was there. But the owner said he never checked in. Why would he lie? That didn't make any sense. And he was supposed to propose. He had bought the ring and everything. Why would he just up and leave before she got there? Doesn't make sense. But the police didn't care."

"Why do you think that was?" I asked.

"Listen, my brother was no saint. I know that. He had his troubles, years ago. But he was clean and sober and we were so proud of him. He had finally gotten himself together. He wouldn't just run off, but they heard 'recovering drug addict' and stopped investigating. That was all they heard. Nothing I said could change their minds."

"What do you think happened?"

He sighed. His fingers twitched and then slid into his pockets. "I honestly don't know. I don't know why Beth Hardwell said he never checked in. He did. I know he did. He wouldn't have lied about that. And nothing of his has ever shown up. It's been a year. The car, engagement ring, his phone…everything. Where is it?"

"His girlfriend, is she still on the island?" I asked,

He nodded slowly. "Yeah, Kitty. We talk from time to time. She's been having a real hard time. She was an addict too, you know. While we were looking for him she started using again. I think she's clean now but I'm not sure. I'll give you her number. I don't have an address for her though."

He took his phone out of his pocket and searched for her number. When he found it, he held the phone out so I could see it.

"Thank you. If we find anything, we will let you know."

CHAPTER EIGHTEEN

KITTY WASN'T HARD TO FIND. SHE WAS, IN FACT, CLEAN and sober and working at a shelter. She seemed like she was both surprised to see us and expecting us at the same time. Like she had been waiting for someone to come to her with news about Elias but thought it would never come. And in a way, she was right. Her face brightened when we said we were with the FBI and there to talk to her about Elias. And then all the light disappeared from her eyes when she asked if we had found him.

"I'm sorry, but no."

Her smile waned and then disappeared completely. She looked like his brother for a moment. So sad and dejected. All hope snuffed out with just one answer. I felt so sorry for the family members of the missing men. They had tried so hard to find them, but they were the only ones trying.

In my mind, I knew we couldn't blame it all on the police. Not right now, anyway. I didn't have their case files. I didn't know what they did or didn't do or who they talked to. I didn't know if they looked at their phone records or credit card statements or if they searched their phone's GPS to get an accurate understanding of their last locations.

I didn't know any of this, and what irked me was that their loved ones didn't either. The officers might have done all those things, but they weren't communicating with the families. I understood that sometimes a case got out of hand, and you lost track of time. It was difficult keeping everyone updated on what you were doing. But they weren't doing anything now.

They weren't searching for the men. It seemed like now was a perfect time to let the families know what was going on.

"I know it's not what you want to hear, but we still need to ask you some questions about Elias and the last time you saw him."

"What about it?" She folded her arms across her chest and sighed. "I told the police everything and look where that got us."

I understood her frustration. I shared in some of it. I was pissed at the police, too. They should have been looking for him or put in more of an effort. But we couldn't change that now. "I understand your frustration. We just have a few questions. For starters, did you see him at the Golden Paradise?"

Her arms fell slightly. "No. I didn't. His stuff wasn't even there. I called him Wednesday morning and told him I'd be on my way after work. He said okay. He said he'd be waiting for me. But when I got there, there were no guests. His car wasn't there. I went to check in, and the woman acted like I had two heads or something with the way she was staring at me. Like she was surprised to see me. And when I said his name... it was like she recognized it. She knew it. But she said he never checked in. Why tell me to come but not be there? It didn't make any sense."

"Did you notice anything strange?"

She looked at Tony. "That woman, for one. It was like she wanted to get me out of there. Like she couldn't wait for me to leave. I tried to reserve a room, thinking maybe he'd come back or something. She wouldn't let me. She told me to leave. I said I wanted to wait for him there and asked for a room. She said I could wait for my druggie boyfriend somewhere else. Now, you tell me, if she didn't know him and had never seen or met him, how did she know he was a recovering drug addict?"

That was a good question. If he were no longer using drugs, it would have been a difficult thing to discern just by looking at him.

"She had to have seen him. One look at his forearm, and you can see the track marks. But only if he wasn't wearing long sleeves, and he mostly always wore them so people couldn't see the scars. How did she know? I asked several times, and I told the police she couldn't have known unless she saw him, but they heard 'track marks' and dismissed it. Looked at my record and figured we were going there to get high."

"What about his credit card? He had to charge it in order to get the room, didn't he?" Surely, the police checked his phone records and his credit card charges. They at least did that much.

"Said it was proof that he booked the room, not that he showed up. And if he never showed up, did she refund his money? No, she did not."

"Figures. Is there anything else you can tell us? Anything the police dismissed?"

"They dismissed everything. They dismissed him, me, and his brother. They only believed Beth Hardwell. It was like they knew her, you know. They walked up, and she offered them glasses of lemonade and asked them about their wives and children. She had them from the start. She was this nice lady, and I was a junkie with a junkie boyfriend. We never got beyond that."

Anger pulsed beneath my skin. How could they do that to them? It was a surprise, but not really. I guess it would be expected. It was also possible. He could have run off to get high. Maybe he had gotten so nervous at the prospect of proposing he needed something to calm him down. Just because something was possible didn't mean it was likely.

We thanked her for her time and left the shelter.

The next morning, we went straight to the computer company where Darius had applied for a position. Sterling Tech was a start-up computer company that was just getting off the ground. They dealt with building apps and security software and something else I didn't understand and didn't ask for further explanation. Tony seemed to understand it, and that was enough for me.

We were taken to HR, which consisted of a young woman with bright pink pigtails and a nose ring. It was a casual type of office. No suits. In fact, there was a sign on the door that said no suits. She smiled at us as she gestured at the two chairs across from her desk.

"I found what you asked for. Darius Gabriel. He did make it to his interview. He was even early. We really liked him. Offered him the job and everything." She handed the job application and the interview notes to Tony.

"You offered him the job?" I asked. His brother hadn't mentioned that.

She nodded. "We did. He was perfect for the position. He had experience building an app that actually worked. He was smart, and he had a good sense of humor. We showed him around the office, and he met everyone. There was another applicant after him, and we told him he'd hear from us later in the day."

"Did you call?" Tony handed me the papers.

"We did. I did. I called him four times and left messages. He never called back or answered the phone." She shrugged. "It was confusing. He seemed so excited about working here. He was asking questions about the area and finding housing. When he didn't answer, for a second, I thought something might have happened to him or something. Like he was in a car accident."

I sighed. "He went missing. That night, we think."

The smile slid from her face. "I see… You think he went missing when he left here? Because he said he was going home."

"He told you where he was going?"

"I told him to look to hear from us that night. And he said he'd be waiting by the phone and that he had no other plans. He was just going to stay at the bed-and-breakfast. I asked him if it was the Golden Paradise, and he said yes. My husband and I stayed there after the renovations but before the fire."

It was like everyone in town stayed there. "What did you think about it?"

She shrugged. "The place was gorgeous and had the most beautiful views. Mrs. Hardwell and her husband were a bit too weird for my liking. They were always watching us. My husband didn't notice it, but he's a man. Men can afford to be unaware of their surroundings. Women can't. Her husband watched us. The way he stared at my husband made me uneasy, and Beth... well, I hate to speak ill of the dead."

"But..."

She adjusted in her seat. "She kept asking me questions. Not weird questions, but there were just so many of them. She wanted to know about our family and if there was anyone waiting at home for us. She wanted to know where our families were from, if we had children, and so on. Once she learned our family lived on the island and that we had two children, the questions tapered off. It was just odd, you know. The way she asked. We were there for a week, and I wanted to have our meals elsewhere so that we didn't have to deal with them. My husband agreed. But the place was beautiful."

"Thank you for your time." She was the first person who also said Beth was strange and could actually tell us why she was strange. It was nice to hear it finally explained.

I walked back to the car slowly, a thousand thoughts and scenarios invading my brain. When I finally got back into the car, I had a partial picture of what had happened. Puzzle pieces finally clicked into place. Whether it was the right place or not, I didn't know. But it was possible.

"You gonna say anything?" The engine roared to life, but Tony didn't pull out of the parking lot.

"She was asking her all those questions to see if there was someone close by who would look for her. For them," I said.

He nodded slowly.

"The men that have gone missing either didn't have anyone that lived on the island to look for them, or they had criminal records or unsavory pasts. Their disappearances wouldn't be taken seriously."

"So, you think she was killing them? You think that's what got her killed and the house burned down?"

I shrugged. "I wouldn't be surprised. It sounds far-fetched, but it feels right." Something about this scenario made me feel like it was worth hanging on to. It was more tangible than the rest. It made more sense. If someone figured out what she was

BREAKFAST IN PARADISE

doing, maybe they killed her and then burned the place down. I took out my phone and dialed Julius' number. He didn't answer.

"That's weird. He's not answering."

I tried calling him again before we pulled into the field office parking lot. The phone rang and rang and rang.

"Hello?"

The voice on the other end didn't sound like Julius. It sounded familiar. "Detective Branson?"

"Storm? Why are you calling this number?"

"Umm... for the case we're working."

"Oh. Well, in that case, you need to get over here. I'm at the Paradise."

She hung up before I could ask any more questions. I relayed what she said to Tony, who immediately stopped the car and backed out of the parking lot. Dread coiled in my chest. Something was wrong. I hoped he was okay. Maybe he found something at the site and got in trouble for looking around the crime scene.

In front of the house that was no longer, there were several police cars and a coroner's van. My heart sank into my stomach. I knew it before I saw it. Jill knelt over a body. Detective Branson stood next to her. She looked up and saw me and waved me over.

"Did you know him? Suspect?"

"Not really. We had just interviewed him yesterday about his brother Darius. He went missing, and his last known whereabouts was the Paradise."

"Oh. What was he doing here?"

I glanced down at the body. Darius looked like himself as long as you weren't looking at his face. The rest of his body was fine and intact. But his head... wasn't a head anymore. It was just a mix of blood and bone and brain matter all mixed together. Bile coated the back of my throat. I pushed it down. "Looking for his brother, I think."

Branson sighed. "I guess he didn't find him, but he found someone else."

I shook my head like if I shook it hard enough, I could wipe the image from my mind. But it didn't work like that. He was still there. Why? It was clear to everyone, at least I thought it was, that Darius's brother wasn't here. If he had been, we would have found his charred bones with Beth's.

Her body was the only body found on the property, so what was he looking for? Was he looking for something we might have missed? We weren't looking for evidence of other bodies. We were looking for evidence of who murdered Beth, not her murders. Maybe we missed something.

"What did that to his face?" I asked. Tony walked past me and wandered somewhere else.

Jill pointed to a claw hammer close to the body. "Judging by the amount of hair, blood, and brain matter on that thing, I would say that was it. I do not see any defensive wounds, so they must have caught him off guard. I see a lot of dirt underneath his fingernails, though. I wonder what he was doing?"

"Storm." Tony's voice was calm and firm.

I looked up, and he stood by a shovel.

"Where did that come from?" asked Branson.

"Your guys didn't leave it?" I asked as I walked toward him.

"Nope. We left nothing behind. Figured the FBI could bring their own shovels."

"How sweet?" A smile tugged at the corner of his lips. "He brought the shovel and looked at this patch of dirt." Next to the shovel was a small patch of dirt. There were no charred pieces of wood or debris on this one strip of dirt. It had been disturbed. Next to it was a little hill. "He was digging."

"I guess he was still looking for his brother," I said.

Jill glanced back at the body. "So, did he find him or not?"

Tony slipped on a glove and picked up the shovel. Lightly, he moved the dirt out of the way. My hand gripped his arm. He stopped when he saw it. Fingers, still a little fleshy but mostly bone stuck out like someone was reaching for the surface.

I swallowed. The unmistakable scent of decomposing flesh wafted into the air around us. "I guess he might have found him after all."

CHAPTER NINETEEN

A LOUD GASP RIPPLED THROUGH THE SMALL CROWD AS Tony slowly unearthed more of the hand. It wasn't what I was expecting to see. Jill looked equally shocked. Detective Branson shook her head. "I can't believe this. Who is that?"

I watched as her eyes roamed the remains of the house, looking for other clues, other hints that there were other bodies underneath the charred earth. It was difficult to tell. We wouldn't know for sure until we dug everything up.

"Well, it looks like the hand is still attached to the body or the arm, at least," said Tony. What was a somber scene turned into chaos in a matter of seconds. Techs swarmed around us, nudging us out of their way so they could get to work.

It wasn't like we could help them. The scene had to be maintained, so we moved to let them get to the hand and whatever else lurked beneath the dirt. I followed Detective Branson to her car and leaned against it.

"He found his brother," I said quietly. "At least, I think that's his brother. It could be one of the other men that went missing."

Branson nodded. "I was not expecting this. Did he know there were bodies under the house, under the rubble? Or was he just looking around and thought let me dig here."

"He might have had his suspicions," said Tony. "He thought Beth Hardwell had something to do with his brother's disappearance. He knew it. And he was tired of no one looking for him, so he took it upon himself to search for him. That was, he kept walking around this property, looking for clues."

"He found them." Jill shook her head. "This might be a while. We have to search the entire property, and then I still have to get Darius on the table. There are probably more bodies."

That was her way of telling us to go away so she could get back to work. So, we did. Branson left first, but I scooted across the street to talk to the neighbors.

Mrs. Nakamura ushered us inside as soon as my feet touched her front porch. She pushed us to the living room, where her husband was still sitting in his recliner. It was almost like he hadn't moved since the last time we saw them.

As if reading my mind, he smiled. "I promise I do get out of this chair." He sat up. "I just have a bad back, and this helps. Now, what's going on over there?"

"Did you see anything strange last night? Anyone walking around the property?"

He looked at his wife for a moment. "I don't think so. It's been pretty quiet around here since that last time. Our camera is on the fritz, though. No matter how many techs they send out to fix it…it'll work for a little while, and then it goes back out. They sent someone yesterday, and an hour after he left… it wasn't working again. It's so strange and infuriating. Wasting money, really."

"That…sounds strange," I said. "Sounds like someone is doing it intentionally."

Mrs. Nakamura gasped. "That's what the tech said. He said it seemed like someone was hacking into our system and overriding it. I think he thought it was us, but we are too old to realize we are doing it. Or how to undo it."

"So, you saw nothing strange last night. Heard nothing?" Asked Tony. He leaned against the door frame with his hands deep in his pockets.

Mrs. Nakamura glanced at her husband. "I didn't see anything…but I heard a dog last night. I didn't think there were any in the neighborhood. But it was like a dog had been hurt. It yelped or something. But that was it. I didn't hear anything until the police showed up."

"Okay. Well, thanks for your time."

"Now, don't do that," she whined. I spun around, and Mrs. Nakamura sat next to her husband mid-pout. "Tell us something."

I looked at Tony, who shrugged. Wouldn't get any help from him. I wasn't even sure what to tell them. True crime addicts, they couldn't help themselves. I shook my head. "We might have found a body buried underneath the building."

Her eyes went wide as she jumped to her feet and clapped her hands. "Seriously? Why? Was Beth a serial killer or something?" She turned back at her husband. They shared a laugh. Tony and I didn't join in.

The laughter died in the room, and they stared at us. We neither confirmed nor denied anything. We left them in the room wondering. I followed Tony outside, mildly annoyed. I wondered as I walked back to the car if the same person who killed Darius also messed with their cameras.

At the field office, we sat at our desks in complete silence. There was nowhere left to go until we knew for certain if there were any more bodies at the scene. I hoped Darius was there so his mother could finally have closure. But I hated that we would have to tell her that both her sons were gone. It'd break her heart. I put the thought out of my mind. No point in worrying about it until we knew for sure.

After a day of waiting and paperwork, I went to the hospital to visit Harrison. The nurse smiled at me when I neared his door.

"He was just asking about you."

Harrison could talk, but his voice was raspy and hoarse. It would be a while before he was back to normal again. But other than the hole in his throat, he seemed to be okay. Upbeat but unwilling to talk about what happened. He didn't even want to write it down. I found it strange at first, but considering how much he cared for his patients, he probably didn't want to get them in trouble. It was something I respected even though I couldn't understand his reasoning. I sat with him in a measured silence. His raspy voice was heard only every five or ten minutes or so. He fell asleep, and I sat in an uncomfortable chair by his bed for a couple of hours before I went home. I couldn't stop thinking about Beth Hardwell. I wouldn't have been good company for him even if he could talk.

A body was buried in her backyard. Was it her husband? Was it one of our missing men? I wanted to know more. I needed to know more. I couldn't stop myself from thinking about it. I was trying to get better at putting things out of my mind. To stop obsessing over my cases. When I had a puzzle, an unfinished one, I could think of nothing else until all the pieces fit together. And here I was with one of the biggest puzzles I had ever encountered, and some of the pieces were missing. I couldn't make them fit together until I had more information, and I dared not call Jill. She would feel like I was rushing her, and that would make her upset. So, I went home, crawled into bed, and watched a home renovation show until I fell asleep.

I woke the next morning ready to call Jill or Tony or anyone who could tell me what I needed to know. It was a little after seven when I got in the shower and then got dressed. I sent a text to Tony to glean where he was and if I had to drive myself to the field office.

While I made toast, he sent me a text saying he would meet me at the morgue. Jill must have called him and said she found something. I finished getting ready, shoved my toast in my mouth, and headed out the door. He got there forty minutes after I did.

"You're late!" said Jill.

I sat on a stool in the exam room surrounded by dead bodies, one of them charred beyond recognition.

"Have you heard anything from her sister?" she asked before Tony could say anything.

I shrugged and then shook my head. I hadn't heard anything from Beth's sister Savannah. I was starting to think I needed to send agents to the house to speak with her. Either she hadn't checked her messages yet, or she didn't care about her sister. Either way, it only made me more curious about their relationship.

"That's odd. If someone from the FBI called me asking about my sister, I'd call them back right away." She sighed. "Anyway, Mr. Walker, you are late! Been waiting almost an hour."

It had only been forty minutes, but I didn't say anything. A smile tugged at my lips as I watched how flustered he was. He kept running a hand through his hair as if he expected it to be messed up. He smoothed down his shirt and stuck his hands in his pocket.

Jill walked toward one of the bodies and then spun around. "You have some lipstick there on your neck." She grinned.

Tony's hand darted up to cover his neck. I laughed, and so did she.

"Aisha?" asked Jill teasingly.

"I was going to say his mother."

Jill smiled. "I don't think that is her shade."

He rolled his eyes. "I get teased enough at home with my family. I don't need it here, too."

I pictured his brother King teasing him about having a girlfriend. He probably did it in front of her relentlessly. The thought deepened my smile.

"Don't ruin my fun." Jill pouted for a moment, and then her smile returned. "Anyway. Now that he's here, let's get started. The bodies have been identified."

My mouth fell open, and Jill smiled.

"While you were home sleeping…" She glanced at Tony. "Well, one of you was sleeping anyway… I was here working and trying to put something together for you when you came in."

"Well, thank you." I raised my hand, affirming I was the only one sleeping. A smile tugged at his lips. He relented.

"I hate you guys so much." He shook his head with a chuckle. "Please continue with your findings."

"Right. Well, anyway... this is what I found. One of the bodies did belong to the brother of our non-buried victim. Four bodies so far, and all matched the men who went missing in the area. We think she might have buried some bodies deeper... underneath the ones we've already found. We will continue searching the entire area to make sure we haven't missed anything." She opened a folder and flipped through the pages before handing it to me. "All victims were bludgeoned to death in the head. Back of the head, to be more specific. The men were fully clothed and seemed to have all their belongings with them when they were buried." She pointed to a table behind Tony that housed several items in plastic bags. "They had their wallets, complete with their ID cards, but there was no money in them."

"You think that all of this was about robbing them?" asked Tony.

Jill shrugged. "The 'how' is my job. The 'why' is yours."

"Her ex-husband did say that when she fixated on something, she had to have it. And she loved money. Maybe she was looking for more funds to finish the renovations." Beth was working on the bed-and-breakfast before she was killed. Maybe she was still looking for money to help pay for it. "So, she killed guests that had no one living close by or who had a history of drug use and then robbed them. She used their money to pay for renovations and buried them under the house or in the backyard."

"For their petty cash?" Jill asked. "I don't know..."

"Hey, like you said, you do the how, not the why. We'll figure it out," I said.

She smiled. "Fair."

"Is Doug there?" asked Tony. That was still a big missing piece of our puzzle. My running theory was that she killed him when he tried to leave her. Tony wasn't sure that was the reason, but he was pretty sure he was dead.

Jill shook her head. "Sorry to say, but so far, Doug Frazier is not among the bodies buried on the property. I don't know where he is, but so far, we haven't found him."

Where could he have been? Maybe she buried him deeper. Or maybe she buried him somewhere else. The pieces weren't fitting into place. They were still up in the air, hovering over my head. Not sure where to land. It was difficult to see to understand how it all fit together.

"As far as Mrs. Hardwell is concerned, the charred body is definitely female and looks to be close to her age. I still can't say definitively that it's her, though. It would be better if I had some kind of DNA or familial DNA."

"What about dental records?" I asked. If we had her records, we could match them to the body and identify her that way. It would make it easier. I couldn't say why her sister hadn't called me back yet. I called her twice and left a message both times. She wasn't dead. At least there were no records of her death. I was tempted to call in a wellness check for her.

"Oddly enough, there are no teeth in her mouth."

"Dentures?"

"Maybe. They wouldn't have melted in the fire, though. Or maybe the killer knocked them out. The techs still have a lot of ash and debris to sort through. I have them on the lookout for teeth."

"Let us know if you find anything," I said half to myself.

Jill stared at me for a long moment. "What are you thinking?"

I shrugged. "I don't know. Not yet, anyway." I didn't plan to tell her I didn't really know what I was thinking until the words were out of my mouth. We left the morgue. I wanted to make a stop before we went to the field office.

Detective Carey and Detective Brockless sat at their desks. Both men had their heads bowed, writing something. Carey was the first to look up. He said something as I walked up that made Brockless turn around. I stopped next to their desks. Tony stood behind me. Anger pulsed in my veins.

"I need the case files of the men who are missing that you aren't looking for," I said. Carey's expression soured.

"He stood up. "Now look here, you can't come up here and take over…"

"First, you don't tell me what I can and can't do. Secondly, we found the men…underneath the bed-and-breakfast, the Golden Paradise. We've identified them and everything. So now that it is an FBI case, I need those files."

There was an edge to my voice. I heard it, but I didn't care. If they had just done their jobs. If they had looked harder or given Beth Hardwell a second glance, then maybe some of those dead, buried men could have been saved.

"We just need the files." Tony's hand gripped my shoulder, keeping me steady.

Carey's face softened for a brief moment as he looked around. Officers and detectives passed by the window, some moving more slowly than necessary. They were watching. Listening. I tried to keep my voice as calm as possible. I wanted to tell them off. I wanted them to know how their nonchalant attitude toward actual police work cost people their lives. I wanted them to feel bad. I wanted to see an ounce of remorse. I saw nothing when I looked at Carey. He was more concerned with what his peers saw when they looked at him through the window.

Brockless, on the other hand, had an ounce of remorse. His shoulders fell, and his eyes searched the floor. He seemed sad, worried even.

"I'll go get the files." Carey walked away, but Brockless stayed behind. He leaned against the wall and sighed.

"I'm sorry," he whispered before walking out of the room. Brockless might have been a great detective if he hadn't been stuck with Carey as a partner. My fist clenched and unclenched at my sides. I wasn't sure Beth had anything to do with it. Maybe it was her husband. Maybe he killed the men and forced her to go along with it. But then, where was he? Did he kill her and set the place on fire to cover his tracks?

The more I thought about it, the more questions bubbled up. Saying it annoyed me didn't do it justice. We couldn't even say if the body was hers or not. What the hell was going on?

Carey returned with the files. "Here." Without another word, he left the room. I snatched up the files.

"Now we can leave."

CHAPTER TWENTY

WHERE WAS DOUG FRAZIER? I had a dream last night that Doug sat on the rubble of the house. He was there waiting for us. His skin was charred like the rest of the house, but his eyes blazed white against the blackened, charred flesh.

He sat near the front step, or where it used to be, and that was it. He was alone and staring at me, waiting. Just waiting. He didn't say anything or make any moves. At first, I thought he was trying to tell me something. Point me in the right direction. But he didn't do anything. He watched me, and I watched him, and we watched each other for what felt like hours until I woke up.

He wasn't trying to tell me anything. He was waiting for me to find him. He was telling me he was there, or at least he had been. That was what I took away from the dream. But Jill said his body wasn't there. They hadn't found it yet, anyway.

So where was he? Why was he hiding? I ran through what we learned from everyone we talked to. So far, we haven't found any evidence that Doug was seen after he left the house. No one knew or saw him with a mistress.

How was that possible? How was that—the identity of the mistress—the best-kept secret on the entire island? It didn't make sense. None of it did. Someone was lying. And I had an idea of who it was.

"I have one more thing that I want to do," I said as we walked back to the car.

Tony's eyebrow lifted slightly. "Oh, really. Where else are we going?"

"Follow me to the neighbors, or do you want to go to the field office with the files, and I'll meet you there."

His eyes narrowed at the files in my hand. "You don't mind going by yourself?"

I shrugged. "Sure. I just have a couple of questions for the Nakamuras, and then I'll be at the office." I hoped they could tell me more about Doug. Or maybe Mrs. Oakley was a better bet. She was closer to Mrs. Hardwell's age, and she lived closer. Maybe she knew or saw something they didn't.

He held out his hand, and I handed over the files. "Be careful. Call if you find anything strange."

"Of course."

I drove to the house and parked in front of the burned down house. There were no police cars or coroner's vans. Jill said before we left that the dig would resume sometime later. They were waiting on equipment that would allow them to see if there were any bodies buried deeper underground.

"I would really like to be there when you use this equipment," I said on my way out. She was supposed to call me when they were ready. Instead of stopping by the Nakamuras, I headed toward Mrs. Oakley's. She sat on her front porch with a cup of tea and a crime novel.

She smiled when she saw me.

"Where's your partner?" She gestured to the wicker chair next to her.

"He went back to the field office. I just had a couple of questions, so it shouldn't take long. Do you have a minute?" I sat and sighed.

"Sure. Not doing anything else today. What do you need to know?"

"Did Mrs. Hardwell ever talk to you about her husband?"

"Doug? She seemed so miserable when he left her. Broke her heart."

"Were you around when he left? Did you see anything?"

She shrugged. "I was surprised when he ran away. They argued so much in the months before he left. Nonstop almost. And it wasn't just in the house. They fought outside. Right in the yard. It seemed so unlike them. I thought they were happy. Or at least they were when he first moved in. I don't know what soured it. Well, it might have been that cook."

"Piper?"

She waved her hand dismissively. "No, not her. She came on after the other one ran off. A week, maybe two, later Doug was gone. Beth thought he ran off with her, and I didn't want to say, but I agreed. It was just too coincidental, you know. The girl gets fired, and then they both disappear... there has to be more to it than that."

I nodded as I listened. This was the first time someone mentioned who the mistress might have been. "Do you remember her name?"

She shook her head. "No. I don't, I'm sorry. I can't even say what she looked like. I just know that she left. I stopped seeing her, and then Piper, the new girl, showed up. She was much more friendly. She always waved on her way into the property. The other girl did not."

"I see. Is there anything else that happened around here? Anything strange?"

She shrugged. "Just you all digging up all those bodies. I can't believe it. How did they get there? I wonder if they were there before Beth took over the property."

I shook my head. "Yeah, I don't think so. Some of the bodies are of men who went missing within the last few years. So, I would say she had to know something."

"I just can't believe it. I won't believe it. Little old Beth, doing that? Granted, she kept to herself a lot, but that doesn't mean she was a serial killer or something. It can't be. Maybe it was Doug."

I sighed. "Maybe it was. But we haven't found him, either, to ask him."

"When he ran out on her, it was all over the island. Everyone was saying he ran off with his mistress. No one said what she looked like or who she was. It was just known he was cheating on her and left to be with the other woman."

"You heard it from her?"

Mrs. Oakley paused for a moment as if she was shifting through her memories, trying to find the right one. "No." I don't think so... She told me about it, and I pretended not to know anything. But I had already heard about it from my hairdresser one morning several days earlier. And she heard it at the grocery store. When I came in for my appointment, she was eager to tell me. She wanted to know if I knew and if I could add anything to what she heard. I didn't know anything. I had noticed I hadn't seen him in a few days by then, but I thought maybe he had gone to see his mother or was doing some work somewhere else."

"I guess gossip travels fast on the island."

She laughed. "Fast is an understatement. It's like living in a small town. If one person knows something, then pretty soon, everyone knows it. It's where secrets go to die, I guess."

Tony had told me that when I moved to Honolulu. Living on the island was like living in a small town. Something happened to you, good or bad, and it wouldn't be long until a bunch of people knew about it.

"Well, thank you for your time, Mrs. Oakley."

"Anytime. Can't wait to figure out what happened." She sipped her tea as I walked away.

I walked back to my car but stopped. My feet moved toward the crime scene. I ducked under the yellow tape. The area smelled like freshly dug dirt and burnt wood. It was a strange combination. I was almost used to the burnt smell. My eyes roamed over the burnt remains. I moved through the remains of the house and walked over to the holes in the ground. I walked by the holes, peering into them as I passed. They were deep. I couldn't imagine Beth digging them herself. She was an older woman, but that didn't make her an invalid.

She probably wasn't in a rush; it wasn't like there was someone paying attention to what she was doing. It amazed me and confused me at the same time. How could living on the island be like living in a small town when all of this happened right under everyone's noses?

No one was paying attention. My ears pricked up when I heard something behind me. The hairs on the back of my neck stood up. I paused for a brief moment.

Pain, hot and piercing, pierced the back of my head. I tried to turn around, but my legs wouldn't move. My body wouldn't move. My legs buckled as the ground rose to meet me.

White dots crowded the edge of my vision, my head throbbed with every breath. Something squeezed my neck, and my vision turned white. I couldn't breathe. I couldn't think. My hands darted up, searching. Hands. Not my hands. My fingers grazed over someone else's fingers, gripping my neck. I scratched, hit, clawed, and kicked my way into the air. I gasped, desperately gulping in air.

I yelled in frustration and pain and shock at the same time. But not fear. I wasn't afraid. I just couldn't see. I flailed wildly, trying to get my attacker off me.

The white dots subsided for a moment, finally allowing me to see a blurry figure rolling over on the ground. I kicked them, and they fell back. The figure was covered in black. Black ski mask, black gloves, and black baggy clothes.

"FBI!" My heart stuttered in my chest. A million things ran through my mind. I opened my mouth; my throat was so dry. My voice cracked. "Stay on your knees."

I reached for my gun, but the figure was faster. They kicked my gun and it skittered away, then kicked me hard in the ribs, knocking the wind out of me and making me double over. I balled my hand into a fist and lunged forward with a punch, trying to push them away. I collided with their shoulder, but they still had the advantage. They countered with a heavy hook to my right that exploded on my temple. Before I could even react, they hit me again, twice, three times, until I staggered, my head spinning. And then they placed their hands around my throat and squeezed—hard.. I opened my mouth, but no words came out. White blanketed my vision, and then nothing.

CHAPTER TWENTY-ONE

THE CONSTANT BEEPING WAS ANNOYING. I OPENED MY eyes, and I immediately regretted it. The bright light stung my eyes for a moment. I closed them instantly and then opened them again. The room, bright and cold, came into view. Tony sat on one side while Harrison was on the other. I closed my eyes.

Tony's voice made me open them again.

"Storm?"

I nodded. "What happened?" I choked out. The words scraped against my throat so hard it felt like they drew blood.

"What happened?" Tony's voice was urgent and worried.

"She should take her time," said Harrison. His voice cracked, but it was better than it was before.

"Water…"

Tony grabbed the water pitcher and filled a big cup that had a wide straw. He brought the straw to my lips. The water was cold. It bloomed in my chest and rippled throughout my entire body. I shivered, but I kept drinking. I gulped down half the cup of water before Tony placed it back on the tray table in front of me.

I leaned back and sighed. My throat felt better.

"They came out of nowhere. From behind and hit me with something. I fought back, but they choked me until I passed out."

"Did you get a good look at them?" Tony leaned forward. He hung on every word. Harrison used his thumb to stroke my hand.

"No. Wearing all black. They ran off. I don't know where they...went."

"Okay. Jill thinks she might have their DNA under your fingernails. She's already taken a scrapping back to the lab." He stood up. "And now you need to get some rest. I don't know if they will release you today because you might have a concussion." He glanced over at Harrison. "He'll take care of you for a little while. I'll see you later." He squeezed my hand for a long moment and then left the room.

Nurses came in and out of the room several times before a doctor entered. He was an older man with grayish-white hair and thick, black-rimmed glasses. He smiled at me.

"I'm happy to say that your concussion is only mild. As far as we can see, your brain and skull are going to be fine. You've got bruised ribs and a pretty nasty cut on your temple, but otherwise you'll be okay. And you can go home in the morning. We want you to spend the night for observation, but if all goes well, you'll be home by noon."

"What about work?" I asked. I was already eager to get back to the case. I wanted to know who did this to me and why. Why was there someone stalking the property? Had they been waiting for me to come back to the scene? I hadn't even seen anything new that the crime scene unit hadn't already pulled up.

The doctor's eyes flicked to Harrison. "Well, I would say you take it easy for a couple of days. And if you feel any dizziness or headaches, you come straight back."

I nodded slowly. If I even stumbled, Tony would drag me back to the hospital and make me stay. He told me he'd come back before I left tomorrow and then left. My eyes closed before he closed the door.

I woke up in the middle of the night. Harrison was still next to me, and a nurse, a young woman with bright pink glasses came in to check my vitals.

"How are you feeling?" Her voice was barely above a whisper.

"A little better." My head didn't throb anymore. I knew it was the painkillers, and I was thankful for them.

She checked my vitals and poured more water into my cup. She brought the straw to my lips. I gulped down the water and then stopped. My throat didn't hurt like it did before.

"Thanks."

"Of course. Your vitals are good. They should release you later today."

"That's good to hear. I need to get back to work."

Her smile wavered. "So soon. Don't you need to take it easy?"

"Working on a case," I said.

"I heard. Everyone is talking about it. The bed-and-breakfast was a favorite on the island. Well, one of them. It was a beautiful spot. I got engaged there last year. And this morning I heard about the bodies they found there and now…we wanted to get married there. Talked to Mrs. Beth about it and everything." She shut her eyes and shook her head. "It's horrifying. She was such a nice woman, and her husband was nice too. Quiet though. Not in a creepy way, just quiet. He let her lead." She glanced at me. "Oh, I'm sorry. Don't mean to talk your ear off. Go back to sleep."

"Did you stay there long?" I asked.

She shrugged. "It was a couple of days. No…three days. We both had time off and really wanted to enjoy ourselves without leaving the island."

"How was the food?"

She cocked her head to the side. "Um…It was good. A little under seasoned for my liking, but still good. The cook—"

"Piper?"

Her right eyebrow raised. "No. That's not it. Umm… Owen…um…Cherrica? Yeah, that's it. I remember because it was such an interesting name. I had never heard it before. She made a special dessert for my proposal dinner. A chocolate soufflé. It was good. I wanted to go to the kitchen to thank her. She was nice and proud of her food."

"Oh." No one we talked to had remembered the first cook's name or even knew her. But now that we had a name, we could really look for her and for him. Find her family and see if they knew him or had seen him lately. I wanted to think of them both in a small town somewhere, living a quiet life on a farm or something.

But something in my gut told me that wasn't going to happen. There was something else going on here, and we still needed to figure it out. I wanted to ask her another question, but my eyes were so heavy, and my tongue felt thick and clunky in my mouth. I closed my eyes, and that was it.

When I woke up, Harrison was gone, but a nurse and Tony were there.

"When did you get here?" Carefully, I sat up. There was a dull ache in my head, but overall, it wasn't so bad.

"A few minutes ago. They had to take Harrison down for testing. If all goes well, he'll be released. The doctor seemed hopeful. Now, back to you. I thought you just had a few questions."

"I did. I talked to Mrs. Oakley, and then I stopped by the scene. I was just walking around, and then I heard something behind me, and before I could turn around, something hit me in the back of the head."

"Well, there was nothing at the scene but footprints."

"You think I could come in today?"

"Mia." The frustration in his voice was loud and clear. But I ignored it.

"Yeah, I know. But we might have a break in the case, and all it requires is a little research at the office. I wouldn't even have to go out in the field unless we find something."

He rolled his eyes. "What did you figure out?"

"Well, no one saw Doug leave with his mistress. No one saw him after the night she said he left. But more importantly, I know who she is."

BREAKFAST IN PARADISE

He blinked, and his back immediately straightened. "Who is she and how?"

I told him about my conversation with the nurse and what I learned. "Only you could get a read laid up in the hospital. I'll do the search. If anything comes from it, I will let you know." He took out his phone. "You'll stay home today, and then tomorrow, you will have to take it easy. We are supposed to be on the lookout for dizziness and headaches."

I nodded. He sent a text and then shoved his phone back in his pocket. "So, Harrison seems nice."

"Thank you?"

He chuckled. "He doesn't want to press charges against the patient that hurt him. I both admire it and question it at the same time." He looked at me for a long moment. "I don't think I could ever be that understanding. You stab me, your ass is going to jail."

"That's what I said."

"I'll see you later. I'll stop by after work."

I rolled my eyes as my arms folded across my chest.

"I'll fill you in when I see you. Take the time to relax," he said on his way out the door. He didn't even give me a chance to respond before he closed the door behind him. I wanted to go to work. I wanted to figure out what the hell happened to Beth. I wanted to find an angle on the case that actually made sense. And we weren't there yet, nowhere near it.

The doctor returned an hour or so later with my test results. "Everything is fine, but I still want you to take it easy. Don't overdo it, and if you feel dizzy or have a headache, have someone bring you right back here immediately."

I nodded. Thirty minutes later, Harrison and Delia walked through the door. She was ready to drive us both home.

"So, who's taking care of you two?" Delia closed the door behind me. Harrison collapsed onto the sofa, and I followed suit. Delia shook her head. "Both of you beat to hell. Your jobs are taking a toll, aren't they?"

I shrugged. I wasn't tired when I left the hospital, but I was when I sat on the sofa. My body sank into it. I let it mold around me. I woke with a start as voices eased into the room. I opened my eyes and saw Tony.

161

"Well, look at you."

"She just woke up," Delia told him.

"She's right here," I groaned, but I closed my eyes again. I guessed I was in worse shape than I thought.

The smell of tomatoes, meat, onions, and garlic surrounded me. Someone was cooking. My mouth watered instantly. I sat up to get a better look into the kitchen. Aisha, Harrison, and Delia looked busy. Harrison was at the stove, Delia was at the sink, and Aisha stood at the counter with a knife and a cutting board.

When did they get here? I blinked, my eyes darting from Tony to them and back again. The doorbell rang, and Delia ran to answer it.

"How long have you been here?" My voice cracked.

He smiled. "I just got here, but everyone else has been here for a while. Just checking in." He glanced back at the kitchen. "They are making dinner, though. Ravioli, I think."

"Sounds good." My head fell back against the cushion. "My mouth is watering."

He chuckled and sat down next to me.

"Smells amazing." Jill and Hattie said at the same time. I recognized their voices instantly. They wandered over to the living room and sat down.

"You two get beat up a lot," said Jill.

Hattie looked at her, mouth open, brows furrowed. Jill shrugged. "What, it's true. They do. Between the two of them, they have been in the hospital way too much."

Tony nudged me with his elbow. We both laughed. There was nothing we could say. She wasn't wrong. We had been in the hospital quite a few times in the last year. At least this was nothing too serious. However, Tony did get shot and was in the hospital for Christmas.

"Now, how are you feeling?" Jill stared at me like she was examining my face. I hadn't taken a look in the mirror yet, so I didn't know what I looked like, but I knew it was bad. The right side of my face felt sore, and my throat was sore when I swallowed. But other than that, I felt all right. I shrugged.

"Sore all over. But I'll live."

"Did you find out who did it?" asked Hattie.

BREAKFAST IN PARADISE

"Well, I tested the skin under your nails, and whoever it was is not in the system, which I found strange. I mean, if you have the gall to beat the shit—no offense—out of an FBI agent, then I expect your prints or DNA to be in the system."

"No offense taken." He hadn't beaten the shit out of me. He just bruised me a little. Or rather a lot. I understood what she meant, though. I thought the same thing. I fully expected the DNA to be in our system. Surely, he had done it before. He was so prepared. Ski mask and black gloves. I felt my fingers slip beneath the cuff of his shirt even though I couldn't see.

"I'm more curious about why they were there," said Tony. He nudged me with his elbow again. "What were they looking for? The bodies? Or something else? It makes me think that we missed something."

Jill shrugged. "We combed that scene before and after we found the bodies. I can't think of what it would be. We found the teeth, but we couldn't say whether they belonged to Beth or not. We are going to do a DNA test on the teeth and the bones, and we will see what happens."

"They were looking for something," I said. "Maybe it wasn't the bodies. Maybe it's something else. Although how would they know what to look for?"

Delia announced the food was ready, and everyone headed toward the dining room. Jill and Tony helped me up even though I didn't really need it. They both stared at me intently when I stood to see if I was dizzy. Satisfied I wasn't, Jill took one arm and Tony the other, and they led me to the dining room. The food was good. Ravioli with a salad and dinner rolls. And wine, but I wasn't allowed to have any.

It was a nice way to end the ordeal. Quietly and surrounded by friends, talking and laughing. Even Harrison joined in on the conversation. His voice sounded better, too.

"It was lucky for you they didn't nick anything like an artery or your voice box," Jill told him. She stared at him like he was on her table, and she was examining the wound at his throat.

Harrison smiled shyly and shrugged. It was clear it was something he didn't want to talk about, so I didn't want to push it. Instead, we talked about what we had seen in the news and TV shows we had watched. However, most of us didn't have the time. The night ended with Delia telling us what we needed to watch, what was boring, and what we could avoid.

It was a good night. A fun night. The kind I needed. We still didn't have the answers, but that was okay. For now, I just wanted to sit surrounded by my friends.

CHAPTER TWENTY-TWO

"I HAD THE STRANGEST DREAM LAST NIGHT." I got in the car, and Tony stared at me, waiting for an explanation.

"You think it was because you were bashed in the head?"

I shrugged. I felt fine. After Tony and the others left, Harrison and I tucked ourselves into bed. We were both exhausted, and he was going back to work the next day. Light work, mostly paperwork and reviewing notes. I curled up next to him and laid my head on his chest. As I listened to him breathe and the steady beating of his heart, I drifted to sleep.

In the dream, I was at the morgue with Jill and Tony, and I was staring at a charred body, bent at a strange angle because of the fire. It felt less like a dream and more like a memory. I had been at the morgue with Jill and Tony, and I had seen Beth's body. But this body was different, kind of. It looked the same. It was even shaped the same as it was in the morgue, but there was something shiny in the bone. Well, it was attached to a bone in her leg. I didn't notice it at first, but as I got closer to it, the silver metal seemed to sparkle. It was so weird.

"Like I said, it seemed more like a memory than a dream. It was so odd. It wasn't scary or anything. It was just weird."

Tony took out his phone.

"What are you doing?"

"Calling Jill and asking her to check the bones."

I blinked. "Why? I told you it was a dream."

Tony shrugged. "You've had weird dreams about cases before. I think it is less about it being a dream and more about your mind trying to make sense of what you saw. You got closer to the body than I did. Maybe you saw something and thought it was debris or something. But if Beth had a pin put in her leg, that's something we can use to identify her."

Jill answered the phone, and Tony asked her to check the body for anything metal, like a pen or a hip replacement or something. Jill said she had just started the process of examining the bones this morning and that she would call us and let us know if she found something interesting.

"So where do we go now? Field office?" The engine turned over, and a blast of cold air hit me in the face.

"Nope. We are on our way to see Cherrica's mother."

I smiled. "You found her. Did you ask her about her daughter?"

"No, I didn't. I knew that if I had questioned her without you, I never would have heard the end of it. I just asked if we could come by and talk to her about her daughter. She said yes. She sounded really sad."

Mrs. Owens's home was a long ride away from our condo building, but it was a nice ride. And it gave us a chance to talk and review the case. We were both stumped about Doug and wondered if he had a role in those murders. Or if he did them and made her play along.

"I don't know. The way her ex-husband spoke about her… she was dedicated to that place. And if killing people and robbing them could make her dreams come true, she would have done it. I think Doug wouldn't have had the idea on his own. If he did it, I think she might have put him up to it."

Tony agreed that could have been plausible. But we were still nowhere near finding the person that killed her. Or finding a suspect. The loved ones of the men buried on her property needed to be contacted, and then they needed to be interviewed. I didn't like the idea of interrogating them. Asking their whereabouts and trying to figure out which one killed Beth, but we had to. Someone killed her, burned down the bed-and-breakfast, and then left the guests to fend for themselves.

What if no one had seen the fire in time? What if they hadn't been able to get out? There would have been more dead bodies. Someone had to pay for that. We pulled into the driveway of a white stucco home with dark green trim. The brightly colored pink and orange flowers in the front flowerbed were striking up against the house. The front door opened as soon as we got out of the car.

A woman with hair so black it was nearly blue stood in the doorway with her arms folded across her chest.

"What do you need to know about Rica?" There was an edge to her voice, but it wasn't sharp. It was worn thin. A tired blade that wanted to be put away. She looked so tired. Her eyes sunken. Her clothes hung off her like she had lost a lot of weight recently and hadn't bought anything new.

I stared at her for a brief moment and realized whatever answers we came to find were not here. We followed her into her home. I closed the door behind me. Her house was small but tidy and well-kept. The living room had white walls, a white sofa, and three small white chairs. The green from the trim outside had been carried inside through the curtains and some of the paintings on the walls. She gestured toward the sofa for us to sit.

"I take it you have no idea where your daughter is?" I posed it as a question, but it wasn't really. I knew the answer from the moment I saw her. She was a mother grieving the loss of her child and was not taking care of herself.

She startled at the question and then shook her head. "I was hoping you were here to tell me something I didn't know."

I sighed. "Well, I'm sorry, but we need your help to figure out where she might have gone."

"I can only tell you what I've told the police," she said.

"That would be a great place to start."

Mrs. Owens recounted the report she filed with the local police. Her daughter had been missing for months. "I told them it wasn't like her to run away. She had a good job, and she truly loved what she did. She loved working at the Golden Paradise. She was happy there."

"What did they tell you?" asked Tony.

She shrugged. "She wasn't really a priority. She was an adult, and she could leave whenever she wanted to and never speak to me again. And they were right. She could, but that wasn't like her. We talked every day. Before she went to work and on her way home, she either called me in the car or when she walked through the door. And we spent the weekends together. She wouldn't just leave and never contact me. And then I started hearing these rumors about her and her boss. Complete bullshit, but the more I argued about it, I think, the more people believed it."

"You don't think she had an affair with her boss, Doug Frazier?" I asked.

She sucked her teeth. "Please. She was…is a devout Catholic. So devout, she was thinking about becoming a nun. She was still looking into it and hadn't made her final decision yet, but she was on the path. And I supported her. Could she have been swayed away from her path? Sure. Most young girls are. But not by him. She didn't like him."

"I thought you said she liked her job."

She shrugged. "You can love your job and not like the people you work with."

"That's true," said Tony. "Did she ever mention why she didn't like him?"

Mrs. Owens sighed and leaned back in her chair. "She said he made her feel uncomfortable. Not in a sexual way. She wasn't afraid he was going to rape her or anything. She said he only had eyes for Mrs. Hardwell. But he had a way of looking at her…it was like she didn't exist. Or better yet, she didn't matter. It was like she was a bug, and he could squash her whenever he wanted. It creeped her out. Apparently, he looked at everyone that way, not just her. She wanted to work somewhere else that was a little warmer. Friendlier staff."

"Most people we talked to said Beth was nice and friendly," I said.

Mrs. Owens nodded. "She was when I met her. But Rica said she had many faces. Her nice face was reserved for people she wanted to impress and people who were giving her money. She said she was a woman who had a mean streak, but it was a quiet one. She didn't yell or curse at you, and she didn't fight. She used her words like a scalpel, using them to make you feel small and unimportant."

"When was the last time you saw your daughter?" I asked. Mrs. Oakley told me that Doug disappeared a week or two after Cherrica quit. This led people to believe that she was the reason he left.

"It was a few months ago. Maybe a week or two before they said Doug Frazier left the Paradise…You know what, I saw her the weekend before she went missing. We went to the farmer's market, and then on Sunday, we went to church. We spent the whole day together, and then that night, she said she would call me Monday. And she did…before work. But she didn't call me that night. She always does to remind me to take my medicine, but she didn't that night. At first, I figured she was tired when she got in and forgot. But she didn't call the next morning either or that night. I don't like to pester her, but I called her Tuesday just to check in, and she never answered. So, the weekend before was the last time I saw her, but that Monday morning was the last time I spoke to her."

"Did you speak to Mrs. Hardwell?" asked Tony.

She sighed. "She was the most unhelpful person I have ever met. She said my daughter left her shift early Monday and never came back. She said she thought because she left so abruptly, it was a family emergency. But she never came back. I asked to look around, and she kicked me out. Said she had guests coming and couldn't be bothered."

"Did you contact the police then?" I asked. I wondered what they had to say about it. Or if they even investigated it.

"I did. And they went over and looked around. Said they saw nothing out of the ordinary. They didn't even find her car. I still haven't been able to locate her car. It doesn't make sense. Not at all."

I wondered for a moment about the bodies found buried in the yard and under the house. Could Rica have been one of them? As if reading my mind, Mrs. Ownes stared at me expectantly. A question on her lips.

"Was she one of the bodies?"

I shook my head. "No. So far, we have only found men buried in the yard."

She sighed. "I don't know if that's supposed to fill me with relief or dread."

I didn't know either. Just because we hadn't found her yet didn't mean she wasn't there. "Can we have a picture of her? Something for our records?"

A smile tugged at her lips. "Of course. I have a really good one over here." She got up and walked over to the bookcase in the corner of the room. She picked up a large book and then sat back down. "I took this our last Sunday together. She's always making fun of me for actually having a camera and not using my phone to take pictures. I took this of her in the parking lot. She was so annoyed, but she let me do it anyway." Mrs. Owens pulled a picture out of the back of the book and handed it to me.

Rica was definitely her mother's child. They shared the same face.

"She's beautiful." I fought the urge to refer to her in the past tense. Her mother talked about her as if she could walk through the door at any moment. She still had her hope, and I didn't want to take it away from her if I didn't have to. And since we still had no idea whether she was alive or dead, I didn't have to.

"She is. She really is. My sister told her that becoming a nun would have been a waste of her looks." She laughed. "But she was determined to do it anyway."

"Do you think it's possible that she just…went and joined a convent?" asked Tony. It was a good question and might account for why no one had seen her. If she really wanted to do it, maybe she felt like the people in her life didn't support her decision, so she had to go off and do it on her own.

She shook her head. "My sister might have disapproved, but I fully supported her. I would have driven her there myself. She wouldn't have run off without saying goodbye."

I believed her. If Rica called her mother every night to make sure she took her medicine, I couldn't picture her running off without a word. "What kind of medicine do you take?"

"Blood thinners and anti-seizure medication. I had a brain aneurysm not too long ago. I also have to take aspirin every day. She called me in the morning to take the blood thinners and the aspirin and then at night to make sure I took the anti-seizure medication twice a day. But I am off of it now. Well, the blood thinners and seizure pills. Still have to take my aspirin every morning, though. Sometimes I forget, but I'm not dead yet, so."

"That's amazing. You've recovered so well," I said. I never heard of someone surviving an aneurysm. People I had heard that had them died instantly. She looked more tired than sick.

"Thank you. I'm trying to keep pushing."

I glanced at Tony, who looked like he was trying not to cry. I was doing the same. We all knew Cherrica was probably dead, but no one wanted to say it. My mother used to say if you spoke about something, it gave it power. Putting words to something gave it weight and meaning. Made it true even if you didn't know for sure it was. So, we shouldn't speak of it until we knew.

I thanked her for her time and told her we would contact her if we learned anything new. She thanked me and walked us out. By the car, Tony took his phone out of his pocket.

"Jill has been calling me for the past five minutes."

My chest tightened. She must have found something. Maybe it was another body. My heart sank as I looked back at the house. We got into the car, and he called her back and put the phone on speaker.

"Hey, you called."

"Yeah, a couple of times."

"Sorry, I was interviewing a witness. What happened," said Tony.

"We are going to talk later about how you knew there was a pin in the leg of our victim. But for now, after examining Beth's medical records, I can definitively say the burnt body in our morgue is *not* Beth Hardwell."

CHAPTER TWENTY-THREE

Beth Hardwell

FOUR YEARS AGO...
 He stared at her like she was the only person in the world. No one had ever looked at her like that. Her first husband never even liked her. He only married her because he needed his family to get off his back. He liked her, or he might have liked her once, but in the end, he hated her. He couldn't stand to be in the same room as her, and she felt the same. He was a small-minded man who could never see the bigger picture.
 He never understood her dream. He never even tried. She blinked the thought away. She was tired of thinking about him. She wouldn't give him another thought. Instead, she stared at

the tall, muscular man eyeing her from the end of the bar and smiled. He took that for what it was, an invitation.

He sauntered over and then sat on the stool next to her. He smiled and introduced himself. But she knew his name. She knew him. She had been watching him for weeks. Months even. She needed someone new. Someone who could understand her. Someone who would at least try.

She watched him the way she watched Victor, and she knew. She knew she could mold him. Bend and break and reform him to fit her and not the other way around. This wouldn't be like her last marriage. She would not bow and scrape and bend and break herself for another person. Not again. All she would have to do was ask, and he would do it.

Doug talked about himself, and she feigned interest, which was difficult. Not only did she not care, she already knew everything. He had a sister, Chelsea, and his mother still lived on the island. They seemed close, and as he talked about them, she realized they were. He loved his family, and it wasn't a broken, transactional kind of love. They actually loved and cared for each other. It unnerved Beth to see it, but she knew she could work around it. In time, he would distance himself and cling only to her. See only her. Love only her.

She smiled as he talked about his work and his friends. He had worked in construction most of his life. He loved working with his hands. She told him about the bed-and-breakfast.

"I would love to take a look at it. I'm not sure what I can do to help you, but if there's anything, I'd be more than happy to."

His kindness made her smile despite herself. Perhaps this would be easier than she thought. They talked well into the morning. The bar closed at three, and they walked around until the moon disappeared and the sun lit up the sky. Talking to him was easier than talking to her ex-husband. It was more relaxing. It wasn't all about money or their savings or the work on the house. It wasn't about his family and how they hated her.

It was about them and only them. That one conversation turned into another and then another. They met daily down by the beach and talked well into the night. A month turned into two and then three, and before they knew it, they were engaged.

"It's too soon! You just met her!" Chelsea was not happy with their announcement.

Beth rubbed Doug's shoulder, keeping a firm grip on him at all times.

"Why can't you just be happy for me?" The sadness and pleading in Doug's voice almost brought a smile to her face.

"Yes, why can't you just be happy for us? Just because your marriage failed doesn't mean ours will."

Chelsea cut her eyes at Beth. "Listen, you little bitch—"

"Don't speak to her that way. She's just saying that you don't have to be so negative."

"You just met her. It's only been a few months. We don't know anything about her, and now you want to add her to the family. And who is she to talk about failed marriages? Wouldn't you be her second husband, or is it her third?"

"Second," Beth spat. She heard the edge in her voice and worked quickly to dull it. "But who's counting?"

"Who, indeed." His mother wobbled her way into the living room. "We don't know her, and now you want to marry her? It's not like you to make such rushed decisions. I would ask if she's pregnant, but she looks a little too long in the tooth for that."

Beth's lips curled into a snarl. She fixed it quickly and pressed her lips into a smile. "No, I am not pregnant. Still possible, though, if he wanted a child."

Doug squeezed her hand. "You don't have to be so ugly. I'm not saying we don't want you in our lives. You can come to the wedding."

"Well, thank you for the invitation," said his mother. "But you've made it clear you don't want us in your lives. You don't even come to Sunday dinners anymore. This is the first time I've seen you in a month. You don't come over anymore to check on us. It's like we already don't exist in your new world with her."

She spat out the word *her* right at Beth. Beth sighed. She never understood why mothers clung so fiercely to their male children. She was far too dependent on Doug for Beth's liking. She wanted him to spend too much time with her. She wanted him to come over for dinner every week and stop by every day to check on her and come over when she needed things done around the house. It was far too much.

"He is an adult," said Beth. She kept her tone low and measured because she didn't want to upset Doug. Not now. "He doesn't have to run everything, every decision in his life by you. He doesn't have to stop by every day. He has a life, and you don't have to be at the center of it."

She rolled her eyes. "He's my son. I am part of his family. Everything was fine until he met you. Now, you consume all of his time. He can't do anything outside of you."

"Stop it!" Doug jumped to his feet. "I didn't come here to ask your permission, nor do I need it. We are getting married. If you want to come, you are more than welcome, and if you don't, that is fine too." He grabbed Beth's hand and pulled her to her feet before ushering her out of the house.

It turned out his sister and mother did, in fact, not want to come to their wedding. Beth wasn't bothered by it, but she could tell it bothered him. He tried not to let it show, but she caught him glancing to the back of the church just in case they walked in. They didn't.

The months following the wedding were quite blissful. For the first time in her life, Beth didn't have to talk slickly or choose her words carefully. She just had to ask for something, and it was hers. Doug would do anything in his power to give her what she asked for. It was a thrilling feeling, and one she hoped would last.

In the months following their marriage, the Golden Paradise saw an uptick in business, especially with couples.

"When is Mr. Trujilo coming?" asked Doug after he slid the final drawer into place. He painted a dresser that Beth had gotten from a garage sale. With her help, he moved it into one of the main bedrooms, and now they both stood back to admire their work.

"He's due to check-in in a few hours. Everything's ready for him when he gets here. We just need to make sure that everything runs smoothly during his stay. He's the only one booked."

"And you checked all of his references? He's a reputable journalist?"

Beth nodded. She had checked everything, including the travel magazine he worked for. His article on their bed-and-breakfast would help to bring in more people. The idea excited

Beth. Sure, they had more guests than when it started, but it could be better. Everything could always be better. And this was a perfect opportunity to get their name out there

"Well, I'll be back tonight. I'm still looking for that tile you wanted in the kitchen, and I think I got a lead on it. I'm headed out there now."

"Okay. Good luck." She kissed him gently on the lips. Doug blushed and smiled coyly when she pulled back.

It was just her in the house when he left. They hadn't brought in enough money to hire full-time staff. She was the cook and did most of the cleaning—with Doug's help, of course. She finished cleaning and baking an assortment of cookies for the welcome table when the doorbell rang.

She did a quick once over in the mirror and smoothed down her apron before opening the door, then pressed her lips in her best smile. "Sean Trujilo?"

"The one and only," the man replied with a smile. "And you must be Beth Hardwell. Nice to finally meet you." They shook hands, and she backed out of the doorway, allowing him to enter. Beth closed the door behind him.

"Wow. Beautiful. I mean, the view outside is just gorgeous, but the inside is great, too. You picked a great spot."

"Thank you. I really liked the view myself, so I knew other people would appreciate it as well. Um…let me show you your room, and then I can give you a tour. You're in the palm room." She took him to a gorgeous room painted with bold green palm leaves on the walls along with the palm leaf-shaped ceiling fan. The room also overlooked the palm trees in the yard.

Sean's face lit up. "Oh, this is perfect." He set his bags on the bed and walked over to the window. From the window, you could hear the waves and smell the water. A light breeze burst through the window and rippled through the curtains. "This is amazing. I see why your reviews are so favorable."

Beth beamed. She was so proud of her bed-and-breakfast, and she soaked up every compliment that was offered. Her reviews had been good. People really seemed to love the place. They just needed more people to know that it was there.

Beth commenced to show him around the house. She even showed him the spots they were still in the process of renovating. "This is the kitchen where the meals are cooked. We will start renovations here hopefully next week. I want to do some upgrades that will make it easier to service a lot of people."

He walked around the kitchen. "It looks good to me. But then again, as long as the stove and fridge work, I'm good."

Beth chuckled. He was only staying for a night, so she had to put her best foot forward. She needed to be charming and accommodating. She had to bend herself and the bed-and-breakfast into what he wanted, just for the night.

"So, do you stay in one of the rooms or…"

She smiled. "Well, we did at first because the house stopped here." She pointed at an empty space. A wall that had once been there but was now gone. "We took that pesky wall down and then added an owner's suite to the back of the house. Come with me." She led him to the back of the house into her private quarters. She couldn't say why she was showing it to him. It wouldn't mean anything to the guests. "We are still renovating back here too. But for now, it is workable. I like it because it gives us our own space while staying close to the guests in case there is a problem."

"Oh, there'll be a problem," Sean said darkly.

Beth spun around; her heart stammered in her chest. "Why?" Her eyes went wide as she stumbled back. He was naked. Why was he naked? Fear coiled in her chest like a snake. She stumbled back and tripped over something on the floor. She fell back with a thud.

He inched toward her. "Don't fight me now. It'll all be over before you know it." He grinned as he fell to his knees. "And then we can go outside and eat some of those cookies you made." He grabbed her ankle and yanked her towards him.

Beth's hand slid across a handle. Her fingers wrapped around it. She brought it up and over and slammed it into his head before she realized what it was. A hammer. She hit him again and again and again. Blood spurted from his head, coating the room in red.

She didn't stop until her arm was heavy and the hammer slipped from her fingers. She sighed and checked to see if he was breathing, and when she was certain he wasn't, she stumbled into the bathroom to clean herself up. By the time Doug got home, Beth had come up with a plan.

She sat in the parlor waiting for him.

"Is he here?" He closed the door behind him and set his keys on the console. "How did it go?"

Beth smiled and stood up. "Follow me." She led him through the kitchen into the back room and stopped. Doug stopped short and stumbled into the blood.

"Why is he naked?"

Beth was startled by the question. She thought his first words would have been 'what did you do?' Or 'did you call the police?' She had prepared for those questions. But this one threw her off.

"Beth?"

His voice snapped her back to reality. "Right. He wanted a tour, so I was showing him around. We got back here, and I was telling him about the owner's suite, and when I turned around, he was naked. He told me to just go with it and not to fight him."

He nodded slowly. "So, what do you want to do with him?" Beth blinked at him. He wasn't behaving the way she had thought he would. None of his questions were right. "I could bury him out back, and you can clean this up."

She nodded slowly.

"That's a plan." Doug stepped over the body and headed toward the linen closet. He found a sheet that didn't have any of its matching set and tossed it on the bed. "I can use that to drag him out once I dig the hole."

Beth nodded slowly. "Wait. She flipped him over and started going through his pockets. She found his wallet. "Two thousand bucks. That'll work." She shoved the money in her pocket before putting his wallet back where she got it. It was one thing for him to be buried in the backyard, but she didn't want any of his stuff to be traced back to her or the Golden Paradise. He didn't arrive in a car but an Uber. So that was something they didn't have to get rid of. "His bag is still upstairs."

"Okay. You get it, and I'll bury him with everything. That way, no one will walk through the house and recognize something of his."

Beth blinked. It was like she thought it, and he said it. "I was just thinking that."

He smiled. "That money will be enough to get that tile you wanted."

Beth grinned. "I'll go see if he has anything else. You should start digging now that it's dark."

He gave a small salute. "Yes, ma'am."

CHAPTER TWENTY-FOUR

WE DIDN'T SPEAK ON OUR WAY TO THE MORGUE. THE silence in the car was defeating but not uncomfortable. After saying the body wasn't Beth's, Jill told Tony we needed to get back to the morgue. She didn't elaborate on who the body belonged to or what else she found. I felt like I already knew, but I swallowed my words. It was best not to say anything until we knew for sure. A million scenarios raced through my head, but none of them stuck. None of them tangible. Nothing felt right enough to stand out.

Who else could the body belong to if not Beth? My heart thudded in my chest and a pit formed in my stomach. Something was wrong, and it was not about to get better.

Jill stood in the middle of the exam room, eying the burnt body in front of her. Her eyes met mine as soon as I walked through the door. "I'm sorry. We should have picked up on it sooner, but we've been pretty backed up. How did you know about the pin?"

I told her my dream and that Tony said I must have seen it and not registered it or something. Jill nodded as if she understood what I was saying.

"Happens to me all the time. I'll be examining a body, and then I go home and have a strange dream about that person. It's like your conscious mind doesn't register it and so your subconscious has to figure out a way to get you to take a second look. It's like reminding you that you saw something strange and you should look at it again. And I do. I usually find something that I missed when that happens, so good on you for seeing it. Can't believe I missed it. But then again, I was focused on other things. The body is female. Our anthropologist said she was much younger than Beth." She walked over to the table and grabbed a folder. "I ran the serial numbers on the pin, and while I was waiting, I finally got my hands on Beth's medical records. I don't know what took so long but anyway…" She flipped through the folder. "Beth never had a pin put in her leg. We examined the bones and this body is not one of a middle-aged woman who had given birth."

My ears pricked up at the last statement. "Given birth? Beth never had children. Her first husband said she was unable to have children because of the several miscarriages."

Jill looked at me and then back down at the file. "There are only two miscarriages in her file and three abortions. She gave birth to a baby boy when she was twenty-five." Jill handed me the file.

I searched through it looking for what happened to the child. There was nothing noted there. Maybe the child died after birth. But her husband said they never had children. I glanced at Tony, the crease between his brow deepening.

"It's an odd thing to lie about, isn't it?" I asked. Why would she have lied about having a child? That didn't make any sense. For a moment I thought maybe she had the child before she married her husband, and she didn't want him to know about it. But she had the child when she was twenty-five. They were married by then and had been for a while. I needed to speak to her ex-husband. I made a mental note before continuing through the file.

Jill shrugged. "Depends on who's lying. Her husband or did she lie to her husband about the baby?"

I closed the file. That was a good question. "Do you know who the body belongs to?"

"Right..." She walked back to the table and grabbed another folder. "Like I was saying I got the serial number from the pin and did a search. The pin belonged to Cherrica Owens."

The folder slipped from my hand. My heart stuttered in my chest. "What?"

Jill looked up from the file, a puzzled look etched into the creases of her face. "Were you looking for her?"

"We just came from talking to her mother. That's where we were when you called," said Tony, a deep sadness in his voice.

"Oh...Oh, I'm so sorry. Do you know how she's related to the case?"

"She was their cook. Everyone except her mother thought she ran off with Doug. That she was his mistress," I said. I shook my head. How were we going to go back to her mother and tell her we found Rica's body? I mentally pushed the thought to the back of my mind. I didn't want to focus on that now. We still needed to find Beth. "So, if we don't have Beth's body, then where is she?"

"Now that is a good question," said Jill. "I hope you guys figure that out. We are still searching the property, but so far we haven't found anything. Now we are searching the remains of the house but we are sifting through everything slowly. Looking for bone fragments and all that. If we find anything I'll let you know."

I thanked her and took the file with me. We walked back to the car in silence. I didn't know what Tony was thinking, but I couldn't stop thinking about Beth. Where was she?

Back at the field office, I sat down at my desk. I planned out a few scenarios in my head. Doug could have killed Beth and Rica. Or Beth could have killed Rica and Doug because they were having an affair. Her mother was adamant she wouldn't have started an affair with Doug, but parents didn't know everything. She could have kept some things to herself. It was possible and yet the idea didn't sit right.

Did Doug kill them? Maybe Rica tried to end their affair and leave him so he killed her. And then he killed Beth because she wouldn't take him back. But then where was her body?

"I keep thinking we are missing something here," said Tony as he sat down. "Where is Beth? Where is her body?"

I nodded. I replayed everything that we had been told. Beth couldn't have been buried on the property because the guests had seen her after dinner. No one could kill her and bury her, and then start the fire without being seen. Even if the hole had been dug beforehand, it didn't add up. And if someone was going to kill her and then start the fire, why take her body with them? That didn't make any sense either.

My forefinger tapped against my desk. There was something missing. Something we weren't seeing yet. I stared at the array of files on my desk. My fingers skimmed over them and stopped at the crime scene photos. I picked it up. After spreading the pictures across my desk, I let my eyes roam over them. I had seen them before, but now I really needed to study them. There was something we were missing.

There was a lot of rubble left over from the fire. Too much?

"What's wrong?"

Tony's voice startled me. I had forgotten he was there, he was so quiet. I shrugged. "I don't know. Something about the rubble of the house doesn't sit right. I think there might be too much."

"So what? You think there was a secret room or something?"

"Maybe."

Hattie caught the tail end of our conversation. "What about a secret room?"

I showed her the pictures and told her what I thought. The house was three stories but for how hot the fire was and the damage done, it still looked like there was something extra there. While I was talking Hattie pulled up the floor plans for the Golden Paradise. She looked from the pictures to the screen on the tablet. "You see that door?" She pointed to the door in the kitchen. It wasn't the back door nor was it the door to the owner's private room. It also wasn't the pantry or a closet.

"What is that to?" I asked.

"I don't know, but it's not in the floor plans. It's not supposed to be there."

I picked up the picture and stared at it. The doorway was still intact, although the door was gone. The wood around the door was still standing. "It's so strange."

"You want to go back to the scene?" asked Tony, who was already on his feet before I could say anything.

I nodded and stood up. I didn't know if this doorway was going to lead us to Beth's body, but there was something so strange about it I had to look into it.

Techs were already at the crime scene, searching it inch by inch. It looked like a painstaking process. One tech was bent over a pile of burnt pieces with a pair of tweezers in his hand. I shook my head. I didn't envy his job. I walked past them and headed to the doorway that shouldn't have been there.

"What's holding it up?" I asked as I neared the doorway. There was nothing behind the wooden frame and nothing in front of it.

"That's a good question. Maybe it hasn't gotten the memo that it needs to fall yet."

I nudged Tony with my elbow. I kicked some of the rubble in front of the door. There was nothing there, just metal and burnt wood. I moved to the other side of the door. What did the door lead to? I kicked some of the rubble behind the frame. Something snagged on my shoe. "What is that?" I bent down and brushed the burnt wood out of the way. Underneath a bulge of burnt pieces and metal, was a wooden door set into the ground. It reminded me of a storm shelter door from the movie *Twister*.

Tony bent down. "Why would that be here?"

I glanced back at the techs, who were still slowly moving over a corner of the house. Tony and I exchanged a glance, and he pulled out his gun. I slowly opened the door. "What the hell?" Stairs. There were stairs that led into further darkness. I looked up at Tony, his eyes narrowed. "Hey!"

The techs looked up. Two of them ran over.

"When did that get here?" asked one of the techs.

BREAKFAST IN PARADISE

My feet were on the stairs before my brain could even register it. I heard Tony yell, but it was so distant and muffled. My feet were moving, and I couldn't stop myself. I drew my gun in the darkness and fumbled for my phone so I could use the flashlight feature. Before I could get it started, a bright light came from behind me. I spun around.

Tony was shaking his head as he descended the stairs. He held up his phone, shining the light ahead of me.

"A door?" A few feet in front of me was a big black door. I looked back at Tony, his gun firm in his hand. I inched toward the door. It was quiet on the other side. I turned the knob, and the door opened. A cloud of dust rose in the air. With Tony's flashlight behind me, I could see most of the room from the doorway. I stepped inside. The room was cold. A shiver ran down my spine. "It looks like a dungeon."

Tony followed behind me. "Yeah, it does. You smell that?"

I nodded slowly. The smell of a decomposing body was unmistakable. It was something that, no matter how hard you tried, you'd never forget. It was strong in the room. I looked around, using my own flashlight. There was nothing else in the room. My eyes scanned the corners and stopped at one. In the far corner of the room, there was a lump of clothing. "I think I found the source of the smell." I pointed at the corner.

Tony moved toward it. I kept my gun drawn, pointing at the pile of clothes. Tony lifted the top of the pile and jumped back. Flies seemed to attack the air, trying to get away from the body. "Yeah, that's the source, alright."

"Can you tell if it's male or female?"

He shook his head. "I think it's male, but don't hold me to that."

We eased out of the underground room and met the techs at the top of the stairs. "There's another body down there for you."

In front of me, the female tech's eyes were as big as saucers. "How many bodies can you find on one property?"

I shrugged. "I think we are about to find out." Tony and I moved away from the remains of the house. "What the hell went on down there?"

Tony shook his head. "I don't know. I can't even think of what might have happened there." He looked back at the door frame. "Why was there only one body? What…" He trailed off. I stared at the door frame.

How did the person even get there? They had to know about the dungeon beforehand. Someone had to put him or her there. Was it Beth or Doug? Or was it someone else entirely?

We waited at the scene for Jill to arrive. It took her fifteen minutes, along with more techs.

"You two find more bodies than anyone I know," she said as she slammed the car door.

I shrugged. "You're welcome."

She laughed. "I guess we did miss something. "

I pointed to the doorway. "Yeah, we all did. Can't figure out what the room was for, though."

"Well, I already told the techs to scan the room for evidence of other dead bodies. I was thinking when I got the call, the room might have been used to store the other dead bodies before they were buried."

I blinked. I hadn't thought of that, but she had a point. The bodies had to be kept somewhere before they could be buried. It made sense and I still couldn't picture it. And who? Doug or Beth? Or both? It was hard to picture. A man was killed and then dragged to the room in the cellar and then a hole was dug. The body then had to be dragged back up the stairs and through the back door and into the backyard. It was a lot of work. I worked through the scenario, replaying the steps over and over in my mind. Picturing the house when it was standing. Unburnt and beautiful. I glanced at the pool that overlooked the cliff. It was several feet away and untouched by the fire. The water was still pristine and sparkling in the sunlight. It was beautiful. A striking contrast to the ashes of the house.

It was a difficult process. Too many steps having to move the bodies around so many times, and what about the blood? It was something that no one could do on their own.

I glanced back at the water. "Maybe they both did it."

CHAPTER TWENTY-FIVE

It took a few days for Jill to get back to us after examining the body. She asked us to join her at the morgue. She sounded tired. She sighed when we walked in.

"Putting in overtime working on this case. Bodies were popping up everywhere. We found another body buried in the yard on top of the one found in that strange room. The body in the room," she backed away and picked up a folder, "belongs to a man named Sam Howard from Boston." She handed me the folder.

In the folder were copies of his driver's license and other items found with his body.

"Like the others, he was bludgeoned to death. The back of his head was a mess, and I don't think we found all the bone fragments. To me, it looks like whoever did this caught him off guard. There were no defensive wounds."

"How long had he been dead?" I asked as I handed the folder to Tony.

"Hard to say. The room is dark, and with moisture, flies, and bug activity, it is difficult to say definitively. And then some of the smoke trailed down there from the fire. He had a receipt in his pocket…can't remember the date, but it's in the file. There was nothing after that day, so…"

"Okay. We need to contact his family," said Tony. "Maybe they can tell us the last time they heard from him."

"Still working on the other body. Male. Also had his head bashed in. But there is nothing on the body to identify him. So, we are still working on that."

"Okay. Let us know when you find something," I said on my way out. Jill looked exhausted. Slight bags under her eyes. She didn't look like her bright and perky self. This case had exhausted everyone. I was so tired. I dreamed about this case. I couldn't stop thinking about it. Where was Beth? Where was Doug?

Every time I closed my eyes, I saw Beth and Doug. Burnt bodies on the ground smoldering. Smoke billowing in the air. When I woke up every morning, I could smell something on fire.

This case had crawled into our brains and made a home there, and we needed to solve it so we could all get some sleep. Back at the field office, I sat at my desk and sighed. I was tired and a little hungry even after seeing the bodies on the slab in the morgue.

Tony handed me the file, and I searched for his name. When I found it and found his next of kin, my heart sank. He had a wife. He had a family, and now I had to tell them that he was dead. I hated having those conversations. It came with being an FBI agent, but I didn't like it.

Having to talk to people on what is most likely the worst day of their lives was not fun. However, you could learn a lot from those conversations. If you really listened. The way a person reacted to the news and what they said afterward was extremely important. Sometimes, they were too stunned to speak. Too busy sobbing to speak. At other times, there was no reaction. And that was important, too.

BREAKFAST IN PARADISE

Grief was a strange thing, and everyone handled it differently. That being said, someone who was too stoic and unfeeling was someone you paid attention to. I called the number and waited for someone to answer.

"Hello?"

"Hello. Is this Mrs. Howard?"

"Yes, who is this?"

"I'm Special Agent Mia Storm with the FBI in Honolulu. I need to ask you a few questions about your husband."

Silence on the other end of the phone was thick and heavy. She drew in a shaky breath. Her voice trembled as she spoke. "What happened to him? Is he okay?"

I sighed. "No, ma'am, he's not. I regret to inform you that we found his body a few days ago."

A sob rippled through the phone. I waited for a long moment, giving her time to get it all out. She sobbed for what felt like long minutes. But it wasn't really that long. She drew in another shaky breath. "What happened to him?"

"Right now, we don't know, which is why I called. When was the last time you saw or spoke to your husband?"

"Well, a few weeks ago. He was there for a vacation and was staying at a bed-and-breakfast."

"The Golden Paradise?"

"Yes, that's it. He was staying there for a week."

"Can I ask why you didn't file a missing persons report or come to look for him?"

"The spouse is always the first suspect. I guess that's true. He was there to get away from me. We...had been...things have been rocky lately, and we were trying to see if we should stay together or not. He thought we needed a break from each other, so he went to Hawaii, and I went to New York. He was supposed to come back if he thought our marriage was worth saving. I came back..."

"But he didn't."

"I thought he decided to end things. I did try calling him. But he didn't answer. I figured things were over. I never thought he was dead. I just thought he didn't want me anymore." Another sob rippled through the phone.

I sighed. "I'm sorry for your loss, ma'am. Thank you for your time. Someone will call you when we know more." The phone clicked, and I exhaled a shaky breath. She was no help, really. They hadn't talked to each other since he had come to the island. If he was having problems with anyone, she wasn't the person that would know.

I hung up the phone, but before I could tell Tony anything, the phone rang. It was Jill.

"So, there was a box in the room. I don't know if you noticed it or not. It was close to the body, probably concealed by all the blankets draped over it. But in that box were a bunch of knives and other sharp tools. There was blood all over them, and some of it belonged to Sam."

"I thought you said he was bludgeoned to death?"

"I said that was how he was killed. Bashing him in the back of the head several times was what killed him. But there were other markings all over his body. Knife cuts and stabbings. But those wounds were too superficial to kill him."

"It was a torture chamber?"

"That was my thought." Jill sighed. "There was blood all over that room. Dried blood. I mean, it was a lot. On the walls, ceiling, and the floor. I just called to tell you that."

I hung up. Tony sat at his desk in front of me with his hands clasped on the table. Waiting for me to say something. I told him what Sam's wife said and what Jill said.

"I guess it was a torture chamber," he said. He leaned back in his chair.

"How tall was Sam?"

He pointed at the file on my desk, and I handed it to him. "Over six feet. 250 pounds."

"That's a big guy for Beth to move on her own."

Tony blinked. "Yeah, she wouldn't have been able to move him anywhere by herself. She had to have help."

"That's why we can't find either of them. It's why we can't find their bodies," I said slowly. "They are doing it together. They killed the men. That's why they aren't on the property."

Tony straightened in his chair. "They aren't dead, and they aren't missing."

"They killed those men together and started the fire…"

BREAKFAST IN PARADISE

"Why start the fire, though? That only brought more attention to them. No one was looking for them until this."

I shook my head. "But people were. The police weren't looking for them. The police weren't doing anything. But their loved ones were. They all believed that Beth had something to do with their disappearances. They just couldn't prove it. But if you believe something loud enough, others might start believing it too."

"They were afraid that the more people talked, the more the police might take a better look at them. Makes sense."

Before I could say anything, my phone rang again. I thought it might have been Jill with something else she found in the creepy torture room, but it wasn't.

"Special Agent Mia Storm. How can I help you?"

"Yes, you called me a few days ago about my sister Beth—"

"You're Savannah!" The words leaped out of my mouth louder than I intended. I couldn't contain my excitement. I thought I was going to have to send agents to her house to find her. I called her right after we thought her sister was dead, but she never called back.

"Yes, I am. I'm sorry this call is so late. I was in the hospital and just got your message. I didn't even know she was in Hawaii. I'm a little surprised."

"Why?"

"She was never the sun and sand kind of person. She was never a fun kind of person."

"I see. Well, let me tell you what—you know what? I need you to tell me about your sister. Everything you remember about her. What kind of person is she?" Initially, when I called Savannah about her sister, I thought she was dead, but now I was pretty sure she wasn't. She was alive somewhere, but we still needed to prove it.

"Oh, um…Well, that's hard to say. It's been so long since I had any contact with her. That was on purpose, mind you. I can only tell you what she was like when she was a child and a teenager."

"That works," I said. So much of who we were as adults was rooted in our childhoods. It sounded cliche, but it was true. Our childhoods were the foundation on which our adult selves were built on. I wondered what her foundation looked like, if it was cracked or shotty.

"Oh, well, she was horrible. She was a spoiled child and mean. Very mean. She thought everything had to be about her, and when it wasn't, it meant that we didn't love her or like her. She was selfish. She never wanted to get her hands dirty."

"Why would she tell her husband that your mother and brother were dead? Are they?"

Savannah gasped. "Are you serious? That lying heifer. They aren't dead! Mama is in Georgia, and she's fine. Hell, she's in better shape than I am. And he's not dead, either. He and his wife are divorced now, and he lives in New Jersey with his son. They are alive and well."

"Wow. I thought so, but I wasn't sure. She had different stories that she told people, and I thought that was odd. Why would she do that? Like, why wouldn't she want anyone to contact you?"

She sighed. "She always was a drama queen. I think it was because she wanted to start over. We weren't the family she wanted. We were the ones she was stuck with. She hated living with us. I think she hated us. She wanted more. More money. Better house. We were too poor for her. Mama tried her best, but...she had three kids, and we all had different dads. She treated us based on how our dads contributed. That might not have been fair...when I think about it now, it really wasn't fair. But...that was how it was."

"So, Beth's father wasn't really in the picture, and your mother took it out on her?"

"It was like this. Mama took the money my father gave her and only used it on me. The same with our brother. But Beth's dad disappeared, so she got our hand me downs. She hated that. I understand why she would have hated it now, but then...it's understandable. She couldn't stretch the money across three kids. Beth resented us."

I swallowed my words. On one hand, I understood why Beth would have been upset and resented her siblings. They always got more than she did, which could cause resentment to fester. It wasn't her fault her father didn't contribute, and yet her mother made it her fault. Made it her problem. That wasn't fair, at least not to me. I didn't want to side with Beth, but I understood why she would have felt that way. "What was she like when she was a teen?"

Savannah chuckled. "She was worse. Much worse. She wanted attention. Everyone's attention had to be on her, or she felt slighted. It was crazy. And then she had this thing… I don't know when it started exactly, but when she became fixated on something, and she had to have it, nothing got in her way. And I mean nothing. She wanted a dress that our mother had bought me for a dance. But she wanted it. Mind you, she had nowhere to wear it, but she wanted the dress. When my mother said no, she not only stole it from the store, but she cut mine up with scissors so I couldn't wear it."

"Wow, that's crazy."

"She was always doing stuff like that. Our neighbor's back carport burned down, and while we could never tie it to Beth, we all knew she did it."

"Why would she have done that?" Might be on to something. The bed-and-breakfast was burned down.

"She had negotiated with the neighbor's son about buying his car. She didn't take into account that the son only drove the car. It was his father who owned it. She was only sixteen at the time. Anyway… when the father got wind of it, he shut it down. He said his son could not sell his car, and Beth was pissed. She wanted that car. The son had basically told her that it was hers if she could come up with the money. I don't know where she was getting the money from. She didn't have a job or anything. But apparently, she got the money together and went to buy the car. When everything happened, she rushed back into the house she was so angry… her face was red, and she was shaking. And then her eyes kind of glazed over, and then she was calm."

"She was calm."

"As a cucumber, honey. It was like it didn't bother her anymore. But I knew her, and I knew she was up to something. Two days later, their back carport, where he kept the car, was on fire. Burnt the car pretty badly, too. If I remember correctly, he couldn't do anything with it after that. He had to get rid of it. They both hated Beth. We could never prove it, but she did it. Mama knew she had. That was how she was when she wanted something. She wanted a puppy after my brother found one. Mama said no, and then next thing you know, the puppy ate something that killed him."

CHAPTER TWENTY-SIX

My conversation with Savannah was enlightening and sad. Beth's mother treated Beth like she was lesser than her siblings because her father wasn't contributing to taking care of her. That must have warped how she saw the world, how she saw her place in it. It might also explain why she was consumed by the thought of making more money, of never stopping at anything to get what she wanted. She didn't have anything and was focused on getting it.

I told Tony everything Savannah said about Beth. Killing animals at a young age was how most serial killers started. It was their testing out phase. They would kill animals to see what it was like and if they could do it. And apparently, she could.

I called Doug's sister and left a message for her to call me back. I wanted to know more about Doug when he was a young boy. Part of me wondered if Doug had always been like this or if

Beth had talked him into it. This behavior didn't just come from nowhere. I mean, no one woke up one morning and thought they were going to kill and rob a bunch of people and bury them in their backyard. There had to be a lynchpin. A turning point.

Part of me didn't think it mattered. They were killers, and we needed to bring them in.

"If we understand why, maybe that will lead us to where they are," I said.

Tony looked up from his computer screen and nodded. He had already called around the airports and marinas to be on the lookout for Beth and Doug and to send over their surveillance footage so we could check it.

Beth and Doug had a head start on us of over a week. The thought made me angry. We had spent all this time looking for Beth's killer, but she wasn't actually dead. She was the killer. She and Doug set the fire and almost killed their guests. I shook the thought from my mind. Or rather, I tried to, but it kept popping up.

Why would they still be on the island? Beth and Doug had to be long gone by now. I would have been. Once I burned down the house, I would have been on a plane before the fire had been put out. Why would they stay?

"You think they are already in the wind?" I asked Tony.

He looked up again and shrugged. "I'm not sure. I mean, I would be. I would be somewhere so far away you'd never find me. So, if they stayed, there had to be a reason. A good one."

"Maybe they are waiting for something," I said. He nodded slowly as he leaned back.

"I'll check their bank accounts. Hadn't had a reason to until now… I think we did when we first found the body. Thought it might have been a robbery or something, but nothing since then." He typed something before leaning forward and staring at the screen. "Yeah, there has been no movement on her account. There was also nothing in her account. It was completely empty."

"Oh." My fingers drummed against the desk. "When was the last withdrawal?"

He clicked something twice. "A week before the fire." He leaned back. "She was planning it. She took all their money out of the accounts to prepare to get away. They've got to be long gone by now."

I nodded slowly. He had a point. If this was all planned in the beginning, then they would have had an exit plan, and it would involve money. "Maybe they were waiting for everything to die down."

Tony shrugged. "Possible. They weren't expecting us to search the ground for dead bodies."

"They might have been expecting us to believe that the body was Beth's and to not look any further," I said. At first, we believed that the body was Beth's. It was burnt so badly it was difficult to tell otherwise until the anthropologist took a look. And neither of them probably knew about the pin in her leg. They must have been expecting things to die down quickly. And it would have had the FBI not been given the case.

If the fire marshal hadn't examined the scene so closely and saw the burnt teeth and knew it was arson. If another person hadn't been killed at the scene. There were many different variables that led us to investigate the case fully. Most of which was out of their control.

My phone rang, snapping me out of my thoughts. I stared at the phone for a long moment before answering.

"This is Chelsea—"

"Right. I did call you. I need to ask you a few more questions about your brother if you have a moment."

She sighed. "Did you finally find his body?"

"No, I'm sorry." I chose my words very carefully. She could have been helping her brother get off the island, although I wasn't too sure about that idea. She didn't seem to hate him, but I didn't believe she would help Beth. Her dislike for Beth was palpable, even over the phone. "Do you know of any place on the island that Doug would go if he needed help?"

She stuttered over her words. "What do you mean?"

"If he was in trouble, is there somewhere or someone he would turn to?" I asked again. I spoke slowly and carefully.

"He's dead! Why does that matter?"

"We have yet to find his body—tell me about Doug." I needed to change my strategy to ease her into this hard conversation.

"What was he like?"

"Yes. What was your brother like when he was young? Did he like animals?"

She gasped. "Who have you been talking to? It was just a bird, and it was an accident."

I blinked. "I hadn't spoken to anyone. Just you. What is this about a bird?"

She sighed. "It was an accident."

"What kind of accident?"

She paused. "He accidentally fed the bird the wrong food. That's all. It wasn't his fault the bird died. He didn't know any better."

To me, it sounded like she was trying to convince herself it wasn't his fault.

"Okay. Did that happen a lot? Dying animals?"

"I don't know what you're getting at. Beth killed him. End of story."

"What if he isn't dead?" I asked. I was trying to find another way to say it or even a better way to say it, but we didn't have the time. We didn't know where they were or what they were planning, and we needed to get to them before they got away if it wasn't already too late.

Her gasp was loud and not faked. "You think he's still alive? Where has he been all this time?"

"That's why I'm asking. Is there anywhere he would go if he was in trouble and needed to lay low?"

She paused for a moment. "I'm sorry. I don't know. There's nothing I can think of. I feel like I don't know him. I don't know where he'd go. I don't think there is a place he could go. He didn't have anything. Once he met Beth, she was everything to him. He didn't have anything outside of her."

"I see. Okay. Please, if you think of anything, call me."

"I will. Please let me know if you find him."

I hung up the phone. "Someone knows something. Someone has to know where they are. They might not know that they know."

"Well, I've got alerts out everywhere. If anyone sees them, or if they show up on any cameras, we should get a call."

"That's good to know. But we need to do something proactive." I jumped to my feet. "Let's go talk to the cook and then the neighbors."

We started with the neighbors. The Nakamuras were standing on the front porch when Tony walked up their driveway. While he was there, I went to speak with Judith Oakley, who was also sitting on her porch watching me come up. A smile bloomed on her lips as I drew closer.

"I was wondering if you'd be back."

"Me too. I thought we had a lead, and now I'm not so sure. I need more information on Doug and Beth."

"I didn't think there was a lot to tell."

I shrugged. "It's been difficult finding people that really knew them. They seemed to keep people at bay. Rightfully so, seems like. But now I need to know if there was someone or somewhere they'd go if they were in trouble. Like if they needed to hide out or something."

Her eyes went wide for a moment. And then confusion took over, snaking through the grooves of her face. "To hide out? Aren't they both dead?"

"Maybe. Maybe not."

She blinked and then slowly leaned back. "I see. So, you don't think that either of them are dead. That's an interesting twist."

A smile tugged at my lips. It sounded like something the Nakamuras would say. I glanced back at the house across the street and wondered what Tony was going through with our true crime enthusiasts. Probably being asked more questions and getting very few answers.

Mrs. Oakley sighed. "Well, I don't know. I can't imagine that they are both still alive. Well, him, maybe. But judging by all the stuff you've found over there, I'd want to hide out, too. To tell you the truth, I would have disappeared by now."

"Yeah, me too. But we still need to trace down every lead."

"Understood."

"If you think of anything that could help, don't hesitate to call." I turned to walk away. I was halfway down the driveway when I heard her voice.

"Wait, a minute."

I spun around. "Yes?"

She tapped her chin twice. "You should contact someone that worked over there. They would probably know more than us."

I nodded. "On our way. You were just the first stop." I threw my hand up and headed across the street. Just as I was walking up the driveway, the front door opened. It was Tony. He hurried to close the door behind him and sighed against it.

I chuckled, and he looked up. "Learn anything?"

"True crime nuts," he said as he followed me back to the car. "They asked me more questions than they answered."

I laughed. Just as I thought. I knew they would do that. This is one of the reasons I opted to talk to Mrs. Oakley instead. But she didn't answer my questions either, or rather, she didn't know the answers to my questions. I told him what she said as we headed to Piper's place. She was home. She looked surprised to see us when she opened the door.

"You have more questions?"

"Yes. I'm sorry. Just a few more."

She nodded and let us in. "I'm not sure what else I can tell you."

Instead of moving to the kitchen, we stayed in the living room. "I understand how frustrating this can be. But I just have a few more questions about Doug. What was he like? Did he seem like the kind of person that would hurt someone?"

"Is this about all the bodies you found on the property?"

We tried our best to keep it out of the news, but it seemed like that was no good. This was before we thought Beth was still alive, so chances were she knew what we found. If I were her, I would have been watching the news, waiting for things to die down. She would definitely be on the move soon if she weren't already off the island.

"Yes. Do you think Doug killed those men?"

She shrugged. "I'm not—I'd hate to say I'm not surprised. I mean, I wish I was. I wish I were surprised. I really do. But... Doug was a good person. I think. I just—"

"What are you not telling us?" I asked.

Piper shoved her hands in her pockets. She opened her mouth to speak and then stopped. "They seemed like nice people, but there was a darkness to them. Yes...I think he could hurt someone. But I don't think he would do it on his own. Not without her."

"So, you think if he did anything, it was at her instance?" asked Tony.

"I'm not saying he can't think for himself. He can. But if she said she wanted something done, he would do it just because she asked."

"So, whatever happened in that house, they were in it together."

She looked at me, a long, hard stare. "I would say so. They were both nice on their own, but together, Beth could be cruel, and he'd go along with it."

"Give me an example of that," I said.

"She would say mean things to me sometimes. Cruel things. But it was only when they were together. It was like she was afraid he had eyes for me or something."

"She was jealous?" asked Tony as he leaned against the door.

"She could be, sometimes. She would make fun of my weight and bring up my son being an addict sometimes and say it was because I was a bad mother. And Doug would just laugh and sometimes chime in. But when it was just us and the other wasn't in the room, they were nice. It was strange, but it was how they were."

I glanced at Tony, whose eyes narrowed at her. Part of me wondered why she waited so long to say this. Why now? People don't like speaking ill of the dead and all that. Maybe after hearing about the men digging up in the backyard, she had a change of heart. She didn't want to protect them anymore.

"Do you know anywhere they would go if they were in trouble?"

"Isn't she dead?" She looked at me, confusion etched into her face.

"No. Probably not."

"Oh."

She didn't look or sound surprised by that new information.

"Um...Doug had a place...a house that once belonged to his grandfather. His father's father. I heard him and Beth talking about it once. He said how nice it was and it would be a nice place to get away. Apparently, there were no neighbors for miles. Why does this matter? Isn't he dead, too?"

"What would make you think that?" I asked.

"All these months, and no one has been able to find him. I just assumed...well, me and everyone else...assumed he was dead. I always thought she killed him when I heard about his mistress. Is that not right?"

"We don't think so," I said. "We don't think he's dead. What else did they say about this house?"

She shrugged. "Umm...Just what I said. I didn't think Beth liked the idea of living there full-time. She said it was too closed off. But Doug seemed like he would have loved it there."

I looked at Tony, who stood up straight.

"I guess now we have a lead."

CHAPTER TWENTY-SEVEN

Beth Hardwell

ONE YEAR AGO...
"You think this will work?"
They had changed and rearranged components of their plan almost every week. Beth stared at the now rough outline of what was to happen in the coming months. A year's worth of work scribbled on a soon to be discarded scrap of paper. She was tired of working on it. Tired of thinking about it, but they need to hone in on a plan that would work. Something they could both do.

"Shut up!" Beth glared at the body on the floor. Her muffled screams and constant movement were getting on her nerves. It was distracting, and she was trying to think. Cherrica Owens was part of the plan; they needed her. Better yet, they needed her body.

The room under the house was cold and damp but quiet and away from the guests so they could talk. So they could really talk, not in hushed whispers and serious looks. She was careful what she said in the house. Guests and their phones, it seemed like someone was always recording around the house.

"I'm not sure," she sighed and pushed the paper away. Her bloody fingers stained the paper and mingled with the ink. "I'm really not sure. It will work if no one looks close enough. We just need to make sure no one looks closely."

"How can we ensure that?" Doug sat at the table across from her.

The plan might have changed several times in the last year, but a few steps stayed the same. Doug would have to leave. He would have to run away with his mistress, and everyone would have to know about it. She had to make sure she said it loud and to the right people. Her neighbors, for one. Her neighbors were nosey, and they talked a lot. Especially Mrs. Oakley. She knew almost everyone's business in town.

Beth had sat on her porch and learned everything about the neighbors that she had seen and ones she didn't even know what they looked like. She had to make sure she told her. Doug ran out on her and had an affair with their cook Rica. And once Rica disappeared, too, it would be like they both ran off.

That part of the plan always stayed the same, but the rest of it was malleable. She hadn't quite figured it out yet. "We'll need money. I know that, so we are going to have to start taking money out of our accounts. Especially you. I don't want you using your card or bank account after the night you leave. No one should be able to track you down."

"Noted. I've already started taking money out and keeping it in a good spot. When do I leave?"

She shook her head. "Haven't decided yet. We need to pin down the dates."

The need for an exit plan had become evident a few months ago when the brother of one of the men buried underneath the house or maybe the backyard—she wasn't sure where his body was—came looking for his brother. He was getting too close and trying to get the police involved.

Beth counted herself lucky that the police loved them. Most of them had brought their significant others to the bed-and-breakfast, and she had given them all discounts. It was always good to have the police on your side in whatever town you lived in. She had learned that from her grandmother, who ran numbers when she was younger.

The local police knew her grandmother. They came over for Sunday dinner, and she always fixed them a plate and a cold beer. She waved when they passed by her house and asked about the family whenever she stopped to speak to them. She knew them by name, their wives, kids, and their parents. For some, even their grandparents. If you're going to be doing something, you should make yourself indispensable to the people around you. Especially the ones in charge.

But the brother didn't care about her or the bed-and-breakfast. He didn't believe that his brother would just walk out and never come back. The police did because the brother, *what was his name?* She couldn't remember half of their names, not that it mattered.

The brother had some substance abuse issues, which made it easier for the police to believe that he left and went somewhere and got high. She counted on that. It was why she chose him. It was why she chose most of them. Men no one would miss. At least, she thought no one would miss. She wasn't counting on him coming all the way to Honolulu to find his brother.

He had surprised her when she saw him at her front door. She didn't know what to say. She wasn't expecting it, and it threw her. She recovered quickly, though, but she wasn't sure he believed her. In fact, she knew he didn't. He kept coming around. She had just seen him this morning, and he wasn't going to stop coming around. She knew that. She sighed as she stared at the paper.

Doug's large hand swallowed hers, and she smiled. This wasn't how she pictured her life going. Her hands were still stained with blood. The thought made her smile. They had done a lot together. Shed so much blood. She glanced at Rica, limp and quiet, leaning against the wall.

She was thankful for the quiet. For the peace. She cocked her head as she stared at her. "Fire."

Doug looked at her, a question forming on his face.

"We could burn it all down."

He straightened in his chair. "But you worked so hard on this place. We've done so much work here. Good work. You just want to throw it all away?"

She leaned forward and took both his hands in hers. "We will never be able to come back here. This place is not ours anymore. Once we finish this plan and get away, we can never come back, not even to visit. So, what does it matter if this place is burned down? It isn't ours anymore. Sure, it will be difficult to see it go, but we can build somewhere else."

He nodded slowly. "I guess that will work. Is that part of the plan?"

"I think so. I just need to tweak it a little. But I think the fire is our best bet."

"Okay. And what about her?"

She looked at Rica. "Well, for now, we can do whatever we want to her. And then we set her on fire."

In the coming months, Beth added and subtracted steps from the plan every day.

"Go away!" She closed the trunk and picked up her groceries off the ground. "I don't know why you keep coming here. I don't know where your brother is." Her voice came out in a harsh whisper. She was tired of having the same conversation with him. She was tired of him coming around. If she were a meaner person, she'd stick him in the ground next to his brother so he could see his decomposing body while he died.

But she wasn't, so she didn't. The man pulled his hat low.

"You know something. I know you do. My brother was here, and now he's gone. That doesn't make any sense. Where did he go?"

"I don't know!" Beth grabbed her bags and rushed toward the house. She slammed the door behind her just as he stepped on the porch. Her heart pounded against her ribs as her bags slipped out of her hands. She leaned against the door as she tried to catch her breath. They had to put the plan into action soon. If he kept coming around, someone was going to get suspicious. She couldn't afford that. They had to get away before then.

"Do you think that's the right position to put her in?" Doug hovered over Beth while she changed the position of her body for the umpteenth time. She had moved Rica into several positions while she was on the floor, but none of them felt right.

Except this one. In the middle of the owner's quarters, surrounded by a bedsheet and a comforter. "I think it might work better here, especially if we add more kindling around the body. It will help with the fire."

The guests were still eating dinner. They had time, but not much. They needed to get everything right so the fire would be noticed by the guests shortly after they finished eating and did their usual after dinner activities. After dinner, most of them went to their rooms to relax.

Mr. Monroe liked to spend time in the library after dinner, staring outside at the water. He did so every night since he had been there. Beth knew he would probably be the first to see the smoke. It was better that way. He seemed like a nice man who cared about others. If he was the first to see the smoke, Beth believed he would try to alert everyone. That gave them a fighting chance.

She didn't really care if they died or not, but if more than one person died in the fire, the police would look a little closer at the fire than she wanted them to.

If it were only her, then they would see it as an accident. A fire that started in her bedroom, and she succumbed to smoke inhalation, and her body was burnt beyond recognition before the fire was put out. That part was crucial. Her facial features and fingerprints had to be gone completely. She needed them to struggle with identifying the body. In fact, it would have been better if they couldn't identify her at all. The harder it was, the more likely it was that they would just accept that it was her. She knew most of the detectives and officers who would work the case, and she knew how they felt about hard work. They strongly disliked it.

They wouldn't look too hard. Sure, they might be sad to see her go, but it wouldn't have mattered to them. It wouldn't have made them look harder into her death. Any investigation they did would be superficial. And once that was done, they could get off the island.

Beth stared at the body and sighed, finally satisfied with the placement. "Might take a couple of weeks for everything to die down," she said mostly to herself. Those two weeks would give them enough time to get the documents for their new identities. Doug knew a guy who could help them, but it would take a few days.

"Okay. I'll get everything set up. When you're done here, meet me at our spot," he said. He grabbed her by the shoulders and pulled her into a deep, slow kiss. "I'll be waiting."

Beth's heart bloomed.

CHAPTER TWENTY-EIGHT

TONY AND I LEFT PIPER'S CONDO WITH A GOOD LEAD AS to where Beth and Doug might be. We still didn't know for sure if they were alive or still on the island, but the house was a good place to start. I was pretty sure Beth was alive, but not so sure she was still on the island. I wouldn't have been. But still, it was worth a shot.

I called for backup while Tony drove. "They will meet us there." Instead of pulling into the driveway, we parked down the road and would walk to the house. No sirens were to be used. We tried to keep it as quiet as possible so as not to alert them. I hoped when I got off the phone, that backup would listen. That everyone would get the memo. It was a quiet area, and the neighbors were so far apart. Noise traveled easily. A siren would alert everyone.

My heart thudded in my chest. It banged against my ribs nonstop. I always got nervous before confronting a suspect. It was nerve-wracking because I never knew how it was going to turn out. The suspects might come with us willingly, or they might start a shootout. One of us could get shot.

I glanced at Tony, who was bent over the trunk, looking for his bulletproof vest. I strapped mine on while the backup arrived. Several cars pulled up next to us. Agents and officers descended onto the street. My heart pounded against my ribs harder. I wiped my palms on my pants.

"Take a deep breath," said Tony. He looked so calm as he finished putting on his vest and closed the trunk. I didn't understand how he could be with all the times he got shot. He should have been more anxious than anyone. "It will be what it will be." He smiled.

The tension between my shoulders eased a little as I took a deep breath. He was right. It will be what it will be. But we still needed to be careful.

"Okay. We'll head toward the house quickly and quietly," said Tony. The scouts we sent toward the house came back and said there was a truck in the driveway.

"It looks like there is someone home. But the curtains are closed, and we didn't see any cameras out front," said one of the plain clothes officers.

"If there were no cameras, they might not see us coming," I told Tony.

He nodded. "Maybe the cameras aren't bulky. They could still have a Ring camera or something."

He had a point. But we still needed to move with caution. Quickly and quietly, we moved down the street toward the house. Doug's home was a one-story farm style home with large windows, white shutters, and a black door. It looked like someone was not taking care of the property. Like someone hadn't been there in years.

The grass was overgrown and wild. The flowers in the front flowerbed had been overtaken by weeds. The white trim around the house was more brown than white. Doug might have liked the idea of living on the property one day, but he didn't try to take care of it. Not that it mattered now. Tony followed close behind as I inched up the driveway, gun drawn and heart pounding.

My heart stuttered as I reached the door. Tony moved across from me on the other side, next to the doorbell. I took a long, deep breath as two more agents walked up, one with a battle ram. Once everyone got in place, Tony held up his fingers and counted down from three. Walking up to a house, time moves so slowly. The seconds dragged on, and it felt like it would last forever.

But once we got to the house, it never failed. Time picked up. Seconds whirled by in a dizzying haze. As soon as Tony got to one, the battle ram burst through the door. There was a loud thud as I was the first to enter. I felt Tony behind me even though I couldn't see him. But I knew he was there. The house smelled of stale sweat. It had clearly been closed up for a long time. If they were there, no one bothered to open the windows.

"FBI! Anyone on the premises, come out with your hands up!" My throat was raw, but I kept screaming. There was no answer. Not that I was expecting one.

A flash of movement! Something moved out of the corner of my eye, and I turned toward it, moving down a long hallway. Tony followed. The hallway opened up to the kitchen. Someone was running toward the back door.

"Stop! Turn around and keep your hands up," Tony yelled. While Tony was focused on the woman by the door, my eyes stopped at the man with the gun.

Doug Frazier, tall with a thick beard, pointed a gun right at Tony, who had his gun aimed at Beth.

"Drop it, Doug!" I demanded.

He looked at me with red eyes and wild hair like it was the first time he had noticed I was even there. His eyes flicked back to Beth and then to Tony. All he saw was Tony and his gun. "Drop it, Doug. Don't make me shoot you!"

He never said anything. Never even blinked. My heart stopped when his finger moved to the trigger. A jolt shot up my arm, and I stumbled back. Doug slumped to the ground. I ran over and kicked the gun both out of his reach and away from Beth. Agents rushed into the room.

Doug groaned on the floor, and Beth screamed. Tony ran over to her and cuffed her before she could resist.

"You shot him. You killed him!" She tried to fall to her knees, but Tony pulled her back to her feet.

"I shot him in the shoulder. He'll live," I said. An agent called for an ambulance, and another took Beth away. Tony and I exchanged a knowing look. We both wanted to look around the house and see what they were hiding, if they were hiding anything at all.

The house was smaller inside than it looked on the outside. We left them in the kitchen and headed down a long hallway with three doors. One was a bathroom, and the other two were bedrooms. The first one was empty. The second was where they slept. The room smelled like sweat and body odor. It was a pungent smell. They must have spent a lot of time in that room. We took our sides and started our search. In the room, we found the luggage they were using. Clothes, toiletries, and money. A bunch of money. I dumped the money on the bed. Tony stopped.

"I guess that's where their money went," he said.

I nodded. "Find anything interesting?"

He held up two plane tickets. "They were set to leave in a couple of weeks for Thailand under different names. Athena and Gerald Whitlock."

"Oh, new names and everything." I figured that was what they were doing. Stayed low until everything died down, and then they could take their new identities, leave the island, and never look back. Or maybe it took a while for them to get their new identities, so they had to wait to leave. They couldn't leave under their names. Especially not Beth.

Along with other agents, we searched the house but found nothing else. When we were satisfied we weren't missing anything, we left. Agents and techs stayed searching the house and dusting for prints. We went back to the field office, where Beth was in an interrogation room waiting for us.

Doug had been taken to the hospital. Hattie found us as soon as we walked onto the floor.

"Doctor called. Doug is alive and will make a full recovery. The bullet went straight through. Beth is in interrogation room waiting for you, and Davies wants to see both of you before you go in."

I followed Tony into Davies's office. She had given us a bit more room during this investigation. We didn't have to report our every move to her anymore now that she was comfortable with my investigation abilities. It was nice not having to tell her our every move and run things by her first. Made me feel more like an agent.

"You wanted to see us?" I closed the door behind me.

"Yeah, I just wanted to check in with the case. Hattie said you brought a suspect in."

I explained everything we knew, with Tony chiming in now and then. Her jaw tightened for a moment and then went slack.

"So, she faked her death and then set the place on fire so she and her husband could get away with murder?" The surprise in her tone brought a smile to my lips.

"It looks that way," answered Tony.

She shook her head. "That's hard to believe but not impossible. See if you can get her to confess. Sure, the bodies were found on her property, but unless you have something more to tie her to their deaths, she could blame it all on her husband."

I paused outside of her office door for a moment. Tony spun around. "What's wrong?"

"We record the interrogations, right?" I asked.

"Yeah, it's standard procedure. Why?"

"Because we might need it to turn Doug. If she blames him for everything, that might convince him to talk to us."

Beth asked for a lawyer, so it made getting things set up easier. We had more time to make sure everything was in place. There was a camera in the interrogation room, but it wasn't automatic. We had to make sure it was turned on before we entered the room, but after she spoke with her lawyer, that someone was there monitoring the conversation.

The lawyer arrived thirty minutes later, and we entered the room fifteen minutes after that. Her lawyer was an older man who looked and smelled expensive. Part of me wondered how she could even afford to speak with him, let alone his retainer.

"My client doesn't understand why you are looking for her. Her house burned down. That is not an FBI matter."

"Well, a burnt body was found in the rubble of her home, and then multiple bodies were found buried underneath it and in the backyard. So that does make it an FBI matter," I said.

Beth blinked. "I don't know what they're talking about."

"Ask your client why she never came back to the bed-and-breakfast. If she had nothing to hide."

He looked at Beth and whispered something in her ear. She straightened in her chair. "I needed a break from the place, that's all. Just a little vacation with my husband."

"I thought you two were no longer together." I rested my elbow on the table. My chin in the palm of my hand, I stared at Beth. "He ran off with his mistress. Isn't that what you told the police?" She opened her mouth to speak, but I waved my hand dismissively. "Before you tell another lie, let me tell you what we know."

I glanced over at Tony, who nodded. "We know that you killed men who came to your bed-and-breakfast and stole their money. And then you buried them on the property. We know that Rica Owens, who people believed was having an affair with your husband, was the burnt body found in your home. We know the names of most of the men found on your property, and we know that they were staying there before they went missing. Now, here's what we don't know."

I placed the folder on the table and took out the pictures of the bodies. I spread them out in front of her and watched her reaction. She didn't have one. She didn't look away from the pictures either.

"We don't know who killed the men. Maybe you killed them, and Doug helped you get rid of the bodies, or maybe he killed them and forced you to help. And because we don't know, you have the liberty of explaining everything to us your way."

"I—"

"Don't answer that."

I studied Beth. I watched the annoyed look on her face while her lawyer forced her to be quiet. It twisted into anger and then back to being neutral. She didn't like to be told what to do. She didn't like being told she couldn't have something or she shouldn't do something. It was clear by the look on her face.

I decided to try something. "Beth, I think you might be tired of other people telling you what to do, especially men."

Her eyes darted from the lawyer to me.

"And I get that. You're tired of people telling you what you can and can't have. So now is your chance to control your fate. You control the narrative. You control everything from here on out."

Her back straightened, and her body turned slightly, no longer angled toward her lawyer.

"So, what do you have to say?"

"Beth, I need you to trust me. Say nothing." The lawyer's voice was a harsh whisper, and it seemed to annoy her even more.

"Get out," she hissed. "I don't need you. I can work this out on my own."

Tony walked over to the door and opened it. "You heard her. She can handle this." The lawyer looked from her to me and back again. He jumped to his feet in a huff and exited without another word.

"I killed those men," she said, leaning forward, a strange look of glee on her face. "He helped, but it wasn't his idea. It wasn't mine either, not really. It just worked." The words tumbled from her mouth so quickly that I was thankful we were recording the interrogation. I was sure I missed a few things by the end.

Beth recounted how it started with a travel blogger coming to the bed-and-breakfast and wanting more than just a free stay for the night and free meals. Killing him had not been done on purpose, but it was the only way to get him away from her. And while that may have been true for that particular murder, she didn't call the police, nor did she tell anyone about him attacking her. Instead, she killed him, buried his body in the backyard, and took his money.

"After that, it just...was easy. When we needed money. I wasn't done renovating the place. It still wasn't how I wanted it, and their money helped. It always helped."

I asked about Doug and his role in the murders. She dismissed it and said he just did what she asked. "He always did whatever I asked of him. He loves me so much. All I have to do is ask, and he does it. That's all."

Doug helped drag the bodies and bury them in the yard. When I asked about the room underground with the body and the sharp implements with blood all over them, her expression changed. Her arms folded across her chest.

"I don't know what you mean." She pressed her lips into a hard line and looked away from the table. I pushed the pictures of the room toward her. She refused to look at it.

"We know that you used the room as a torture chamber." She didn't look at me, but I knew she was listening. I could have stopped talking. I probably should have. Regardless of what she said, no, we still had her on all the murders on her property, but still. She wouldn't take credit for the body in the room. Why? Because it didn't go with her, it just happened, right?

"What about Julius Gabriel? Why kill him?"

She sighed. "He kept looking around the property for his brother. He just wouldn't go away, and then he found something. Doug had seen him digging something up. He had to kill him and then cover it all backup. But then you found it anyway. A lot of good that did."

I sighed. I knew that was what he was doing there that night. He had found the body before we did. Or maybe it was the hand he found that Tony unearthed later.

"And the attack on me?"

"We weren't expecting you to be back there that night. We had some things to take from the wreckage. You just got on the way."

Grumbling, I slid over a pad and pen. "Write down everything in your own words, and we will see if we can get the prosecutor to make you a deal." I tried to say it in my most sincere and empathetic tone. But I didn't feel sorry for her or Doug, and I doubted any prosecutor would make a deal.

I felt sorry for Julius, whose search for his brother was what got him killed.

I felt sorry for Rica, who just wanted to live her life.

I felt sorry for all the victims whose lives were taken, and for what? Nothing more than petty greed.

CHAPTER TWENTY-NINE

"SHE WON'T CLAIM THE TORTURE CHAMBER," SAID Tony as we walked to our desks. Another agent was in the room babysitting Beth while she wrote her statement.

"Did you see the smile?" When I slid over the pad and paper, she glanced at the picture of the body in the strange, dark room. The corner of her mouth curved slightly before she took the pen out of my hand. She smiled at that picture but not the others. "I want to talk to Doug."

Tony nodded. "Okay. I'll stay here in case she gets chatty again." He handed me the keys, and I left the building in search of more answers.

Doug was in a hospital bed with his shoulder bandaged up and an officer sitting outside his door. When I entered, he rolled his eyes.

"You've already shot me and taken Beth. What more do you want?" His voice was soft and not what I was expecting at all. Almost childlike.

"I wanted to get your statement since I've already gotten hers. She told us everything."

He laughed. "She wouldn't do that."

I played a snippet of the audio from the video. His eyes went wide, and I stopped the tape. "She told us about the travel writer who was supposed to be writing an article on the bed-and-breakfast. She told us how you helped her bury the body after he attacked her and she killed him. How would I know all that unless she said something?"

He sighed. "So, what do you need from me?"

"I need to hear both your versions of what happened in that room. We found knives and other sharp objects, a body, and blood all over the walls and ceiling. I'm wondering why that body was tortured. Why not the others?"

He stared across the room at the window that was closed with the curtains drawn. "It was just to see if we'd like it. I wasn't expecting her to take to it like she did. But she did. She liked hurting people. She always smiled when it happened. That was her room. Her happy place."

I blinked. "I see. Yeah, that's what I thought. So, you two would torture them and take their money and then kill them?"

"Sometimes it worked out that way. Sometimes it didn't."

I nodded as I handed him a pad and paper. "I need you to write down your statement so I can compare it to hers and make sure you both are telling us the truth."

He nodded and took the pad and pen. "Can I see her before you take me to prison?"

"Don't count on it." He was facing life in prison, and yet his only thoughts were about her. Not about the men they killed or their families. Just her. It was like he was obsessed. It was weird to see and hear. I shoved the repulsion from my mind. They both liked killing people and torturing them. He had to like it too, even though he tried to put it all on her.

Part of me believed it was mostly her. Like if he had never met her, he might have had a chance. But his eagerness to please her… he just wanted to make her happy. And he would do whatever it took to do that. It was sweet, in a demented and deranged kind of way.

Once Doug finished writing his statement, I left the room and headed to the field office. I showed the pad to Tony, who was both surprised and happy that I got his confession. "I should have known you were there getting him to say something."

"Well, thank you." I gave a curt bow. I relayed everything Doug had told me in his hospital room. "They liked it. I mean, he said it was more about Beth than anything else, but... it was about him too. He liked it and went along with it. They beat the men who were bad guests or mean to them in some way and then took them to the room, where they tortured them for hours. Sometimes days depending on how Beth was feeling."

"Damn," said Tony as he looked over the statement. "I can't help but think if they never met each other, these men might still be alive."

I nodded slowly. I had the same thought on my way back to the field office. If only they had never met, then Julius would still be alive. It was a hard thought to process, and I didn't want to think about it anymore. I didn't want to think about anything anymore. There was a slight pounding in my head. I didn't know if it was because I was hungry, tired, or tired of thinking. Or all the above.

"Let's go get something to eat," said Tony.

"How do you read my mind?" I jumped to my feet.

"When you haven't eaten, you get a very pensive look on your face."

"No, I don't." I didn't know how I looked when I was hungry, but I was hungry, and I really needed something to eat. Aunt Mai's was packed, and I didn't feel like waiting, so instead, Tony and I went to a Vietnamese restaurant. It was a small place with limited seating. Dark wood tables and dark blue chairs. There were two available tables, and we sat in the back. The smell of onions, ginger, and meat consumed me. My mouth watered before I even saw the menu.

A waitress with long black hair walked over to our table. "Is this your first time here?"

I nodded.

"Oh, okay. Do you want more time?"

"What would you recommend?" I asked as I glanced over the menu.

"Well, I would start with our spring rolls. My favorites are the Sugarcane prawns, fried chicken wings, and Beef pad Thai." She pointed to where the items were on the menu. Instead of searching for anything else, we decided to go with her recommendations. I was too hungry to think or make any decisions. She took the menus and walked away but then came back and asked us for our drink orders. Tony ordered limeade while I got the sweet tea.

I sank into my chair. Pressing my back into the cushion behind me. It was super soft, but it was better than the chair at the hospital or in the interrogation room.

"You okay?"

I looked up from the table and caught Tony staring at me. Eyes narrowed, the creases between his brows deep. I gave him my best smile, and he shook his head. The corners of his mouth curved slightly.

"Have you talked to Harrison?"

My eyebrow raised slightly. What did he mean by that? I talked to Harrison a lot. "About what exactly?"

"About him getting stabbed by a patient."

"You know something I don't?"

He threw his hands up. "I'm not getting involved. But I just... I was curious about what happened that led to it. Why does someone stab their therapist? He was lucky it wasn't too serious. It could have been worse."

I nodded. "He didn't really want to talk about it. He didn't want to betray his patient's trust. He takes that very seriously. I don't think he wanted to press charges either." I was trying to give Harrison the benefit of the doubt. His patients... his job was his business, and I needed to stay out of it for my own sanity. If I searched too hard for a puzzle, I wouldn't be able to focus on anything else.

Tony sighed. "He should probably talk about it to someone. Does the therapist have a therapist?"

I shrugged. "Probably. I would hope so. I think they all need someone they can talk to that can't say anything about what they talk about."

"A therapist's therapist. Like priests who also have to take the confessions of other priests. I think that's how that goes."

I chuckled. I understood what he was saying. Being stabbed was a traumatic experience. He would need to talk to someone about it. So far, that someone wasn't me. He didn't want to talk about it any time I tried to bring it up. I didn't know if there was an investigation or if someone was arrested. I was trying to stay out of it. It wasn't my case either way. But staying out of it was easier said than done.

"How are you feeling?" he asked.

I frowned. "I'm fine."

He tapped his temple. "I mean your head, dummy."

"Oh," I said. I had almost forgotten about my injury. "It's fine. No lasting damage."

He grinned. "How would you be able to tell?"

"Shut up!"

The food arrived, and my mouth watered instantly. The scent of onions, garlic, and ginger filled the air. Without another word, we both dug in. The fried chicken was crispy and salty. We shared bites of everything. The sugarcane prawns and Beef pho were delicious.

"We should come here again," I said.

Tony nodded and smiled as he finished the last chicken wing. "Yeah, we should. We find the best places when we are starving."

"Yeah, we do. Surprisingly, or maybe we are just really hungry, and that's clouding our judgment."

"Yeah, we will have to come back when we are starving and then try it." Tony laughed.

"Speaking of relationships and trying things again..."

"Good pivot." He rolled his eyes.

"How are things with Aisha?"

He shrugged. "We've just fallen back into how we used to be but without any expectations. I'm still on the fence about getting married ever. And she's too wrapped up in her work to think about it."

"So...you haven't really dealt with your issues with each other. You're just too busy to focus on them?"

"Pretty much."

"And that's working?"

He shrugged. "Seems so. Now, for how long, I don't know."

"And you're okay with that?"

His eyes met mine for a long moment. Silence stretched between us.

"I guess for right now, it's something. We can't all have what we really want. We just have to make do."

I opened my mouth to say something, but I didn't know what. The waitress returned with the check, cutting me off. Just as well. Judging by the look on his face, he didn't want a follow-up comment. We paid for dinner and then headed back to the field office in a comfortable silence.

Hattie was waiting for us by our desks. "I was wondering when you'd be back. Where did you go?"

"Dinner. We were starving," I answered. "What happened?"

"Nothing, really. Finished up with Beth, and she's on her way to jail. Doug is expected to make a full recovery. But someone called you. Her first husband, Victor. He said you called him."

I slumped into my chair. I had forgotten I called him but didn't get an answer. It didn't matter now that we found her, but I still had a nagging question for him. I called him back.

"Hey, I was returning your call. I saw a lot of stuff on the news since then, so you might not need to talk to me anymore."

I chuckled. "Yeah, it's been a busy day. Um... I'm sure now you know we've found your ex-wife alive and well with her second husband."

"I did hear that. I'm surprised but not surprised. All the bodies found on her property were a hell of a shock. Are you sure they weren't there before we moved? I mean, it's possible right?"

I sighed. "I'm afraid not. The men we found were all guests of the Paradise. And she's confessed, so we know that she and Doug killed them."

He exhaled slowly. "I see. Okay... but what did you want to ask me about Beth?"

"Did you have a child together? I just ask because we got a look at her medical records while trying to identify her body, and she had given birth when she was twenty-five or so."

The silence on the other end was deafening. I immediately regretted the question. It wasn't my place to ask or my business to share.

"No. We didn't have any children. She had several miscarriages. The records must be mistaken."

"Right. They must be. Thank you for your time." I hung up the phone before he could ask me another question. I sunk deeper into my chair. She had miscarriages, but she also had abortions before and after she had the baby. Beth didn't want to be a mother, so what did she do with the child?

"Let it go, Mia. You don't need to know everything. And you probably never will. It's his turn to start asking questions and figure it out for himself."

I nodded slowly. Tony was right. Beth and the mess she made of her life and others was no longer our problem. It was time to put everything to rest.

CHAPTER THIRTY

I FOLLOWED WHAT TONY SAID AND PUT THE CASE OUT OF MY mind. We found the killers of Cherrica and Julius and his brother and the other men that had gone missing. I didn't need to know anything else about Beth, her husbands, or the rest of her family. The puzzle had been solved, and now it needed to be put back in the box. I still had so many questions but swallowed them one by one. I swallowed them whole and prayed they never came back to bite me in the ass.

They both took deals. Not wanting to claim their innocence. I was thankful for that because I didn't really feel like having to exhaustively find the conclusive evidence to convince a jury. Beth took some responsibility, but she still tried to put most of it on Doug. Doug went along with it because it made her happy. He did any and everything that made her happy. His life revolved around her. It was sad.

Made me wonder what was going to happen to him in prison. They both got life and would never see each other again. I doubted they'd be allowed to write to each other. Half of me hoped not. They didn't need to contact each other anymore. They didn't need to contact anyone anymore.

The weeks after they went away were quiet and peaceful. It was nice to have some downtime to relax and file paperwork. I knocked on Mrs. Owens's door and waited. I hadn't called, but I was just stopping by to check on her. Tony and I went to her daughter's funeral. It was a great turnout. So many people loved her. So many people hadn't believed she was having an affair with Doug.

After a long moment, the door opened. She looked startled when she saw me. "You too?" She opened the door wider and moved out of the way. As I walked past her, I saw Tony. He smiled and helped up a mug.

"I didn't know you were coming," I said. She closed the door behind me, and I handed her the dish I had been carrying. It was the only thing I knew I could make and not mess up. And something most people liked. "It's just scallion pancakes. I hope you like them. They go with everything."

"Thank you so much."

"Of course. It was the one thing I could think to make and not mess up."

She laughed as I followed her to the living room. I sat down while she went to the kitchen. "What are you doing here?"

"What are you doing here?" I asked.

He smiled. "I just came to check up on her. Remind her to take her meds."

I leaned back on the sofa. "Me too."

Mrs. Owens came back into the living room with another mug. On the coffee table was a tray with a tea kettle, sugar, cream, and cookies. I could smell the butter and sugar and a hint of vanilla. "Thank you."

I poured cream and tea into my mug and stirred. "How have you been?"

She sighed into her chair. "I'm doing all right. She had been gone for so long I think deep down I knew. I knew she was gone. It's still hard, though. Sometimes, I pick up the phone to call her, and then I remember. I remember she's gone and not going to answer, and then I hang up." She smiled faintly.

My heart ached for her. In this mess, her daughter and Julius had done nothing wrong. Rica just worked for the wrong people. Julius was looking for his brother so he could take him home. They were innocent, and they were gone. Tears pricked my eyes, but I blinked them away. She didn't need to see me crying.

"I'm so sorry," I said.

She nodded slowly. "What happens to the property?"

I glanced at Tony. I had no idea what would happen to Beth's property. "It will probably be sold once we are done searching the ground for more bodies."

"You think she killed more people?"

"Wouldn't put it past her," said Tony.

She nodded again. "That was what I thought. I hate to think of someone building a house where she... Probably be better off if it was a park or something."

"That would be nice. If it was a park overlooking the water," I said.

"Maybe if you petition the state or something. I'll look into what we can do to make that happen, and I'll get back to you," said Tony.

We stayed with her for a few hours, drinking tea, eating cookies, and gossiping. She told us all about her neighbors and the strange things they do.

"And one of them, just last week," she shook her head, "I never would have believed it. The family was so nice. I had met the son and the daughter. I can't think of her name right now. But she killed her parents and her brother."

"Really?" Tony and I said in unison.

She nodded and then sipped her tea. "I never would have thought it. She always seemed a little fragile, you know. I know she was in therapy."

"Guess it didn't take," said Tony.

"I remember talking to her mother, Naomi Ross, one day. I had just come home with groceries, and she came over and helped me with them. She said they finally found her a good therapist that she liked. She was making progress with her depression. I would never have thought she would have killed them, herself, maybe. But I guess you never know people."

I hadn't seen anything about it on the news. If she was a minor, they probably wouldn't have wanted to release her name. It made me think about another case we had worked on. I wondered how those kids were doing. They thought they were in love, and it turned out they were related. It was a shock for everyone, us and them. I couldn't say who was shocked more.

Their parents had kept the secret from them their whole lives. And instead of telling them why they didn't want them to date, they clung to their secret. They were more concerned with protecting their secret than they were with protecting their children. He killed his family, and she killed hers. And then they ran off together.

Mrs. Owens was horrified by my reveal of that case. She shook her head. "This is why parents shouldn't lie to their children. I wonder if they regretted it when they were dying. It's a horrible thought. A horrifying thought. If they had just told the truth, then maybe they'd still be alive. They ruined so many lives. Oh, that's hard to think about."

She was right. It was difficult to think about.

I had dreams about that case that lingered for months. I never thought I'd get over it. I wondered how they were doing. After the tea was gone and Tony picked up the cookie crumbs with his forefinger, we decided it was time to go. She looked tired, and I needed to get home.

We said goodbye, and I hugged her. I made a mental note to call her in the morning to remind her to take her medicine. I would add it to my calendar so I didn't forget.

"So, what are you doing for the rest of the day?" asked Tony as he walked me to my car.

I shrugged. "Just going to stay home and hang out with Harrison. You?"

He mimicked my shrug. "Going over to Aisha's place. Think we might go out to dinner or something."

"I'm thinking about ordering in. I don't really feel like going out. You should take her to that Vietnamese place we went the other day. She might like it." I opened my car door.

He shook his head. "Probably not. I guess we'll just keep it." He stepped back. "Drive home safe, not like you usually do." He walked back to his car in the driveway.

"I'm a safe driver!" I yelled after him. He waved his hand dismissively and got into his car. A smile tugged at my lips. He was so annoying. I got into the car, stuck the key into the ignition, and rolled my eyes. I went home. Harrison sat on the sofa with his arm in a sling, staring at his computer. He jumped when I walked in.

"Sorry. Didn't mean to scare you."

He closed his computer and shook his head. "I just wasn't expecting you back so soon. I thought you had to work today or something."

I shrugged. "In between cases at the moment. I was just checking up on a victim." Mrs. Owens was a victim just as much as her daughter. Her daughter was stolen from her, and then she was made to feel like she was crazy. Like she didn't know her daughter like she thought she did. And now, because no one listened to her, she had to live the rest of her life without the one person she loved most. "What are you doing?"

"Just reviewing some patient files. Going over my notes."

"How are you feeling?" I set my purse on the counter and grabbed a bottle of water out of the fridge. I collapsed onto the sofa and relaxed for a moment before tucking my legs underneath me.

"I'm okay. My shoulder is a little sore, but overall, I think I feel better."

I nodded slowly. "What about the patient? I mean, what's—"

He sighed. "I told you, Mia, I can't talk about the case or what happened with my patient."

"I know you said that, and I think I understand, but someone stabbed you. They barely missed an important artery. You could have died. You need to talk about it or press charges or something."

His sigh, this time, was louder and more exaggerated.

I sat up. "What if they do it again? Let's say that you stop being their doctor, and they get another one. What if they get so angry that they do it again to their new therapist? Have you thought about that? I get trying to protect their privacy, but you need to protect yourself, too. And others in your profession." I sipped my water while I waited for a response.

"I'm not their therapist and have already transferred their files to a colleague. They are going to jail, but that's all I can say about the incident." He sighed. "I have to keep the confidentiality of my patients sacred. I have to. It's the law. This is how I gain their trust, and if anyone, even one of my colleagues, believes that I talk about my patients with my girlfriend, who just so happens to be an FBI agent, I'll never gain their trust back."

I blinked. This was the first time he had ever referred to me as his girlfriend. It just rolled off his tongue like he said it every day. Like he had said it before.

"Girlfriend, huh?" A smile pulled at my lips, but I forced my face to stay neutral.

He smiled. "Yes. My girlfriend."

I nodded slowly.

"Am I wrong?" He slid off the sofa onto his knees and crawled over to me. A smile bloomed on my lips as I shook my head. He snaked his hands around my waist. His hair tickled my nose. "Have I not said that before?"

I shook my head.

"Oh. I've said it. Not to you, but I've said it. But yeah, I call you my girlfriend. I thought that was understood."

I shrugged. "We've just never said it to each other. That's all. Surprised me."

He nestled his nose in the crook of my neck and took a deep breath. "Didn't mean to surprise you." His lips brushed my skin, sending a shiver down my spine. My fingers stroked the backs of his arms.

"It's good to be surprised every once in a while." Heat pooled at the base of my spine, and my fingers tightened on his arms.

"What are you doing now?"

I blinked. "Shit... I have a poker game tonight."

"When?"

"In a few hours."

He pulled away, the heat of the moment leaving with him. He cocked his head and checked his watch. "I can work with that."

§

Detective Branson opened the door and grinned. "Look at you. Finally accepting an invitation."

"I'm sorry. We were a bit busy."

She smiled. "Yeah, stealing our cases."

I rolled my eyes as she opened the door wider to let me in. Her home was beautiful. The front door was a vibrant emerald green. The green was carried throughout. Light gray wood floors, black trim, and black doors on the inside with pops of green everywhere. It was a classic look and not what I was expecting from her.

"Come on in." She closed the door behind me and led me into the dining room where other female detectives sat at a large round table. "Everyone, this is Special Agent Mia Storm."

I waved. Meeting new people as an adult was awkward. I was very aware that I was the only person in the room that didn't know everyone. I was also having a hard time figuring out what to do with my hands, so I stuck them in my pockets.

"Nice meeting you. I'm Detective Amyra Kahale." She shook my hand and led me to the table. She seemed nice enough. She looked about my age, maybe slightly older, with big brown eyes and brown hair. "This is Detective Amy Dumas, Detective Jamie Anderson, Detective Maggie Stevenson, and Officer Delphine Jackson."

"Nice to meet all of you."

"You, too. Call me Del," said Delphine Jackson. She was beautiful. Dark skin, smooth and perfect. Light brown eyes and dark hair. She had the most perfect cheekbones. She was sitting down, so I couldn't make out her figure, but she looked like she could have been a model.

BREAKFAST IN PARADISE

Maggie had almond-shaped hazel eyes that lingered over everything. She gave everything and everyone at the table a lingering look.

"You're the one that worked that weird ass case at that bed-and-breakfast," said Del.

"Yeah, that's me. And it was weird." I sat next to Amy Dumas, who was Branson's partner. She nodded.

"Yeah, Liz and I heard about everything, and we were glad you guys took it from us. Saved us on the paperwork," said Amy with a chuckle.

"I can't tell you how many times we wanted to give it back."

She laughed. "I couldn't believe it when they started digging up all those bodies."

"Yeah. They still think they are more. Still digging. Beth and Doug won't cop to any more bodies. There's no point in it now. They're both serving life regardless." I shook my head. "It's sad, though. If there are more bodies, and we don't know about them, they're just out there decomposing and losing their identities."

The table groaned.

"Oh, she's a bleeding heart," said Del.

Amy shook her head.

"It's good to have a heart," said Amyra. "Especially in this line of work."

"Be that as it may, don't let it ruin you," said Del. "You led with your heart in this line of work, and it's going to get broken."

"Or stabbed," said Amy.

They had a point. But it was easier said than done. "I know. But some cases just pull at your heartstrings."

"Cut the strings before it pulls out your heart," said Del.

I blinked. That was a good line. A smile tugged at my lips. Branson returned to the table with drinks and snacks. Chicken wings and fries and fruit because she said we probably all needed some type of fiber. The wings were good, sweet and spicy, and crunchy around the edges.

It was less a poker game and more a talking session. Sure, we played cards, ate, and drank, but mostly we talked about our cases. The ones that stuck with us. I listened as they talked about rescuing children from their abductors and molesters. And walking into gruesome crime scenes.

I talked about the Wheeler and Vega families case and how the teenage couple were half-brother and sister and didn't know it. I talked about how the daughter was pregnant with her half-brother's child when we found them and how they killed their parents.

The table was stunned into silence.

"Damn, that's crazy," said Branson.

"Yeah, it was. And that's not how I saw the case ending. Not at all. I still think about it from time to time. Like their parents were so focused on protecting their secret, they weren't thinking how it affected their children."

"This is why you don't lie," said Del.

Amyra shook her head. "That's horrible. I hate cases with children. I have one now with the missing children who were dropped off at the precinct."

"Yeah, I saw that in the news," I said.

She explained what they were going through while trying to find the parents of the children, how difficult it had been for some of them, and how they were waiting for DNA testing to come back on two of the children.

The night finished around one. It was fun, and Tony might have been right. I didn't know if I'd come back and do it again, but it was nice talking to other people like me. People who dealt with difficult cases and had a hard time letting them go.

They all talked a good game about letting things go and not getting too wrapped up in your cases, but they found it as difficult as I did. And that was comforting in some way. I went home and crawled into bed next to Harrison. He wrapped his arm around my waist and pulled me close. The perfect spot.

The next morning, I met Tony at the field office.

"What did you do last night?"

The elevator doors closed, and I pressed the button for our floor. I shrugged. "I ended up going to a poker game."

His jaw twitched. "With whom?"

"I was invited by Detective Branson. I wasn't sure I was going to go until last night. But it was fun. I got to meet a few of the other detectives, and we had a good time. Or at least I did."

"That's good. Look at you meeting other people. I'm proud of you."

The doors slid open, and I rolled my eyes. Hattie stood next to my desk. She looked up, saw me, and pointed toward the conference room. I craned my neck to see who she was pointing at.

"Who is that?" asked Tony.

"Detective Kahale. I met her last night. I walked into the room with Tony following close behind. "Hi?"

"Nice to see you again." She glanced at the back of the room. "This is my partner, Detective Lister."

"You guys have amazing coffee." He lifted his coffee cup. "Much better than we've got."

"What's going on?" asked Tony behind me.

"Detective Kahale, this is my partner—"

"I know who he is." She smiled tightly. "I, um... I just have a couple of questions, and then I can get out of your hair. You two worked a case involving Dane Wesley and Yumi—"

"Yeah, we did. I mean, it wasn't the same case, but yeah, we worked cases involving them. What is this about?" The room was still for a moment. For a long moment, we all stared at each other.

"Well, I was telling you about the case I was working on and how we were waiting for DNA on two of the children. One came back early this morning. It matched Dane Wesley as a familial match. He's her uncle."

"Yumi had a daughter?" The surprise in Tony's voice was exactly what I felt. "Why wouldn't she have said anything?"

I noted how Kahale didn't look at Tony as I talked. She only looked at me. "So, are you looking for Yumi? Because we don't know where she is? She's in witness protection."

"Right. I just wanted to know more about the case you guys worked on involving her and her brother."

I explained how her brother was a serial killer who killed people related to a child trafficking ring and how she was taken by the ring when she was young and then worked her way up. She became a procurer for the ring.

"I see. Any family?"

"Nope. The only family she had was Dane, and I think he believed she was dead," said Tony. 'They didn't have any other family."

"I see." Kahale kept her eyes on me. "Well, thank you for your time. If you ever figure out where she went, please let me know." She handed me her card and left, careful not to touch Tony. Lister followed after her.

"What was that about?"

Tony shrugged. "I don't know. I can't believe Yumi had a daughter."

I shook my head. For a moment, I wondered why she never told us about her daughter. She could have made a deal for the girl. They could have joined witness protection together. But the more I thought about it, the more it made sense. She didn't know what had happened to her daughter.

If they were raping and pimping her out as a child, she could have gotten pregnant, and they would have taken the child. She probably didn't know where the girl was or what happened to her. That was probably how they kept her in line. I wished there was a way we could let her know her daughter was safe. I wondered if she thought about her ever. Or if she even knew where she was. Who did we know that could tell her that her daughter was safe? But if she was already caught up in a murder investigation, how safe could she have been?

What other secrets were there out there that we didn't know about?

It wasn't my problem. But I couldn't help but feel like somehow, it was all connected. I just didn't know how.

AUTHOR'S NOTE

Thank you so much for reading *Breakfast in Paradise*! Mia's adventures have reached more readers than I ever could have imagined, and as a new indie author, I am incredibly appreciative of all of the support you have shown me. This is why I want to share some heartfelt news with you. The next book in this series, A Girl's Farewell, will conclude Mia's journey. I am already hard at work crafting this story and I promise that our cherished characters will find their resolution, bringing the series to a satisfying close.

Your reviews and word of mouth recommendations have fueled my passion for writing and for bringing these stories to life. I'd like to ask you once again, If you could spare a few moments to leave a review for Breakfast in Paradise. Your feedback makes a world of difference. Thank you for being an essential part of my creative process!

If you're looking for more mysteries to capture your curiosity, I have something I know you will love. You can now get all six books of my *Glenville Small Town Mystery Thriller* series as a bundled set for an amazing reduced price! Through these stories, you can experience Detective Heather Bishop's escapades as she navigates the seemingly peaceful facade of a small town, uncovering mysteries that shatter its tranquility. I sincerely hope you will decide to check out these stories and lose yourself in the twists and turns of this gripping saga.

Thank you again for your support. I can't wait to share the final chapter of Mia's adventure with you in *A Girl's Farewell*.

Warm regards,

Cara Kent

P.S. I will be the first one to tell you that I am not perfect, no matter how hard I try to be. And there is plenty that I am still learning about self-publishing. If you come across any typos or have any other issues with this book please don't hesitate to reach out to me at cara@carakent.com, I monitor and read every email personally, and I will do my very best to rectify any issues that I am made aware of.

Get the inside scoop on new releases and get a **FREE BOOK** by me! Visit *https://dl.bookfunnel.com/513mluk159* to claim your **FREE** copy!

Follow me on **Facebook** - *https://www.facebook.com/people/Cara-Kent/100088665803376/*

Follow me on **Instagram** - *https://www.instagram.com/cara.kent_books/*

ALSO BY CARA KENT

Glenville Mystery Thriller

Prequel - The Bachelorette
Book One - The Lady in the Woods
Book Two - The Crash
Book Three - The House on the Lake
Book Four - The Bridesmaids
Book Five - The Lost Girl
Book Six - The Good Marriage

Mia Storm FBI Mystery Thriller

Book One - Murder in Paradise
Book Two - Washed Ashore
Book Three - Missing in Paradise
Book Four - Blood in the Water
Book Five - The Case
Book Six - Hidden in Paradise
Book Seven - Breakfast in Paradise

An Addictive Psychological Thriller with Shocking Twists

Book One - The Woman in the Cottage
Book Two - Mine

Made in United States
Troutdale, OR
03/28/2024